WESTERN PURSUIT

JOHN ALEXANDER

This book is a work of fiction. All characters, places, and incidents are either the product of the author's imagination or are used fictitiously. Any resemblance to places, incidents, or actual persons, whether living or dead, is purely coincidental.

Copyright © 2020 by John Alexander Joboulian

Reproduction, or storage and retrieval, by any means is prohibited.

Cover Design by Tim Barber, Dissect Designs

Formatting by Sweet 'N Spicy Designs

This book is dedicated to my wife, Kimberly, who always said I could be a writer, and who encouraged me at every step. *Western Pursuit* was written over a span of many years, with interruptions for active duty tours in the Navy and Air Force, and the corresponding uprooting and relocations. Yet Kim never complained when I went off by myself to write after being away from her at work all day. When I was tired or discouraged, she urged me to keep writing. Without her, *Western Pursuit* could not have been written.

My success is her success.

ACKNOWLEDGMENTS

I want to thank Kimberly Joboulian, Michelle Dingman, Robert Mathews, and Westerns novelist Robert Broomall for reviewing the manuscript. Their input is most appreciated.

CHAPTER ONE

With a heavy heart Ray Halstead watched the slender young man struggling to hoist the last bale of hay up onto the clumsy stack he'd built near the barn. It was an awkward position for him bent at the waist with arms outstretched and baling hooks sunk into the ends of the bale.

"Billy, you better go help Zeke with that hay bale or by the time we get to town we'll be ordering breakfast instead of supper." Billy came up out of his chair next to Ray on the shaded porch and ambled casually through the yard scattering three chickens pecking at the hard, bare earth.

Even at this distance Ray could see the boy's left knee quivering as he strained mightily to lift the bale, which remained at mid-thigh, neither rising nor falling, a foot short of the waist-high stack.

Ray watched the struggle intently. No matter how many times he'd seen it, it still pained him to watch his son struggle with simple chores on a bad leg. "COME ON, ZEKE, GET IT UP THERE!" he yelled, more out of frustration than encouragement.

It didn't budge.

Finally, Billy arrived and the two of them lifted it to place. Ray shook his head and spat in the dirt.

A few seconds later Zeke walked up to him and said, "I sure am hungry, Pa."

"Couldn't you have lifted that bale by yourself?"

A momentary stab of pain flashed in the boy's eyes. "I do the best I can, Pa."

"Well hurry up and get ready; we've been waiting on you and we're hungry, too."

The Kansas sun blazed in the western sky, still a few hours from the horizon, as the three farmers rode into Wattersville.

They'd had lunch hours ago, and Zeke had worked hard in the sweltering heat all afternoon; his stomach was as empty as a dry well. "Uncle Billy, do you think we'll have to wait again like we did last week?" he asked.

"Chadwick's is always busy on Saturday night," Billy replied.

Ray glanced at Billy. "I see you're all duded up again. Hoping to bump into Mary Lou or Doreen?"

"I'm hoping to bump into both of them—just not at the same time."

"I see an angry girlfriend in your future if you're not careful."

"*Careful* is my middle name," Billy said with a grin.

Swinging past two wagons loading up at Miller's General Store, the three men rounded a corner and Chadwick's Restaurant came into view. The hitching rails in front were occupied, so they stopped at Albert's Barber Shop and tethered their horses to the empty rail in front.

The stench of fresh manure baking in the sun filled Zeke's

nostrils as he carefully sidestepped the abundant droppings and mounted the woodwalk.

As usual, Zeke soon trailed behind the two men. Mrs. Terwilliger and her daughter Thelma came out of the millinery just ahead of him. There wasn't room for them to pass, so he stepped into the street and tipped his hat as they walked by.

Billy turned back looking for his nephew and saw him standing in the street. "Come on, Zeke, try to keep up."

"Save your breath," Ray said.

Zeke mounted the woodwalk again and did his best to close the gap, but Ray and Billy easily beat him to the doorway. His stomach growled as he wedged in behind them unable to see if all fifteen tables were occupied.

Anxiously, Zeke peered around Ray's back and was immensely pleased to see that there was one table available. Before they could move to it, Timothy Chadwick came over to greet them.

"Looks like we got here just in time," Ray said shaking hands with Chadwick.

"I'll say you did. Fifteen minutes ago people were standing outside waiting for a table," Chadwick replied with a smile full of tobacco-browned teeth. "We've been getting good comments on the chicken if you're undecided about what to have." Again he smiled. "Well, enjoy your dinner." He turned to walk away when two men came in, walked past them and sat down at the empty table.

Unlike the other diners, who wore their best town clothes, these two were filthy. One man was short and had three-day whiskers and a belly that pushed at the buttons on his plaid shirt and hung precipitously over his belt. The other was reed thin, a whipcord of a man with a jagged two-inch scar on his right cheek. Taller than his friend, he had an unkempt moustache and scraggly whiskers.

Both wore six-guns.

As Chadwick approached, the taller one beat his weathered hat against his left arm spewing road dust into the air to the disgust of nearby diners. "You can't sit here. These other people came in ahead of you and this is their table," Chadwick said pointing in the direction of the three men near the door. "And there's no guns allowed in here, either."

The tall, thin stranger looked up, then turned his head and stared at the three farmers by the door. Zeke shivered as two black, reptilian eyes fastened on him.

The other stranger said, "We just got into town and we're hungry. Bring us a couple of steaks, mashed potatoes, and bread—if it's fresh. I don't want no stale bread." Then he turned to his friend and said, "You need anything else?"

The thin one turned his attention back to Chadwick. "Yeah, some whiskey. Bring us a bottle, and quick."

"I wish I had my forty-four with me," Billy said in a low voice. "We wouldn't be waiting for no table. I'm just glad my pa ain't here to see this." He stared at the two strangers, then glanced away quickly when the short one looked over.

Zeke's heart raced and his empty stomach churned. He, too, stared at the men. They were sitting at *his* table. He wouldn't do that to someone else. Why should they do it to him? He took a couple deep breaths, his fists clenching and unclenching at his sides.

The short one shifted his gaze to Zeke and their eyes held for a brief moment. The stranger snickered and looked away.

Then Zeke turned to his right; Uncle Billy still averted his eyes from the two strangers. Chadwick walked past Zeke's father and shrugged in resignation: what more could he do? Zeke scanned the room as the diners ate quietly. Bert Watson, the town's blacksmith, mopped the back of his neck with a blue kerchief; a few women fanned themselves with paper fans.

Zeke cringed as a drop of sweat fell from his damp hair and cut an icy path down the center of his spine to the small of his back. He pulled at the front of his shirt in a vain effort to get air inside. The aroma of chicken and steak assailed his nostrils, tormenting him. Zeke glared at the two strangers as they sat at his table while he stood in the doorway waiting for another one.

This ain't right, Zeke thought. It ain't right at all, and nobody's doing anything about it. As he watched the strangers, anger surged and the thought came to mind: they ain't eating ahead of me!

Suddenly he started across the room toward the two men. His right boot heel clomped solidly on the wooden floor, the left one less so as his damaged knee buckled and his left shoulder dipped with each step. The sound of his boot heels against the plank floor unnerved him but he kept going.

CHAPTER TWO

A board creaked underfoot and the two strangers looked up at Zeke's approach. Off to the left Erich Haufmann's chair squealed in protest as he swung it around for a better view. The room fell silent as Zeke arrived at the table.

The thin one's eyes blazed, but it was his friend who spoke in a low growl. "What you want, gimp?"

Zeke clenched his fists, took a deep breath, then said, "This here is our table and we aim to have it."

"Oh, yeah?" the fat one said. "If it's your table, how come we're sitting at it and you and those other two grubbers are standing by the door?"

"We were here first. It's our table."

The thin one looked up at Zeke, his dark eyes two bottomless pits. Despite the heat, Zeke shivered. The stranger's right hand moved toward the six-gun on his hip. "Well, Mr. Colt here says it's our table. You want to argue with him?"

A strong hand rested on Zeke's shoulder. He hadn't heard the steps come up behind him. "Here, now, there's no call for any of that," Ray Halstead said. "My son's been working all day and he's hungry, that's all." The stranger's hand didn't move from his hip. "He's just a kid," Halstead said. "Barely eighteen."

"The way he runs his mouth he ain't going to make it to nineteen."

"You ought to feed that boy more," the fat one said. "Put some meat on him."

"Your friend here ain't much more than a string bean himself," Ray said.

The two men glared at Ray, then the thin one said, "I wasn't always this way."

Chadwick stepped between them wringing a towel. "I have a table for you now, Ray," he said. "If you'll come this way, please."

Zeke whirled around and saw three suddenly-empty tables. Odd, he thought. He hadn't heard anybody leave.

Ray glared at the tall one a moment longer, then with a strong hand on his son's shoulder turned him around as they followed Chadwick to one of the empty tables. Zeke saw Billy standing in the shadow of the doorway with his left leg on the woodwalk outside.

"Next time don't send a cripple," the fat one yelled, then guffawed as Zeke and Ray walked away.

"Hey! Where's that bottle of whiskey?" the tall stranger called out.

Chadwick returned, struggling to contain his anger. "This is a restaurant, not a saloon. We don't serve whiskey here."

The thin gunman said something to his partner as Chadwick walked away, then the fat one got up and left.

The other diners remained quiet as Billy joined Zeke and Ray at a corner table. Zeke sat with his back to the wall in the corner so he could see the entire room.

Ray said, "What the devil's the matter with you, Zeke,

talking that way to two strangers, especially ones wearing guns?"

"They was laughing at us, Pa."

"They're a couple of drifters. They'll probably leave town tonight or tomorrow and you'll never see them again. Does it really matter what they think?"

Zeke didn't answer. He looked from his father to the two strangers, his mouth set, jaw muscles bulging.

"I asked you a question, son."

Zeke looked at his father for a few seconds, then said, "I don't like people pushing me around, Pa."

His anger abating, Ray studied his son for a few moments, then his face softened to one of abject resignation. "What could you have done, anyway?" he said. "Even if they didn't have guns, what could you have done?"

Though seething in frustration, Zeke held his tongue. They wouldn't shoot an unarmed man, he thought, and even if they whipped him it'd be worth it just to get in a few licks of his own.

Just then Lydia, the waitress, came over to take their orders. She placed a hand on Billy's shoulder and gave him a wink when he looked up. "No good saddle tramps," she said. Then she smiled. "What'll you folks have to eat?"

She took their orders and bounded off to the kitchen giving the strangers' table a wide berth.

Zeke's eyes never left the tall stranger for more than a few seconds at a time. The shorter man, who'd gone out earlier, returned with a whiskey bottle about half full. Zeke strained to hear them and was just able to make out their conversation since they talked much louder than everybody else.

"What's this, don't they have full bottles at that saloon?" the tall one asked as the short, fat man handed over the bottle.

"The bartender said he'd have to go out back to get one

and I didn't feel like waiting. We can go back for more when this is gone," Zeke heard him say.

"How dumb can you get? I send you out on a simple job like bringing back a bottle of whiskey, and you can't even get that right."

"Aw, Ledyard, I ain't so dumb. I remembered these, didn't I?" he said as he pulled two whiskey glasses out of his pants pockets and put them on the table.

So the thin one's name is Ledyard, Zeke thought as he turned his attention back to his father and uncle.

Billy said to Ray, "I've been thinking about putting in a few weeks working for that new railroad that's laying track from Leavenworth. I hear they're looking for men. Figure I could make a few bucks—if you and Zeke can spare me at the farm."

"Seems to me I heard something about that," Ray said. "What's it called? The Kansas Central Railway?"

"Yeah, that's it. What do you think?"

"Sure. Me and Zeke can run things while you're gone." He looked at his son and frowned. "Too bad Zeke couldn't handle a job with them. A little pocket money's good for a boy."

"I can do it, Pa," Zeke said. "I can work just as hard as other men can."

"You think you can swing a sledgehammer all day, or carry cross-ties around by yourself?" Billy said. He started to laugh but a glare from Ray cut it short.

Zeke turned away and after a few moments Ray and Billy resumed their conversation. Zeke put his attention back on the gun-toting strangers. Were they gunfighters, or just cowboys? He'd never seen a gunfighter before. The tall, thin one looked like he could be a gunfighter. Had he killed anyone?

The strangers' food came and they wolfed it down, but it hardly slowed their drinking. They talked and laughed, and the more they drank, the louder they got. Zeke noticed that people made a conscious effort not to look at the two men, although that was becoming increasingly difficult.

Soon the bottle was empty and the short man got up to leave. He's probably going for another bottle, Zeke thought.

With his friend gone, Ledyard looked around lazily. People turned away from him as his eyes scanned the room. All except for Zeke, that is. As Ledyard's gaze came around, Zeke felt their eyes meet and lock in. A cold chill ran through him as neither he nor Ledyard attempted to break the stare.

After what seemed an eternity, but was actually only a few seconds, Zeke pulled his eyes away. Too late.

"Hey! What're you looking at?" Ledyard bellowed.

Zeke didn't look up.

"Huh? You! I mean you!" he said pointing at Zeke.

Now everyone was looking at Ledyard except for Zeke, who continued to look down at the table.

"Ignore me, will you!" he roared in a drunken rage.

Still, Zeke wouldn't look at him. Ledyard picked up his whiskey glass and hurled it at Zeke. It missed his head by inches and slammed into the wall just behind him.

A few women cried out, and chairs shrieked against the hardwood floor as people lurched at the sound of breaking glass.

Zeke jumped at the loud crash as shards of glass rained onto his neck and cheeks. Startled by this unknown assault, a flash of fear surged through him; his heart raced and the breath caught in his throat. What was that, he wondered? Zeke brushed a hand down his neck but felt no wound or pain.

He looked up to see Ledyard glaring at him even as Ray leapt to his feet and charged the stranger bulling past the Kennedy family at the table between them. Grabbing the edge of Ledyard's table before he could react, Ray violently overturned it onto the stranger knocking him off his chair and pinning him to the floor as dishes and glasses crashed all around him.

Women screamed and men jumped to their feet.

Pressing the table down with his left hand, Ray used his free right hand to drive a heavy fist into the side of Ledyard's face. Ray flung the table aside and jerked Ledyard to his feet. He drew back for another blow, but seeing the blood pour from Ledyard's left nostril and his glassy eyes roll around, Ray dropped his arm.

Instead, he picked the stranger up by his shirtfront and flung him several feet across the room as if eager to be rid of him. The stranger landed heavily and crashed into the base of the wall near the entrance.

Ray straightened up and said to Zeke and Billy, "Let's go, supper's over." Then he turned to Chadwick. "I'll get with you on the damages next week."

Still shaken, Zeke got up with Uncle Billy. Just then he saw Ledyard's hand move. A split-second before comprehension, then, horrified, he screamed "NO!" as the stranger drew his six-gun.

Two deafening, startling blasts from the gun, and then smoke poured from the barrel clouding the room. The slugs slammed into his father's chest driving him backward to the floor. Acrid gunpowder assailed Zeke's nostrils and his stomach churned.

Zeke rushed over to him just as Billy took a step toward Ledyard.

"You want some, too?" Ledyard asked as he slowly got to his feet, the revolver in his right hand. Billy stopped in his tracks and shook his head, his hands in the air.

"Anybody else want some?" Ledyard asked as he swept the room in a wide arc with the six-gun and moved slowly toward the door wiping the blood dripping from his nose with the back of his left hand. As he reached the entrance, his friend came in, bottle in hand.

"What's all the shooting?"

"Let's get going," Ledyard said to him. In a moment they were gone with the sound of hooves racing off in the night even as more people crowded into the restaurant.

Zeke reached under his father's head and lifted it off the hard floor. Ray struggled for breath, his mouth full of blood that spilled down the right side of his face in a red line that ended in front of his ear and dripped onto the dusty floor.

He looked up despairingly at Zeke. "Who'll watch out for you now?" he said. His gaze shifted to his brother-in-law. "Help him, Bil—". Then his eyes were vacant and he moved no more.

CHAPTER THREE

It was almost six o'clock when the funeral ended. The late-afternoon start was so the deceased's father-in-law, Henry McNichol, could arrive from Topeka in time for the service. Close to fifty people attended as Ray Halstead had had many friends in the community. In addition, many of the patrons who witnessed the cold-blooded killing at Chadwick's felt obliged to go as a way of putting the matter to rest in their own minds. People shook hands with Zeke and Billy as they left, most offering some awkward words of condolence.

None paid any attention to the thin man with the shock of gray hair sprouting from under a dusty, sweat-stained hat. His Mexican boots made him look taller than his five-foot-nine frame, and the leather vest he wore covered the six-pointed star pinned to his shirt. United States Marshal Henry McNichol, the deceased's father-in-law, was clean-shaven except for a long, scraggly gray moustache that trailed past the corners of his mouth. Silent throughout the proceedings, his eyes had moved constantly over the crowd, taking in everything.

Finally, all the guests had left. "Well, let's get some

supper," Henry said joining Billy and Zeke, "and then you can fill me in on exactly what happened."

In a few minutes they were tethering their horses at the rail by Chadwick's. "This where it happened?" Henry asked.

"This is the place," Billy said.

After receiving condolences from Mr. and Mrs. Chadwick, they took the same corner table Zeke, Ray and Billy had taken the night before. Besides themselves, there were two cowboys at a table in the middle of the room, and a young couple in another corner. The remaining tables were unoccupied.

They ate in silence. Zeke was surprised that his uncle and his grandfather had nothing to say to each other. Grandpa rarely visited them, and looking back on those visits, the two hadn't spent much time together. But why wouldn't a father and his son be close?

Zeke knew his own father had been disappointed in him, but he also knew a lot of that was because he'd worried about Zeke making it on his own in a harsh world. He'd even heard his father tell Uncle Billy he didn't know how a weakling could survive on his own. Still, Zeke never doubted his father's love for him.

For as long as Zeke could remember, his father had included him in almost everything he did, patiently teaching him how to use the stars for a compass, start a fire with no matches, or tell a forty-dollar horse from a ten-dollar horse. And they'd spent many hours together fishing, telling stories at night on the front porch, or racing their horses behind the barn. In the end his father gave his life protecting him. A tear formed and Zeke wiped it away with the back of his right hand, his grandfather noticing but saying nothing.

Finally the old man took a big drink of water and wiped his mouth with the large red-checked napkin hanging from his shirt. "So tell me, Zeke, exactly what did happen here last night?" His voice was gruff, as though it passed through gravel on the way out, but his manner was straightforward, if not gentle, as he cast his slate blue eyes on Zeke, patiently waiting for his grandson to answer.

It struck Zeke as odd that his grandfather would rather hear it from him than from his own son, who was sitting right there with them. He looked at his uncle, but Billy's eyes were on the empty plate before him and he didn't look up. Slowly, Zeke told his grandfather all that had happened, leaving nothing out. The old man listened quietly, taking it all in.

When Zeke had finished, Henry turned to Billy. "And what were you doing while all this was going on?"

"Me? What could I do?" Billy said, his face suddenly crimson.

"Seems I have heard that answer from you before," Henry said. "Ain't you got any new answers?"

What's he talking about, Zeke wondered. What's going on?

Henry glared at Billy. "Well, where was your gun then? Were you even wearing it?"

Billy shook his head slowly, his eyes on the table before him. "No," he said softly.

"Well, why not?" Henry demanded.

"Town ordinance against wearing firearms," Billy said.

"I thought as much. Well, you're not going to have that one to hide behind anymore." He reached inside his vest pocket and pulled out two badges, throwing them onto the table. They made a metallic scraping sound as they clanged together before skittering across the wooden tabletop.

Zeke leaned over to get a closer look. They were plain, six-pointed stars just like Grandpa's, only the writing was a little different.

"Now raise your right hands," Henry said. "Do you swear to defend the Constitution of the United States and to uphold the laws of this great land?" He looked at both of them. "Say 'I do'."

"I do."

"I do."

"You're both now Deputy United States Marshals."

"I don't understand," Zeke said. "Why are you making us deputies?"

"It's so we can wear our guns anywhere, whether there's an ordinance against it or not," Billy said.

"What do we need guns for? Pa's already dead."

"We're going after the man who did it, Zeke," Henry said.

"You mean us three?" Zeke asked. "What about Marshal Ryan? I thought he went after them—but then I saw him in town today." Zeke looked confused.

"By the time he got a posse together it was pretty late. He lost their trail in the dark a few miles west of town, so he came back," Henry said. "Anyway, Ryan's just a town marshal—he wasn't even wearing a gun when I talked to him at the funeral. He lacks the authority and the experience to go out on what could be a long and dangerous hunt."

"Who's going to watch our place while we're gone?" Zeke said. "Someone's got to feed the animals, milk the cows, and make sure no one breaks in and steals things."

"Already talked to Marshal Ryan about that. He said there's some newlyweds staying at the hotel until they find a place to live. He said they'd be glad to stay at your house and do the chores. You can pay them when we get back. Hopefully, that'll be soon, but you never know how long it takes when you're chasing someone."

Billy said, "What about your duties in Topeka?"

"At least that part worked out all right. I was getting bored in Topeka. The town's gotten too civilized—all I did was push paper or stand around in court all day. So I asked for a transfer to someplace further west. It turns out they need a marshal in Cheyenne, in Wyoming Territory, so they offered me the job. I told them I'd take it, but I asked for some time off. I didn't know this was going to happen, of course. Anyway, I don't have to be in Cheyenne until September first, and there's a couple of deputies in Topeka that'll run things there until my replacement arrives."

"You left Topeka?" Billy said, surprised.

Henry nodded. "All done with Topeka."

"What chance would Zeke and me have against a gunfighter?" Billy said.

"I doubt that he was a gunfighter. Any drunken bum can shoot an unarmed man standing right in front of him."

"But I don't even have a gun," Zeke said.

"We'll take care of that," Henry said. He looked at the two of them, disgusted with their excuses. "The man he killed was your father," he said to Zeke; "your brother-in-law," he said to Billy; "and my son-in-law. That makes it a family matter. We don't need strangers doing our business for us. It don't make no difference that I'm a marshal because we'd be going after him anyway. This just makes it legal, that's all."

Zeke was confused; this was all so sudden. As he took in what Grandpa said, he thought back on last night. If he hadn't started that quarrel by going to Ledyard's table, and if he hadn't stared back at him, none of this would have happened. Pa would be alive right now.

Zeke's stomach lurched. He would have cried, but he was all dried up.

"What's the matter, boy?" Henry said. "You look a mite peaked."

"I couldn't sleep last night. Every time I closed my eyes I saw Pa lying on the dirty floor with blood pouring out of his mouth. Even now I can't get that picture out of my head."

"A murder's a terrible thing, Zeke," Henry said. "You're

young, and seeing your father gunned down makes it much worse."

"What can I do?"

"You ain't going to get over it for awhile, but eventually it'll fade. You'll never forget it, but you'll be able to deal with it."

Zeke said in a soft voice, "It's my fault pa's dead. I killed him."

"What?" Henry said, taken aback. "You mean because you told them two critters to get up from your table? Because one of them threw a whiskey glass at you later?"

Zeke said nothing. He stared at the tabletop.

"There's nothing wrong with standing up for what's right. You used poor judgment in approaching two armed men without a weapon yourself, but at least you had the sand to do it." He shot a contemptuous glance at Billy, then looked back at Zeke.

"It's still my fault."

"People don't survive out here by tiptoeing around so's not to bother anybody. But if you want to blame yourself, well, now you got the opportunity to do something about it." Then he stood up. "I got to step outside, but I'll be right back. Then we'll find the gunsmith so he can open his shop. I want to get started tonight while the trail is fresh."

After he left, Zeke picked up the badge and turned it in his fingers, studying it. It was cold and harsh. Yet what was he to do, go back to the farm and pretend nothing happened? No, he couldn't do that. He laid the badge in the palm of his hand and studied it a moment longer, then pinned it to the outside of his vest.

For the first time since last night, he felt better. Not good, but better. This was the right thing to do. It wouldn't bring Pa back, but it would set things straight. Besides, like Grandpa said, Ledyard's not a gunfighter, he's just a drifter.

They should be able to bring him in easy. Zeke looked down at the badge, suddenly proud at this supreme symbol of manhood.

"Don't wear it like that, you idiot," Billy said. "Pin it to your shirt so your vest covers it."

"But then no one can see it."

"That's the point. He made us deputies, but that don't mean we have to tell the whole world about it."

"So what's wrong with people knowing?" Zeke asked.

"We're not lawmen, we're farmers. You flash that badge around and people are going to come to you for help, or worse, take a shot at you. Lots of men would love to shoot a lawman."

Zeke knew his uncle was right: putting on a tin star didn't change anything. He wasn't a lawman. Reluctantly, Zeke took the badge off his vest and pinned it to his shirt, so no one would know that he was a Deputy United States Marshal.

CHAPTER FOUR

Before leaving town, Henry dragged the gunsmith away from his supper and bought a .44 Remington New Model Army for himself, and gave his Colt .44 to Zeke. Billy already had a .44 Remington. Henry also bought a used belt and holster for Zeke, and ammunition for all three of them.

Fortunately, the Halstead farm was west of town so they stopped there without losing much time. Zeke quickly put together a bedroll. Then he scooped up his money from a dresser drawer and jammed the bills and coins into his left front pants pocket. Then he put several pairs of clean socks, some underwear, leather gloves, and a spare shirt and pants into his saddlebags. He spied his Bible atop the dresser and seeing that he still had room, stuffed that into his saddlebag as well. On the way out he took Pa's Winchester .44 rifle off the wall above the fireplace.

They loaded everything onto an extra horse Henry had insisted they take. Henry said they could rotate riding the four horses so every fourth day each horse got a break as the pack animal, not having to carry a rider. It would also provide a spare horse should one of the other three go down.

Billy led the way to Gooseneck Creek, where Marshal Ryan had lost the trail the night before. They arrived just as the sun dropped below the western horizon. "We'll camp here for the night," Henry said dismounting. "I want to be up at dawn to look for sign and pick up their trail, so we'll turn in early."

It was a very warm, muggy night and since they weren't cooking or making coffee, no fire was made. Billy went right to sleep, but Henry sat down next to Zeke, who was spreading his bedroll near a cottonwood blackened in the twilight. "You ever shot a handgun before, Zeke?"

"No, only a rifle, but I'm a fast learner if you'll teach me," he said, eager to master the six-gun he'd owned for little over an hour. Then he smacked a mosquito feeding off the back of his left hand.

"It's too dark to show you how to load it, but there are a few points I'd like to go over with you." Henry then showed Zeke how he had to cock the gun before each shot because it was a single-action revolver. He went on with the lesson:

> Never load all six chambers. Always leave one empty to set the hammer on. That way, if something bumps your gun, or you drop it, it won't discharge.
>
> Never bluff with your gun; if you're not prepared to use it, don't draw it. And don't get too fancy with your aim. Go for a big target like his chest or stomach, not his arm or his head.
>
> The most important thing is accuracy, not speed on the draw. You must hit what you're aiming at, and you must do it on the first shot. You can't get off an accurate shot if you rush yourself. So I want you to practice your draw so that you get faster and faster with it. The idea is that the more

you practice the draw, the faster you can get your gun out and cocked without rushing yourself. Be sure the gun is unloaded, then practice drawing, cocking the hammer, and squeezing the trigger. Do that over and over and over till it becomes second nature to you.

When we get a chance we'll do some practice shooting, but it's been my experience that good shots are born and not made. Some fellows are good shots and others ain't no matter how much they practice. If you ain't a good shot then it's important that you get as close to your target as you can. We'll know soon enough what kind of a shot you are.

"Uncle Billy's a real good shot," Zeke said. "I've never seen him use his handgun, but I've seen him use a rifle to pick off rabbits on the dead run many times."

"I got my own opinion of Billy, but you're right, he is a good shot. He's almost as good with a six-gun as he is with a rifle." Henry paused for a moment, looking off into the distance in the twilight.

Zeke said, "I'm really nervous about this, Grandpa. I don't mean the shooting so much, but what I mean is the whole business about being a lawman. I don't know the first thing about it. Ledyard's a killer, probably a gunfighter, and I'm just a farmer. Once I get close enough to shoot him, I'll also be close enough for him to shoot me. I ain't afraid of getting shot, but I wonder if I have what it takes to bring him in or kill him if I have to."

"A little fear is a good thing, Zeke. It gives you that edge you need. And you're right about Ledyard. Once you get close enough to capture him, he's close enough to put a bullet in you. Always remember that when you're tracking someone. Likely as not it'll be in the back, or from behind a tree, or when you're sleeping. Outlaws are like that. Indians, too, of course."

Henry studied his grandson for a few seconds. "You thinking on turning back?"

"No, I was just thinking this may not be as easy as I thought it was going to be."

"Assuming Ledyard doesn't get away," Henry said, "there's three possible outcomes: one, we capture him; two, we kill him; or three, he kills all three of us."

Zeke joined Henry and Billy for a breakfast of coffee, biscuits, and jerky. He hadn't acquired the taste for coffee yet, but it was hot and chased the morning chill and washed the dry biscuits and tough jerky down. The sun peeked over the edge of the eastern horizon while they ate, and in a few minutes the whole countryside was visible. Henry poured himself another cup of coffee, then rode his horse across the shallow creek. Zeke watched him move off to the left and then back to the right, all the while staring at the ground.

Finishing his coffee, Zeke walked to the edge of the creek to wash out his cup and rinse the bitter taste out of his mouth. "See anything yet?" he called out.

Henry nodded. "Yep, I think we got them. You boys get your stuff together and get on over here. And don't take all day about it; we got some catching up to do."

Five minutes later Zeke and Billy joined Henry on the far side of the creek. Henry pointed to the ground. "There's two of them all right. Whether they're the two we're after or not I don't know, but I'm thinking it's them. Looks like one of the horses has a shoe coming loose."

Zeke stared at the ground, the patchwork of hoof prints

meaning nothing to him. "You can tell all that by looking at those hoof prints?" he asked.

Henry looked at him in surprise. "Shoot, that ain't nothing. I learned all I know about tracking when I was a Ranger for a few months. They had some boys in that outfit that could look at a set of prints like these and tell you what color the horses were."

Zeke and Billy laughed at that, and even Henry had to smile at his own joke.

"So you think they're heading for a town?" Billy said.

"If they don't know it by now, they'll soon discover that they need a blacksmith for that loose shoe."

They followed the trail for mile after monotonous mile of flat, grassy, treeless prairie shimmering in the summer sun. Except for the path, the land looked the same in every direction. All around them, knee-high grama grass and little bluestem grass swayed gently in the wind.

Every once in a while the three lawmen came upon the cold remnants of a campfire, or a broken chair, a torn dress, an empty whiskey bottle, or other discards.

They made good time and followed the tracks for several hours, being careful not to go so fast as to wear out the horses. Periodically checking his gold pocket watch, Henry called a halt every fifty minutes. Then he'd time a ten-minute break, and they'd loosen the saddle cinches so the horses could breathe freely.

Finally, Henry decided to stop for lunch. "I'll start a fire and put on some coffee," he said. "Why don't you two see if you can't get us some meat, but don't be gone too long. I want to get back on the trail."

Zeke and Billy tethered their horses and removed the saddles, then set off into the brush looking for a rabbit or two. They came to another clearing and moved along its edge looking deeper into the woods for any sign of movement.

"I sure hope we get something," Zeke said. "That jerky's too tough for me."

"Well, you find it and I guarantee you I'll shoot it," Billy said.

Zeke followed Billy further into the woods. The sweat ran down his face from under the soaked liner of his hat. It dripped from the tip of his nose and from under his chin. His shirt was all wet under the armpits and as they moved deeper into the brush the buzzing of the gnats about his face was stifling. As Billy moved ahead of him, the leaves and branches whipped back raking his face and neck. Zeke enjoyed working out in the open on their farm, but tramping through the brush like this was not at all to his liking.

Billy stopped a few paces ahead as he emerged from the woods into an open area surrounded by trees. "Let's just sit here and see what comes along," Billy said. The ground dropped away so that they were able to look down into the clearing. "We'll get a good look and a wide-open shot from up here."

This was the first time Zeke had been alone with his uncle since supper after the funeral. "What do you think about us being Deputy U.S. Marshals, Uncle Billy? It's exciting, isn't it?"

Billy looked at him and then looked away shaking his head in disbelief. "I'd rather we were back on the farm and my pa was on his way to Cheyenne."

"Why? Don't you want to get the man that killed my pa?"

"Listen, if that outlaw showed up here right now what would you do? You wouldn't do anything, that's what. He'd kill both of us. You think wearing a badge makes you a lawman?"

"Maybe I ain't a real lawman, but I ain't yellow, either."

Billy was on him in an instant. Grabbing two handfuls of Zeke's shirt, he pulled him so close their noses were almost touching. "Don't ever call me yellow again. Ever! You hear?" He pushed Zeke away and resumed his seat, staring off into the distance.

Zeke tugged at his shirt, straightening it. "What are you getting so worked up about? I didn't mean anything by it. What do you expect me to think when you talk about going home?"

Billy continued to stare off into the clearing. "Maybe I seen death before. Maybe I ain't ready to die yet. Does that make me yellow?" He turned to stare at Zeke.

"I don't know what you're talking about."

"My pa thinks I'm yellow. That's why he made us deputies. He wants me to be a man like he is." He paused for a few moments to collect his thoughts. "Ain't you ever wondered why I live with you instead of with my pa?"

"I figured you came to help out after my mother died," Zeke said.

Billy shook his head. "I came to live with you before your ma died. You was about two years old at the time." He turned away again. Several seconds passed. Billy plucked a blade of grass and stuck it in his mouth.

"I was twelve years old when pa turned me out of the house," Billy said. "Being my sister and all, Louise took me in and I came to live with you and her and your pa. A couple of years later your ma died having a baby. The baby was born dead. Your pa probably told you about that."

Zeke nodded that he had.

"Well, after Louise died I became more valuable than ever and just stayed on helping your pa even after I was old enough to be on my own."

"Why'd Grandpa turn you out of the house?" Zeke asked.

Billy continued to stare off into the distance. Pain creased his face. Finally, he shook his head. "I don't want to talk about it," he said.

Suddenly, a rabbit appeared at the edge of the clearing. Billy scooped up his rifle and drew a bead. As it scampered across the center of the clearing, he squeezed off a shot and the rabbit flipped over and lay still. Billy looked at his nephew and said, "Come on, we better get back. We've been gone too long already."

CHAPTER FIVE

Early in the evening Billy said, "We've been riding quite a spell, Pa. Do you want to stop and make camp?"

The question surprised Zeke. After all, Uncle Billy was the one who had wanted to cover as many miles a day as possible. *Maybe he's bored, too, or his butt hurts as much as mine does.*

"No, Junction City's up ahead about five miles," Henry said. "Used to be I'd just as soon sleep under the stars as indoors, but ever since my bones began to creak and I got used to my bed back in Topeka I try to find a hotel when I'm out of town. Besides, I want to ask around and see if anybody's seen this Ledyard fellow."

Zeke breathed a sigh of relief and said, "Should we pick up the pace a bit since we're so close? I'm starving."

"No, we'll let the horses walk into town. We got to ride them tomorrow, so there's no point in running them when they're tired already."

Being raised on a farm and not traveling much, Zeke was beginning to understand how important a horse was to a man out on the prairie. His grandfather did nothing without considering how it would affect his horse. Zeke would have to remember that in the future. Henry not only rested the animals, he paralleled the river as much as possible so the horses would have water, and he'd brought plenty of grain along to feed them in the days ahead, and would no doubt buy more as needed.

The last rays of the setting sun cast barely enough light for Zeke to read the signs on Junction City's buildings. There was a general store, a dress shop, a restaurant, a blacksmith, and five saloons that Zeke counted. There were also several buildings with no signs on them leaving Zeke to wonder what they were. The temperature had dropped considerably and Zeke turned his collar up against a trailing breeze. He was surprised when his grandfather stopped in front of the blacksmith shop. "I thought we were going to get some supper. I'm starved," Zeke said.

"Horses come first," Billy said. "You know that."

They dismounted and went inside. Zeke was immediately hit with a strong odor of horses that made him think of the barn back home and how it smelled the same way whenever he first went in. The shop was dark. A single lantern hung on the back wall; its yellow light barely illuminated the heavyset man sitting in a rocking chair beneath it. He had a thick black beard, bib overalls, a bottle in his left hand and a pistol in his right. "Shop's closed! What do you want?" he said, his voice a mild roar.

"You can put that gun away," Henry said. "We're peaceable."

"I said, what do you want?" he demanded.

"Name's Henry McNichol. I'm a United States Marshal. These are my deputies." He moved closer, his hands in the air. Then he leaned in and slowly pushed his vest aside displaying the badge.

The blacksmith set the bottle down, rose from his chair

and turned up the wick on the lantern throwing yellow light all around the shop. Bushy black eyebrows danced above two blazing eyes as he squinted at the badge. He lowered the gun. "I always get a bit jumpy when people come around this time of night—me being here alone and all," he said.

"I can't fault a man for being careful," Henry said.

"I was getting ready to turn in when I heard your horses stop out front. I get up with the roosters and try to get my work done before it gets too hot. The summer heat's bad enough without standing in front of a blazing forge all day. Got me a room on the other side of this here wall," he said jerking a grimy thumb at the wall behind him. "Is there something you want, Marshal?"

"I didn't see a livery on the way in, but we sure could use a place to put our horses up for the night. They could use some tending, too, if there's anyone around to do it," Henry said.

"I run the livery, too. It's next to my shop. I never got around to putting up a sign since I didn't see a need for one. I can take care of your horses for you."

"We'd be obliged if you'd water and feed them and rub them down real good," Henry said. "Give them an extra ration of oats." Zeke and Billy turned to leave, but then stopped when they saw that Henry wasn't through just yet. "And one other thing. You seen two men come through here? A short, chubby one and a taller man, real thin?"

Fire blazed in the smith's eyes and he moved a step closer. "They was here early this morning. My first customers, in fact. They wanted to swap horses with me for some fresh mounts. I could see that theirs had been rode hard. I didn't like the looks of those fellows and didn't want nothing to do with them, so I told them I didn't have any at the moment.

"So then the fat one swore and the other one said his horse had thrown a shoe. Told me to take care of it and then went down the street for some breakfast." Agitated, he reached for the bottle and took a long pull.

"That's them," Billy said. "They got a day's head start on us."

"All right, so they went down the street," Henry said. "Then what happened?"

"It wasn't an easy job. The hoof needed some work, and then I had to make a new shoe and the forge wasn't hot yet. Anyway, I wasn't done when they came back. So the skinny one starts to cursing me. I tried to ignore him and finish the job, but he wouldn't let up. So I reached out and grabbed him by the shirt and jerked him up in the air like this," he said thrusting his left fist above his head. "I don't let no man talk to me that way in my own shop. This is my shop! I built it and I own it and no one curses me in my own place!" He was breathing hard.

"What happened then?" Billy asked.

"The next thing I knew the yellow dog had a hogleg jammed under my chin. So I let him down and finished the job while he sat and watched me, the whole time telling me to hurry up. Didn't even pay me for my work!" His eyes shifted back and forth between the three men. "You after them?"

Henry nodded. "They leave right away?"

"Soon as I finished they lit out of here heading west."

"Well, thanks," Henry said. "We'll be by early to get our horses so I'll just pay you now." He handed over some coins. "By the way, is there a hotel in this town?"

"Yep. They still ain't got around to putting up a sign, but it's easy enough to find. Just go three doors down from the restaurant in the opposite direction from the Full Keg Saloon." He watched as they turned to leave. "I hope you catch them," he said.

After the three men ate a quick supper Henry started

toward the hotel. He stopped when he realized that Zeke and Billy weren't walking with him.

"We ain't ready to turn in yet, Pa. Me and Zeke are going over to that saloon to see if we can get into a poker game."

"All right, but don't stay up too late—we're leaving at sunup. And stay away from them saloon gals." He moved off toward the hotel, his boots banging on the wooden deck.

The two deputies were soon disappointed. There was no card game in the saloon, only a couple townsmen off in a corner talking quietly, and a bartender anxious to close up and go home. They left without even having a beer.

Ten minutes later they were in their hotel room and in their beds. Zeke's legs and buttocks ached so badly it hurt him even to lie still and he wondered how he could survive more days in the saddle. He didn't want to think about that. Maybe he could get some horse liniment or something to rub on his legs: anything to just make the pain go away.

Their room had a musty odor to it, but it was warm and dry, and to Zeke the clean sheets and soft mattress were infinitely better than the hard ground of the night before. Now, if only he could find a way to get comfortable....

Billy reached for the kerosene lamp on the nightstand between the two beds.

"Do you mind if we leave the light on for a little while?" Zeke asked.

"What for?"

"I'd like to read a little bit," Zeke said.

"Read? Ain't you tired?"

"Well, yeah, but I'd like to stay up for a few more minutes if the light won't bother you." He looked at his uncle for a reaction, but there was none. Zeke continued, "You know how my pa used to read the Bible to me?"

Billy nodded.

"Well, now that he's dead, I just feel like reading it since it was something that we did together. I'd feel like he's close by, even though he's gone."

"You thinking about being a preacher or something?"

"No, nothing like that," Zeke said. "I just remember how he'd read a Bible passage to me and then we'd talk about what the meaning was. Ever since we started this search I keep thinking about this one part that Pa once read to me: 'Vengeance is mine, sayeth the Lord'. It makes me wonder if Pa would approve of what I'm doing out here."

"I remember my pa reading the Bible to me, too," Billy said. "He liked the part about 'an eye for an eye'."

"That's what I mean," Zeke said. "Even reading the Bible can get you mixed up. I don't think God wants killers running loose shooting people."

"Well, I wouldn't look to the Gospel according to Henry for answers," Billy said.

"What's wrong with Grandpa?" Zeke asked.

"He's about the most pig-headed, stubborn man I've ever met. Don't get me wrong—there's a need for lawmen like him out here. Without them this country wouldn't be fit for decent people to live in. I just wouldn't look to him for understanding and guidance."

Zeke sat up in bed and looked directly at his uncle, listening intently.

"He wants me to be a lawman like he is," Billy continued, "but he ain't asked me how I feel about it. There's nothing about marshaling that I like; I'd much rather be back on our farm."

Zeke thought about how he felt wearing his badge. It made him feel proud, there was no denying that. But at the same time, he couldn't see himself being as good at it as his grandfather was. Still, he couldn't dismiss the possibility from his mind the way his uncle could.

"You were saying this morning that you came to live with

us before Ma died, when I was about two," Zeke said. "Why? Why didn't you stay with Grandpa?"

"I told you I didn't want to talk about it," Billy said. "Besides, it's a long story, and I'm tired."

"Yeah, I reckon I'm pretty tired, too." Zeke reached for the lamp. For a few moments he lay still in the darkness, then said, "Uncle Billy?"

"What now?"

"Is your butt sore?"

CHAPTER SIX

Loud pounding awoke Billy. "Come on, boys, rise and shine," he heard Henry growl through the thin door.

Billy jumped up and stubbed his toe on a piece of furniture in the dark. "Ow!" he said limping to open the door. He was met by Henry's grim face.

Henry stepped into the room and let up the window shade, flooding the room with early morning sunlight. Zeke opened his eyes. "What's going on?" he asked sleepily.

"Up and at 'em, boy, we got things to do. You two get dressed and go on down to the restaurant and order up some breakfast—and order some for me, too. I already paid the hotel clerk for your room. I'm going over to the general store and pick up a few things and I'll meet you for breakfast. We'll get the horses after we're done." Then he was gone.

"This bed sure feels good," Zeke said pulling the covers up around his neck.

"I could have used a few more hours myself," Billy said, "but if we don't get down to that restaurant there'll be the devil to pay. Don't want to start the day off getting the old man mad at us."

Zeke threw the covers off and jumped out of bed in a single motion.

Billy filled the basin on the bureau with water from the porcelain pitcher, and quickly shaved while Zeke pulled on his pants and shoes.

"Pa never let me use a razor," Zeke said. "I went to the barber every Wednesday and Saturday for a shave."

"I know," Billy said.

"What do you think I should do?"

"Well, we ain't got time for you to go to no barber." There was a long pause as Zeke stared at his uncle. "And I ain't going to shave you, if that's what you're thinking."

"No, I was thinking maybe I should wait and see if we don't come to some other town when we have time for me to get a shave."

"We could be on the trail for a long time yet, and there may not be any barbers where we're going, so unless you're planning on growing a beard, you better learn how to shave yourself."

Zeke pondered that for a moment or two, then asked if he could use his uncle's razor. Billy nodded.

Zeke lathered up his face real good and had only taken a few strokes with the razor when he let out a yelp and grabbed for a towel. Blood flowed freely down his right cheek into the white cream. He held the towel in place not wanting to see any more blood flow.

Billy let out a whoop. "Boy, you're supposed to scrape them whiskers off—not dig 'em out by the root." He shook his head, still grinning. "You got to be one of the bravest men around to use a straight razor knowing you're just going to carve yourself up with it." He sat down on the bed and watched as Zeke held the towel in his left hand and crossed his right over and scraped away at the left side of his face.

Zeke didn't see what was so damn funny about it. His face

hurt and he had only just started. Slowly he pulled the razor down the left side when it caught again and a sharp pain shot through his left cheek. "Damn it to hell!" he bellowed. When he looked in the mirror again he saw that blood was now flowing on both sides of his face.

Billy got up again. "I can't bear to watch anymore of this," he said. "I'll see you outside." He left still grinning as he closed the door behind him.

Very carefully he finished shaving, not being too particular about making it a close shave, but still gashed himself several more times. The towel was a mess of red blotches and foamy cream; his face was a mixture of blood and lather smeared all over, and resembled a bizarre strawberry shortcake.

Zeke then rinsed all the remaining lather off into the basin and inspected the damage. He had four red, swollen gashes and several smaller red blotches where he'd only nicked himself. In some places the whiskers had been cut close, while in others patches of hair stuck out here and there. His face resembled a field of grass after a herd of cattle had finished with it.

Zeke put on his shirt and joined Billy outside the hotel. Already people moved about on the street and wagons were lined up at the general store awaiting their owners inside. The air smelled much cleaner and fresher than it had when they arrived the night before. Zeke always wondered why mornings were like that.

The restaurant had about ten tables of various sizes, most of them occupied. It was a homey place with gingham curtains and a scrubbed wooden floor. No sooner were they seated than a smiling blond woman of about twenty-five came over with a pot of coffee and two mugs. She had smooth skin, full breasts and a tight waist.

"I can see why this place is so crowded," Billy said.

37

She placed the mugs on the table and filled them to the brim.

"We'll need another cup; my pa will be here directly," Billy said.

She smiled again and said, "Whatever you say, cowboy." Then she turned and saw Zeke. "My word! Did you do something to get the barber mad at you?"

Zeke flushed a deep crimson.

"No, believe it or not, he did that to himself. Saw it with my own eyes just a few minutes ago," Billy said, thoroughly enjoying Zeke's misery.

"If I were you I think I'd seriously consider growing a beard," she said shaking her head sympathetically. Then she looked back at Billy. "You boys want something to eat?"

"What do you say, Zeke? Scrambled eggs, ham, biscuits with honey? That all right with you?" Billy asked. Zeke nodded his approval. "We'll have three orders of that," Billy said to her.

A few minutes later Henry arrived. "Did you order for me?"

Billy nodded. "Should be here in a few minutes. The waitress will be right back with some coffee for you."

"Well, eat up because we've got ground to make up on those two."

"Where do you think they're at?" Zeke asked.

"I figure they're still heading west, and they got a full day's head start on us, so they're probably near Abilene. We need to close the gap today. No matter, though, we'll catch them." He looked over at Zeke. "Say, what'd you do to your face?"

∽

Thirty minutes later they were back on the trail, moving west out of Junction City. There were no tracks to follow, so they kept the sun at their backs and their eyes open.

"How far ahead you figure they are?" Billy asked his father.

"Well, that depends," Henry said. "If they think someone's after them they'll keep going so as to put as much distance behind them as they can. But if they're feeling secure, they'll stop running and hole up somewhere."

The endless prairie passed in mile after monotonous mile. A breeze rippled the knee-high grass as Zeke followed the two riders ahead of him. The sun rose toward its zenith and brought rising heat with it. Already his hatband was damp with sweat, but at least the sun was still behind them.

Zeke pondered the approaching confrontation with Ledyard. He disliked the long, painful hours in the saddle pursuing the outlaw, and he felt queasy at the thought of actually seeing him again. How would he act? Zeke didn't want to show fear in front of his grandfather, but he didn't know what would happen, and the uncertainty gnawed at him. What if Ledyard killed Grandpa and Uncle Billy both? Then what? Would he have to fight Ledyard by himself? Would he get shot down, too, or worse, turn tail and run?

Two scenes kept running through his mind. In one, he and Ledyard faced each other in the street, six-guns at the ready. Ledyard would go for his gun, and it always seemed that Ledyard's gun cleared the holster and was leveled at Zeke before he could get his out. There would be a thick cloud of smoke from Ledyard's gun, and then the picture stopped.

He needed to be faster, Zeke thought, and made a mental note to practice his draw when they stopped for lunch.

In the other scene, a scene that ran through his mind almost constantly, they were in Chadwick's and Ledyard pulled his gun and shot Pa. Pa fell to the floor, blood pouring out of his mouth as he struggled to tell Uncle Billy to watch out for him. It was a horrifying scene that made him sick to his stomach every time.

If only he hadn't gone to Ledyard's table. They would have gotten another table in a few minutes. Oh, how he wished he could go back and do it over. If only he hadn't made such a big thing about them taking their table. If only....

Henry turned and looked back over his right shoulder at Zeke. "How you doing back there, Zeke?" he said. "Ain't heard a peep out of you for quite a spell."

"I'm good, Grandpa. Just thinking."

"Sometimes a man can think too much and get confused if he ain't careful," Henry said, then turned back around to the front.

Zeke moved his vest aside and looked down at the six-pointed star on his shirt. What did it really mean? Was it a symbol that he was no longer an eighteen year-old kid, but a real man, or was it just a piece of metal on a young farmer's shirt? How would he react when the moment came and they caught up with Ledyard?

A wave of guilt washed over him. Did he lack the guts to avenge his father's murder? Did he really want to catch up with Ledyard, or deep inside, did he hope that they never did? Was he afraid that next time *he'd* be the one with Ledyard's bullet in him as he lay on the ground with blood pouring out of his mouth?

To Grandpa, the badge was a symbol of all that is good and right. It identified him as a force against evil. So why didn't Uncle Billy feel the same way? He looked upon the badge as though it was something terrible that he couldn't wait to get rid of.

Grandpa's desire to catch Ledyard was absolute. The thought of giving up the chase would never occur to him, nor would he accept such a suggestion from his two "deputies". On the other hand, Uncle Billy had already come right out and said that he'd just as soon be back on the farm and forget the whole thing. So Zeke was somewhere between the two: he wasn't sure he wanted to catch Ledyard, but he wasn't ready to quit, either.

Like a falling leaf tossed by autumn winds, Zeke's emotions changed from one moment to the next, swept along by forces beyond his control. He didn't know who was right, Grandpa or Uncle Billy, but he envied them both for the strength of their convictions.

This was just one of a lifetime of outlaw pursuits for Grandpa, Zeke thought. He did this all the time. Zeke was so confused he didn't know if he could follow through with catching Ledyard, and *he* had killed his father!

The thought of actually staying a lawman and continuing to do this sort of work was more than Zeke could comprehend. Why would someone want to chase killers all the time and put his own life in danger? He looked up ahead at his grandfather. Grandpa ain't afraid of nothing, Zeke thought. That's why he's a United States Marshal.

CHAPTER SEVEN

It was almost noon when they finally stopped for a leisurely meal of biscuits and ham brought from the restaurant in Junction City. Billy was anxious to get started again, but Henry said the horses needed a break.

Once back in the saddle they rode for hours amid nothing but tall grass shimmering across a treeless prairie. Finally, on the horizon, a brown speck appeared that grew to be Abilene. As Henry had suspected, their quarry had given the town a wide berth; no one had seen the two outlaws, including Henry's friend Wild Bill Hickok, the marshal in Abilene.

That night Zeke fell asleep in his hotel room thinking of matched pearl-handled six-guns worn backwards in their holsters. How could he draw them that way, he wondered?

The three lawmen arose early the next morning, had breakfast in the hotel dining room, then left town. They rode in silence for the rest of the morning taking regular breaks, then stopped for a quick meal near a creek under the shade of some cottonwoods.

The horses grazed nearby, and Zeke got in some practice draws while Billy and Henry watched. It came natural enough to him, but no matter how fast he got, he wanted to be quicker. Henry must have read his mind as he watched his grandson practicing.

"You're fast enough. The thing to remember is to hit what you're aiming at. Make your first shot count—you may not get a second one."

Zeke squared off against a sapling near the creek they were stopped at. He was perhaps twenty feet from it when he drew and fired. The middle of the tree exploded into chunks of bark and wood chips.

"That's the idea," Henry said nodding his approval.

Billy jumped up, pushing his plate of beans to the ground. He lined up in front of the same tree. Bending his knees slightly, he went for his gun. His hand was a blur, the .44 fired once, and a tiny branch fell to the earth. Billy turned to look at his father.

"Not bad," Henry said, "but you've been shooting a lot longer than the boy has."

Billy's face drew into a tight scowl. Without a word he picked up the near-empty plate of beans and washed it out in the creek. Then he filled his canteen and mounted up. "Well, are we going or ain't we?" he asked.

The Great Plains stretched before the three lawmen as they moved steadily westward, the sun straight overhead. Seemingly endless, the land rolled gently, tall grass shimmering in the midday sun.

It was well past noon when they came upon a lone farmhouse. They hadn't dismounted or even hailed the house when an elderly man appeared on the porch, shotgun at the ready. "What do you want?" he growled.

Henry held his hands up, palms facing the man. "Just some information, friend. You seen two riders, a thin one and a husky fellow?"

The man stepped closer, still on his porch. "What do you

know about them?"

Henry eased his vest aside, displaying the badge. "They're wanted for murder."

The man lowered his weapon. "They came through here early yesterday. Swapped horses with me. Took my best two and left me theirs." He looked down and shook his head. "Their horses were plumb wore out. They won't be any use to me for at least a week."

"Why'd you swap then?" Zeke asked.

The man's eyes shifted quickly to Zeke, and he snickered. "You think I had a choice?"

"They head west?" Henry asked.

The man nodded.

"Thanks for your time," Henry said. He turned to leave.

"Marshal?" the man said.

Henry turned back. "Yes?"

"I figure they're heading for Ellsworth, or at least, thereabouts."

"That thought occurred to me," Henry said.

"What I mean is, there's a water tower about three miles from here. The train stops there everyday around two o'clock. You could catch it and be in Ellsworth later this afternoon. You'd make up ground on those two and rest your horses at the same time."

"You reckon those two outlaws caught the train there yesterday?" Billy said.

"Not unless they knew about the water stop. They'd have to be from around here or else stumble upon the depot by accident. And I can tell you they ain't from around here."

Henry tipped the brim of his hat. "Much obliged."

The three lawmen were waiting at the water stop when the train pulled in. They boarded their horses in an empty cattle car and then found seats with the passengers. According to the conductor a different crew had worked yesterday's train, so he didn't know if the two outlaws had been aboard or not.

About an hour's daylight was left when they came upon a fair-sized settlement. They entered a wide street divided down the middle by railroad tracks. Most of the establishments were one or two-story wooden structures, and the buildings faced each other across the railroad tracks. They even saw a brick building with a sign that read

MINNICK AND HOUNSON'S DRUG STORE on the other side of the tracks.

Horses tied to hitching rails paid no heed when they occasionally stepped into one of the myriad piles of horse manure that dotted the street and fouled the air.

"Look at all the mud," Zeke said.

"Yeah, they must have had a real downpour here today," Billy said. "Glad we missed it."

The train eased to a stop at the depot and the three men got off the train and retrieved their horses.

They rode at a walk past the Ellsworth *Reporter* Office and Zeke eyed the large, neatly lettered sign reading GRAND CENTRAL HOTEL on the building next to it.

"You ever been to Ellsworth before, Grandpa?" Zeke asked.

"It's a fairly new town, but I have been here a few times. More than I'd like to, actually."

"There's a livery stable up ahead on the right," Billy said. "Why don't we leave the horses and get something to eat?"

They boarded their horses, and the livery owner, Mr. Nagle, recommended a hotel called John Kelly's American House for supper and a room for the night.

The three men crossed the railroad tracks to the south side of the street, walked past Nick Lentz's Saloon and entered the American House, which was next door. Zeke noticed that on the west side of the hotel was Jake New's Saloon.

The three men crossed the railroad tracks to the south side of the street. The American House was between Nick Lentz's Saloon on the east, and Jake New's Saloon on the west.

In the hotel's restaurant they got a table by a window that looked onto South Main Street. It was a nicer restaurant than Chadwick's. The lower half of the windows had red-checked gingham curtains affording diners a measure of privacy from the passerby on the woodwalk outside. As usual, Zeke was ravenous. The smell of food cooking in the kitchen made his mouth water and he could almost taste the steak and fried potatoes he was about to order.

Just as the waiter came over, there was a loud crash; Zeke jerked his head toward the sound and pushed the curtains away to peer outside. A man had been thrown through the window of Nick Lentz's Saloon and now lay in the mud amidst shards of broken glass. Two hulking men came out of the saloon and stared down at him. People crowded out onto the woodwalk or stood in the doorway peering out.

One of the men grabbed the fallen man by the shirt and pulled him to his feet. Then he drove a large fist into the man's face, which seemed to explode with the impact. He fell back into the mud, not moving. The second man leaned in and drove a boot into the victim's midsection.

"You got any law in this town?" Henry asked the waiter.

"Yes sir," the waiter said. "Just this month got us our first town marshal. He's probably out on his farm just outside of town. Do you need the marshal for something?"

"*I* don't, but he sure does," Henry said jerking his thumb toward the man lying in the street. "We'll be back in a few minutes. Keep our table for us," Henry said to the waiter. Then he turned to Zeke and Billy. "Come on, let's go."

"Where we going?" Zeke asked. "He said they got a town marshal."

"You see him around anywhere?" Henry's voice had a hard edge to it. "We're lawmen ain't we?" he said, glaring at Zeke.

They stepped into the street. "You men! Hold it right there, he's had enough," Henry said.

All eyes turned to Henry, who stopped about five feet from the two men standing in the street. Men were three-deep on the woodwalk, and others leaned out of the batwing doors of the two saloons flanking the American House.

Zeke's heart raced. He stood two paces behind and to the left of his grandfather. Billy stood at Zeke's right. The men seemed huge to Zeke. One of them had long, stringy dark hair. The other had flowing blond hair and stared at Henry with steely blue eyes. Zeke didn't envy his grandfather's position, and wondered what he would do next.

"Mind your own business, old man!" the dark-haired one said.

"This is my business. I'm Marshal Henry McNichol."

"We already got us a marshal. You got no authority here," the blond one said.

"Reckon I didn't make myself clear," Henry said calmly. "I ain't no town marshal. I'm a United States Marshal, and I got authority everywhere." Henry looked the two men over. "Suppose we head over to the jail. I believe you two need to learn some respect for the law."

"Suppose you go jump in the lake, old man," the dark-haired one said.

Zeke's mouth went dry.

Henry drew his .44 Remington. "I'm through fooling with you two. Now move!"

The dark-haired one held his hands in the air. "We ain't armed. What are you going to do, old man? Shoot us in front of all these witnesses?" He took a step forward, his hands moving toward Henry.

With a quick move, Henry stepped forward to meet him and at the same time raised his gun high into the air. Then he slammed the barrel down over the man's head. His eyes rolled back, his knees buckled and he crashed to the ground splattering mud onto Henry's boots. Without hesitating, Henry took another step forward, pushed the .44's barrel under the second man's nose and cocked the hammer. The loud click of the hammer coming to rest in firing position was heard up and down the suddenly quiet street. "You ready to go to jail yet?"

"Don't shoot, mister. I'm peaceable," the blond-haired one said, his hands in the air.

Still keeping the gun in the man's face, Henry turned toward the men crowded around. Pointing to the victim with his free hand, Henry said, "Why don't some of you men take this one inside and see if you can help him? A few more of you can drag this other one over to the jail."

A flood of relief washed over Zeke when the men obeyed his grandfather. With the help of one of the townsmen, they crossed the railroad tracks and found the brick courthouse and jail on North Main, a block east of Arthur Larkin's hotel. They put the two men in a cell; the dark-haired one had come to and was rubbing his head. The cell key was on the marshal's desk and Henry took it with him after locking the cell door. Once outside again, Zeke saw that the townspeople had followed them down to the jail. Zeke didn't know what to make of that, but it didn't seem to bother Henry at all. "When your marshal gets in tell him I've got his key and that I'm in the dining room at the American House," Henry said to no one in particular.

Fifteen minutes later they were eating supper. Zeke ate like a starving animal, his appetite whetted by all the excitement. His grandfather seemed to have already put the incident out of his mind.

"Didn't you feel strange breaking up a fight when you don't know any of the men involved or what the fight was about?" Billy asked.

"The fight was over before I got there. The man was on the ground and made no move to get up. I wouldn't let a man beat an animal that was down; why would I let a man do that to another man? Besides, I never cared much for two against one."

"But what if the other man started it and we jailed the wrong ones?" Billy asked.

"First of all, I don't care which one started it. I'll let the town marshal figure all that out. I just wanted to restore the peace. I can't have two men kill someone out in the street in front of the whole town. What kind of a lawman would I be if I did that?

"And secondly, I didn't put them in jail for fighting. I put them in jail for not obeying my orders after I identified myself as a United States Marshal. I won't tolerate people who don't respect the law."

Zeke said, "Those two were big and tough. I can't believe you just waded in there like you done."

"Big muscles don't make a man tough. It's what's up here that makes a man tough," Henry said tapping his forehead.

CHAPTER EIGHT

Their conversation was interrupted by the arrival of a tall, lean man of about thirty, who stopped at their table. He had brown hair, a bushy moustache, and a gaudy badge that was highly polished and pinned to the outside of his vest. He stuck his right hand out and smiled at Henry. "I understand I owe you a debt of thanks. I'm Albert Steele, the marshal here in Ellsworth."

Henry shook hands with him, then introduced his deputies. "Won't you join us? We're just having a late supper," Henry said.

"Thank you, I believe I will. I was just sitting down to supper when I was summoned back to town. It's cold now."

Henry handed back the cell key. "I don't know what the ruckus was about, but if you ask around I'm sure you can get some answers," Henry said.

Steele nodded. "I'll take care of it. Obliged for your help." He signaled for the waiter and ordered supper.

"So what brings you to Ellsworth?" Steele asked.

"We're after two men. One of them killed an unarmed man."

"What'd they look like? Do you know their names?"

"The killer's name is Ledyard. Don't know if that's his first name or his last name. He's a tall, lean one with dark hair," Henry said. He turned to his son. "What was he wearing? Did you notice?"

Billy shrugged. "No, I can't say as I did."

"He has a scar on his right cheek," Zeke said making a diagonal slashing motion near his right cheek.

Henry said, "The other one was shorter and had a big belly."

"He was wearing a plaid shirt," Billy said.

"What color?" Henry asked.

Billy shrugged again. "Green, I think—or maybe it was red."

"That sounds like two men I saw leaving town early this morning," Steele said. "They was a ways off, but it could have been them. I know everybody in these parts, so I took notice when I saw riders leaving town just as I was coming in." His supper arrived and he took a forkful of meat. "Of course, I didn't know they were wanted or I would have stopped them. I ain't seen any posters."

"It just happened," Henry said. "Besides, I think we can catch them ourselves."

"Yeah, the man he killed was my father," Zeke said. "We're all in the same fam—." He stopped cold. His grandfather was staring at him with fire in his eyes.

"All in the same what?" Steele asked.

Zeke refused to look at him, but kept his eyes on his dinner plate. No one said anything.

"You know," Steele said breaking the awkward silence, "I didn't get a wire on these outlaws, either."

"Didn't send a wire," Henry said.

"We got a telegraph just up the street; you could alert all

the lawmen in the area. Who knows, you just might find your killers sitting in a jail up ahead waiting for you."

"Ain't going to be any wire," Henry said.

Steele studied him for a few moments. "So that's how it is," he said at last.

"That's how it is."

Steele shrugged. "Suit yourself."

Zeke turned a puzzled face to his uncle, who shook his head slightly for him to remain quiet.

"I can help you some," Steele said. "They were heading west when I saw them this morning."

"That figures," Henry said. "We've been trailing them west since Wattersville."

"What I was going to say was that the trail forks about five miles west of town. If they stay to the right they'll keep heading due west and run into Hendersonville. If they go left they'll veer southwest to Rockford."

"How far away is Hendersonville?" Billy asked.

"About ten miles past the fork."

"What's past Hendersonville?" Henry said.

"If you keep heading west another fifty miles you'll hit Hays City. Past that is Buffalo Station, Fort Wallace, then Colorado."

"What about Rockford?"

"That's about ten miles southwest of the fork. From there it's another fifty-five miles to the Arkansas River and Great Bend, then another seventy-five miles or so south to Medicine Lodge; just beyond that's the Indian Territory."

"You said south from Great Bend," Billy said. "What if they kept going southwest out of Great Bend?"

"That's another possibility," Steele said. "Fort Dodge is about eighty miles southwest of Great Bend; I doubt they want to go there. Another fifty or so would put them in No

Man's Land. That might interest them." He eyed Henry. "You know about No Man's Land?"

Henry nodded. "How do you know all this?" he asked. "Ain't a lot of people living in those parts, and that's dangerous country for a man to be traveling."

"That it is, for a fact. I used to drive a stage on the Santa Fe Trail. Got to know the territory firsthand."

"All right, let me get this straight," Henry said. He took the sugar bowl and put it in the center of the table. "Let's say this is Ellsworth." Then he took the salt shaker and moved it about a foot away. "This is Hendersonville." Then he placed the pepper shaker about eight inches away in another direction so that they formed a triangle. "And this is Rockford." Henry studied it for a minute. "Is there a trail connecting Hendersonville to Rockford?" he asked looking at the salt and pepper shakers on the table.

Steele shrugged. "If there is it ain't much of one. Probably just enough to mark the way to go."

"That's all we need," Henry said. "Appreciate the information, Albert."

Steele nodded to him, then pushed the last of the meat into his mouth and drained his water glass. "I got to be getting home, gentlemen. Nice to have met you, and I thank you again for your help earlier this evening. I just started this month and am still learning the ropes. The town said they'd let me hire a few deputies to help me out, but it hasn't been approved yet and I can't be everywhere at once."

He seemed embarrassed and looked down at his plate. "I'm just a farmer, really. When the town said they wanted to hire a marshal, I figured I could use the extra money, what with a wife and three kids and all. I was hoping to spend most of my time on the farm, but I've been needed in town a lot more than they said I would."

He paused for a few seconds, absent-mindedly stubbing the toe of his boot on a dead cigarette butt at his feet. When he spoke again it was as if he was finally admitting what he'd feared all along. "I'm afraid being a lawman in Ellsworth is a full-time job." He stubbed at the cigarette butt again, then said in a soft voice, as if to himself, "I can't keep neglecting my farm."

He looked up and managed a weak smile. "Well, good luck catching those two men you're after," he said rising to his feet. He pushed a coin under his plate and shook hands with Henry. Then he was gone.

So Marshal Steele had no experience, either, Zeke thought. It must be tough for him upholding the law here with no help. "What advice would you give to a new lawman like Mr. Steele, Grandpa?" Zeke asked.

"From what I know of this town, the only advice I'd give Steele would be to stick to farming."

Zeke's laughter was cut short by Henry's icy glare.

"What do you think we should do, Pa?" Billy asked. "Figure they kept going west?"

"If that's the wrong fork we'd put them behind us," Henry said. "We could keep going until we hit the ocean without running into them. It is a good sign that they stayed in town last night. Most likely they don't think anyone's after them."

"What should we do, then?" Billy said.

Henry glanced out the window as dusk settled over Ellsworth. "We'll ride out to the fork in the morning and see if we can't pick up their trail; it's too dark to do it now."

"Come on, let's get out of here," Billy said.

"I believe I'll have another cup of coffee, then go on up to bed," Henry said. "I don't suppose you boys are ready to turn in yet?"

"We thought we'd go have a beer or two," Billy said. "We'll see you in the morning."

"Well, don't stay up too late. And stay away from them saloon gals."

Billy went up to the hotel room, but Zeke went to Seitz's Drugstore at the corner of North Main and Douglas and bought a bottle of liniment. When Zeke returned, they decided to go to next door to Jake New's Saloon instead of Nick Lentz's next to the hotel on the other side, since Lentz's had a large broken window.

On the way down, Zeke said, "What did Grandpa mean when he told the marshal he wouldn't send a wire? Why not?"

"He meant he didn't want anybody's help. He aims for us to catch these killers ourselves."

Zeke nodded, but didn't understand. Why not get some help?

They had reached the wood walk in front of Jake New's Saloon. Piano music and tobacco smoke spilled over the top of the bat wing doors and into the street.

With a big grin, Billy took a step toward the entrance but Zeke's hand on his arm stopped him. "Can I ask you another question, Uncle Billy?"

"What is it?"

"You remember when Grandpa hit that man over the head with the barrel of his gun?"

"Yeah, he buffaloed him."

"Buffaloed him?"

"That's what it's called when you whack a man over the head with the barrel of a six-gun."

"Why not use the butt of the gun—kind of like hitting him with a hammer? That seems more natural to me," Zeke said.

"Let's try it. Get your gun out and cover me with it." Billy put his hands in the air while Zeke drew the Colt and pointed it at his uncle. "Now you're going to hit me over the head with the butt of it," Billy said.

Zeke transferred the gun to his left hand and grabbed the barrel with his right. He was just raising it above his head when he realized that he was now staring down the barrel of Billy's six-gun.

"Any more questions, or can I get a beer now?" Billy said.

CHAPTER NINE

Pitch black. Utter darkness all around. Couldn't see a thing. Where was he? Hard to breathe. What's happening?

Then he heard it: a loud, prolonged wail of agony. Ma! Got to help her! No, stay where you are. Nothing you can do. Moldy dampness enveloped him, closing in, suffocating him. Struggling mightily, he managed a breath of dank, stale air.

Another long, tortured scream. They're killing her! Get out of this hole and do something! But he couldn't. As if stuck in a shallow vat of glue, his feet wouldn't move. Clawing blindly at the crumbling dirt, he strained for the cellar door, but couldn't reach it. Sweat beaded his face as he vainly struggled to raise his leaden feet and continued to claw at the walls, but still he couldn't reach the door. Finally, he sagged back down and lay in the boggy darkness at the bottom of the pit. More screams. Stop the screams. He must stop the screams! He jammed his hands over his ears, but the cries of agony persisted. Would it ever stop?

Another scream, different this time. Who was screaming?

"Uncle Billy! Wake up! You're having a nightmare."

He came awake with a start to find Zeke shaking him roughly by the shoulders in the dark hotel room. Then a match was struck and Zeke lit the kerosene lamp on the nightstand. Billy looked down at the crumpled covers at the foot of the bed where he'd kicked them off. What the hell?

Zeke brought over a glass of water. "Same bad dream again?" he asked.

Still groggy, Billy rose to a sitting position on the edge of the bed and nodded that it was. He looked awful. His face was drained, his hair a rumpled mess, his nightshirt soaked with sweat. He took a big drink from the water glass, shook his head and laughed ruefully. "Ain't this something, though? I got my pa judging me in the daytime, and I do it to myself at night."

"Judging you for what?"

Billy just shook his head. He ran his hand through his hair and stared at the floor.

"Does it have anything to do with why you moved in with me and pa after your ma died?" Zeke asked. "You know, when Grandpa turned you out of the house?"

Billy sighed, then took another drink of water. "I told you before I don't want to talk about it."

"Something's eating you up inside. Why don't you let it out?"

Billy continued to stare at the floor. Long seconds passed and it seemed he would never speak.

Zeke eyed the empty glass and said, "Do you want some more water, Uncle Billy?"

Billy ignored the question, as if he hadn't heard it. Several more seconds passed and he continued to stare at the floor, the empty glass in his hand. A sad, pained look came over his face and the full force of the burden he carried in his heart showed in his expression. Billy spoke softly, measuring his words as the horror danced before him once again in his mind's eye. He spoke as though Zeke wasn't there.

"I was twelve years old when they came. We were living in Texas. Ma was out in the front yard doing laundry in a big barrel. I was about a hundred yards away carrying two buckets of water from the creek when a band of Indians came over a ridge and swept down onto our land whooping and screaming"...

∼

... The Comanche came at a full gallop as they lay low on the backs of their horses, the wind whipping their long, black hair.

Horrified, Rebecca frantically looked around until she spotted her son and called out, "RUN, BILLY, RUN. GET INTO THE CELLAR. NOW!"

Dropping the buckets, he turned and ran for the shelter. Just before he passed the corner of the house he saw his mother reach for the rifle on the porch.

Driving their hooves into the earth, the Indian ponies surged forward like rolling thunder. The cries of the savages grew louder and Billy's heart pounded deep in his chest and his head swam with confusion as he reached the storm cellar. What to do?

Suddenly he heard shots from the front of the house. The loud report of the rifle panicked him and he threw open the twin doors to the cellar. In two quick bounds he was at the bottom looking up at the open doors. Terror-stricken, he reached up and slammed them shut almost hitting himself in the head. The faint light streaming in through cracks in the doors allowed him to find the board to bar the doors from the inside. Straining to see in the dim light, he rammed the thick board home between the two inside handles so the doors couldn't be opened from outside.

Billy sat back pressing himself into the cool, damp dirt as far as he could. He heard another shot, this one muffled by the hole he was in. More whooping and yelling, closer now. He couldn't breathe. Suddenly they were at the storm doors, trying to pry them open, then pounding on the boards.

He closed his eyes and pressed his hands against his ears. "Go away, go away, go away," he whispered over and over, sobbing. He felt that at any moment the doors would fly open and he would be dragged out, or worse, killed where he sat, run through with a lance. He could almost feel the sharpened point penetrate his stomach and then the push as the wooden shaft was driven through him.

Tears ran down his face and he stifled his sobs by jamming his forearm against his mouth. The pounding on the storm doors ceased. Then he heard the long, tortured cry of a woman in agony. Her single scream seemed to go on forever.

The Indians whooped and yelled some more. Then it was quiet. Billy sat deep in the corner of the black hole, unable to move. He strained his ears, but heard nothing.

It was getting warmer. He wanted to get out and look around, but still he was unable to move. Where was pa? He should have been back from the McIntire place by this time. Several minutes went by and it grew hot inside the cellar. Sweat poured down his face and soaked his shirt. Still he could not move.

Suddenly there was more pounding on the storm doors. "Billy, open the doors! It's me, Pa!"

Billy scrambled up and pulled the board out of the handles and pushed the doors open.

"Come on out of there, boy, before you roast alive," Henry

thundered. Billy stared into the wild eyes of his father and couldn't move. A strong arm grabbed him and pulled him up. Billy stepped out of the cellar and jumped forward a few steps reflexively in response to the searing heat at his back.

He turned to face a wall of fire. Orange-red flames fanned by the wind off the prairie engulfed the entire house. The vice-grip on his arm pulled him toward the front of the house. "Come on, boy, I want to show you something," Henry said.

The front yard came into view as they rounded the side of the house. His mother lay on her back, a bloody lance sticking straight up from where she'd been impaled through her stomach. The grip pulled Billy closer. The top of her head was gone. The sandy hair on top was replaced by a smear of dried blood clumped with torn skin and patches of hair.

"She was alive when they scalped her," Henry said.

Billy's stomach knotted and he turned away and vomited. Woozy, he wanted to sit down, but still the grip on his arm held him fast.

"Why didn't you help her?"

"I wanted to. I ran to her, but she told me to get in the cellar."

"You should have stayed with her."

The boy stood silent, staring at his dead mother's mutilated body. Several seconds passed before he spoke. "It all happened so fast. I didn't know what to do, and then Ma was yelling at me to get in the cellar. So I did. There was nothing I could do."

"You could have stayed with her. You could have fought by her side."

"We only had the one rifle. I'd be dead, too."

Henry had continued to stare at his dead wife and burning house as he spoke to his son. "It happens out here. I could be proud of a son who stood by his mother and fought the

Comanche." He had turned to face Billy. "Any boy who would hide in a hole in the ground and leave his mother to fight the Comanche by herself is no son of mine...."

∼

... Billy reached for the water pitcher, filled his glass, then took a long drink. He faced his nephew. "Pa never threw me out, but he stopped talking to me. I got the message soon enough, and when your ma offered to take me in, Pa didn't object. That's when I knew I had to leave."

"But what did Grandpa expect you to do when the Indians came? What's he judging you for?"

"For hiding in the ground instead of dying alongside my mother when the Comanche attacked."

"I ain't heard Grandpa say a word to you about it the whole trip."

"Zeke, every time that man looks at me he's passing judgment."

"But I still don't understand."

Slowly, Billy rolled back into bed and pulled the covers up. "Turn out the light, Zeke, and get some sleep. We got a long day ahead of us."

Obediently, Zeke turned out the lamp. He lay quietly for a few moments, then said, "I've had the same nightmare twice since we left Wattersville. We're in Chadwick's Restaurant and Pa turns around just as Ledyard raises his gun to shoot. I try to warn him by yelling, but I'm too late. The gun roars twice and I see Pa fall to the floor with the two holes in his chest gushing blood. It's horrible." He looked over in the direction of his uncle in the darkness. "The same dream twice in less than a week. And I think about it all the time when we're out on the prairie, or when I'm lying awake in bed. Does it ever stop?"

"I don't know, Zeke. I wish I could tell you that it would, but I've been having the same nightmare off and on for sixteen years." He paused for a moment, then spoke so softly Zeke could barely hear him. "Sometimes I wish I had died with her."

CHAPTER TEN

The trail they followed was nothing more than a few wagon wheel ruts and worn grass where horses had beat out a tattered stripe. The searing heat of the midmorning sun bore down on them out of a cloudless blue sky. Zeke's shirt was already soaked through, and beads of sweat stood out on his face and neck. He reached for his canteen and took a long swallow feeling the warm water wash over his dry mouth and throat.

His legs and buttocks chafed with each step again today. This morning he'd rubbed liniment over the raw skin for the first time. It had burned like the dickens, but his legs and butt didn't hurt as much as they had the day before. Maybe the liniment had worked, or maybe he was just getting used to long hours in the saddle. Either way, he sure hoped his legs would stop hurting soon.

He thought of the farm back in Wattersville. Days like this he'd be out in the field and he'd peel his shirt off and let the sun bake him as he worked. He didn't mind the way his body poured out sweat all day long. He'd just keep drinking out of the big canteen he always carried with him and work all the harder. The end of the day would find him tired and yet invigorated, caked with dirt and yet feeling cleansed somehow. He wished he was back there, working with Pa and Uncle Billy, the three of them making the farm a success and looking forward to their weekly dinner in town.

A great sadness washed over Zeke. Not the devastation he had felt in Wattersville that made him bawl uncontrollably, but the empty kind of sadness that comes with knowing things will never be the same again, no matter what. He'd never see Pa again. Not in this life, anyway. Tears welled up and he stifled a sob.

His grandfather's waving arm brought him back to the present. Henry was looking back at him, signaling for him to move up. A few quick strides and Zeke's horse had pulled up alongside Henry's sorrel.

"I got a feeling we're going to run into those fellows today," Henry said. "I've seen you practicing your draw. It's gotten so you're right quick with it. How's the accuracy coming? Can you hit what you're aiming at on a regular basis?"

"Yeah. To tell you the truth, Grandpa, using a gun seems pretty easy to learn."

"You mean drawing and shooting is easy to learn. That's 'cause you got McNichol blood in you same as me and Billy. Still, drawing and shooting at trees is not the same as shooting a man.

"Now remember, we ain't in Wattersville anymore. This territory's full of outlaws, Indians, and all sort of drifters that'll shoot you in the back for your horse or your gun. I'm going to keep an eye on you like I've been doing, but you got to learn to look out for yourself, too. Don't be too trusting of people you meet, and if the need arises, don't hesitate to use your gun. That's what you got it for and why you've been practicing with it." He looked at his grandson to be sure his message had sunk in.

A half hour later they arrived at the fork in the trail. The path to the left was narrower and not nearly as worn. Stunted grass, hoofprints, and a few old wagon wheel ruts were the only evidence that others had come before them in any significant number. Zeke welcomed the chance to get down off his horse, even for just a few minutes. Henry and Billy remained in the saddle.

"This is where we split up like I said this morning," Henry said. "If they take the right fork and go through Hendersonville they could be heading toward Hays City and then the mining towns in Colorado. If they take the left fork and head to Rockford they could continue south past Great Bend toward Medicine Lodge and into the Indian Territory. Or, they could veer southwest from Great Bend and head for No Man's Land. Lots of outlaws go there to hide out."

"Instead of splitting up, why don't we all go together?" Zeke asked from where he sat in the grass. "If we don't see them in one town, we can just double back and then try the other one."

"That's a waste of time," Henry replied. "We can check both towns at the same time by splitting up, and then all we have to do is come back together on that trail that connects Hendersonville to Rockford. Then the three of us will go back to whichever town they've been to. If there's no trace of them in either place, the three of us will just keep going west."

"Why do it that way?" Billy asked. "Why don't whoever finds them arrest them? They might get away if we leave them to go and meet out of town first."

"I thought of that, but the risk is too great. It would be safer to have all three of us present when it's time for the arresting to be done."

"Don't tell me a seasoned lawman like you needs me along to help you make the arrest. You expect me to believe you can't handle it by yourself?" Billy said.

"It ain't that at all," Henry replied.

"What is it then? You don't think I can handle it? Is that it?"

"You ain't got no experience in these matters. It would be better if I was along to make the arrest."

"I don't need your help," Billy said. "I've been getting along just fine without it all these years. I sure as hell don't need it now."

"I'm your father! You watch how you talk to me, boy."

"My father. Now there's a joke if ever I heard one."

"What do you mean by that?" Henry said.

"I lost my father sixteen years ago during a Comanche raid." He looked over at Henry with fire in his eyes, and he spoke bitterly as he continued. "You blame me for the loss of your wife in that raid, BUT SHE WAS MY MOTHER!" he screamed at Henry. "You made me feel like it was my fault she died, as though anything I could have done would have made a difference. I was a boy then and I believed you, but I'm not a boy anymore, and I know better. Ma knew it, too; that's why she told me to hide in the storm cellar. You blamed me for her death so you wouldn't have to blame yourself for not being there when we needed you. Well, I'm through being the scapegoat. *I* was in that hole in the ground, not you. *I* was the one who heard her screams as she lay dying with a lance in her leg and a heathen taking her scalp."

Billy was breathing hard as he stopped for a moment and continued to glare at Henry. "I've heard her screams everyday of my life since then, and I hear them in my dreams at night. Yeah, I lost my mother because of that raid, but when you turned me out of the house, I lost my father, too."

Henry replied in a calm voice. "All I ever said was that a

good son, a brave son, would have stood by his mother and fought with her. You didn't do that. You hid in the ground. Nothing you say can change that, and I can see by what you've just said that you ain't learned a thing about being a man since that day, even though you are twenty-eight years old now."

Henry continued, his voice rising. "How come you didn't join up to fight in the war? You were eighteen when it started. Ray couldn't go because his wife was dead and he had little Zeke to look after and a farm to run. But you could have gone. You could have done your duty and joined the Union Army, but instead you stayed home and let other boys fight and die in your place.

"So don't shift the blame for your failures on me," Henry said. "I could never have acted the way you did. Never. No matter what my ma might have said, I would have stayed with her and fought till the end—not hid in a hole."

"I wanted to enlist, but the farm was too much for one man to run," Billy said. "Saving the farm and helping Ray with Zeke were more important to me than some big ruckus a thousand miles away that didn't concern me none anyhow."

Billy glared at his father, then said, "You think I don't know why we're out here? You got Zeke fooled, but you ain't fooling me none. You talk about justice and upholding the law and all that, but that's just a lot of hogwash. You're out here because you take it as a personal insult that some outlaw would have the gall to kill your daughter's husband. You, a United States Marshal, and someone killed your son-in-law.

"And if that ain't enough, you got to drag me and Zeke along as 'deputies'. Deputies, my ass! You want us along so you can have a go at whipping me and Zeke into the kind of men you want us to be. You don't give a hoot-in-hell about either one of us."

"If that's so, then what in tarnation are you doing out

here?" Henry demanded. The vein on his neck was sticking out again, and both he and Billy were red-faced.

"You want to know why I'm out here?" Billy said. "I'll tell you why, but it would be obvious to any other man. When I left your ranch, Ray took me in and made me feel like one of his family. Oh, I know he married Louise, but he didn't have to do what he done. And he was so good about it: he never once resented me being there, and always made me feel like a younger brother. If it hadn't been for him I don't know what would have happened to me.

"Ray made me see the simple joy in a hard day's work, and then seeing the crops come in and the work paying off. He taught me the value of family, but more that anything he made me feel like I belonged somewhere. I don't know that he'd approve of me and his son being out here tracking his killer all over hell, both of us risking our lives trying to do something that won't bring him back no how. But since I knew you'd drag Zeke along I had to come, too, to keep an eye on him. I owe Ray that much."

"You're wasting your time being a farmer, Billy. You should be in politics the way you twist the truth," Henry said. Then his eyes grew hard and his face became like stone. "Now that you got that off your chest, let me tell you how it's going to be. Me and Zeke are going to Hendersonville, and you're going to Rockford. Look around, ask a few questions if need be, and then keep going out of town and we'll meet on the other trail later this afternoon. That will give us time to double back and grab them if they're in either town. If we don't spot them at all, then we can use what daylight is left to keep after them. Maybe we could pick up their trail again."

Then he turned to Zeke, who was still sitting by the tree. "Come on, boy, get mounted up. We're leaving."

"I still say whoever finds them ought to arrest them on the spot," Billy said.

JOHN ALEXANDER

"You do like I told you to do," Henry said.

Billy said nothing, but turned his horse and cantered down the left fork toward Rockford.

Henry yelled to him, "YOU HEAR ME? DO LIKE I TOLD YOU TO DO!"

Billy kept riding without turning to look back.

Zeke watched quietly as his uncle rode out of sight. Then Henry said, "Let's go," and they started off on the right fork to Hendersonville.

They had gone about three miles before Henry broke the awkward silence. Zeke noticed the red was gone from Henry's face, and that he spoke in a surprisingly calm voice. "You probably think I don't care much for Billy. I know Billy thinks I don't. The truth is he's my son and nothing can change that. I'm afraid it's too late for me to help him, but there's still hope for you. Learn as much as you can from me. Watch how I do things and handle people. You got the makings of a fine lawman."

"I don't want to be a lawman, Grandpa. I like being a farmer."

"Nothing wrong with being a farmer, but this country needs more good men to uphold the law. It's men like me that make this land safe for people like your father to settle and build farms."

"My father was shot right inside the town. Where was the law then?" Zeke asked.

"My point exactly. Like I said, this land needs more men to wear badges and keep the peace. I reckon most anybody could work a farm, but it takes a special kind of person to keep the law."

"I don't know. I feel so strange wearing this badge, and the thought of actually performing the duties of a deputy marshal without you or Uncle Billy there with me is something I can't even imagine."

"Anybody who ever wore a star probably felt that way at first. You'll do fine. What I want you to do is not only keep your eyes open for yourself, but for Billy, too."

"For Uncle Billy?"

"I'm afraid for that boy. He's too headstrong to listen to me, and he hasn't got the gumption to survive out here. I see now that is was a mistake bringing him along."

"If you feel that way, why don't you send him back to Wattersville? He's told me he'd rather be back there than out here with us.

"Too risky. I don't want him traveling alone in this country. Like I said, there's outlaws and drifters all over the territory. There's hostile Indians still roaming about these parts, too. I don't suppose you've ever seen what those savages do to a white man they catch alive?"

Zeke shook his head. "No, I ain't."

"Well, I hope you never do." He watched his grandson for a few seconds, then said, "You look upset, Zeke. Something eating at you?"

Zeke hesitated, then said, "It just pains me to hear you talk about Uncle Billy like that, and he talks the same way about you. I wish you two could get along."

"Listen, Zeke, I know how close you are to your uncle—much closer than you are to me, and I can appreciate that. But I want you to understand something that's very important. Don't pay any heed to the way Billy is conducting himself out here. He's going to get killed one of these days the way he's going. I knew he was like that and that's why I wanted him on this trip. I had hoped that I could still make a man out of him, but he's resisting me. I don't want you resisting me, too. It's a rough land out here, and I didn't get to be fifty-five years old by being a darn fool. You watch me and do like I do and not like your uncle does. You hear me, boy?"

The old man was up close to him, his steely eyes boring right through him. "Yes, sir," Zeke said not letting on to his grandfather the turmoil churning within as he struggled with the two conflicting viewpoints he had just witnessed.

He wanted to drop the matter and just leave, but Zeke couldn't do it. After a moment's hesitation he said, "Do you ever just give up the chase because it's too dangerous, or maybe it wasn't that important in the first place?"

Henry gave him a long look. "I see Billy *has* been talking to you."

Zeke dropped his eyes. "Maybe Pa wouldn't want me risking my life chasing after his killer."

"Your pa was a peaceful, law-abiding man, but he never backed down from anyone and he never quit on anything in all the years I knew him. I thought you were just like him. Maybe I was wrong."

Zeke still looked down, not saying anything.

"Anybody can quit and go home, Zeke. Problem is, once a fellow starts quitting on things it becomes a habit right quick. A real man does what needs to be done. You think about the kind of man your pa was, and then decide what kind of a man you want to be."

CHAPTER ELEVEN

Like many of the early establishments in Rockford, O'Brien's Restaurant was a thrown-together wooden structure with a false front. It first opened for business when the town was nothing more than a few pitched tents and two saloons that served the hunters and trappers passing through the area. At the time, O'Brien didn't know how long the town would last, so he opened for business with a few tables and chairs he made himself, and nothing but a dirt floor to put them on.

But the town continued to grow as ranchers moved in, and soon wood-frame buildings began to appear along the town's four intersecting streets. O'Brien's business grew with the fame of his Irish stew and his reputation for serving thick steaks.

Soon the homemade furniture was replaced with twelve sturdy tables and sixty matching chairs he had shipped in from Kansas City. Wooden planking replaced the dirt floor, and he installed a counter near the entrance where diners could look over a selection of cigars, cigarette tobacco and papers, and jars of hard candy while paying for their meals.

The proprietor of this thriving business was Sean O'Brien himself. Fifty-three years old and a bit stooped at the waist, he stood a lean five foot seven. A corncob pipe usually dangled from the right side of his mouth, though he rarely lit the bowl. Instead he clenched it between his teeth so that it bobbed up and down when he talked. A perpetual stubble of gray-flecked whisker covered his hollow cheeks, and no matter the weather, he wore a blue woolen watch cap with the bottom edge rolled up. A white apron hung around his neck and swept down over the front of his body wrapping around the legs and secured by two long ties, which he knotted behind his back.

He moved happily among his lunchtime diners, most of whom were regular patrons, exchanging smiles and handshakes. Only the two strangers sitting at a small table near the front door failed to return his smile when he greeted them and took their lunch order.

Probably a couple of saddle tramps, he thought. Along with hardworking farmers, ranchers, storekeepers, carpenters, and lawmen, the West attracted every kind of human driftwood as well. He just hoped they didn't cause any trouble.

O'Brien did think it a might strange when the thin one asked for a bottle of whiskey with his meal; after all, it wasn't even noon yet. He had to send Thad down to the Bald Eagle to get it since he didn't sell whiskey himself. Not that he had any objection to the request; he had learned long ago that the way to make money was to give the customer what he wanted before he went somewhere else to get it.

O'Brien wandered into the back room of his restaurant where Mrs. Finnegan was busy stirring a big pot of stew. He emerged a few moments later with two heaping bowls, which he placed before the two strangers.

"Hey! What happened to the whiskey? You send that kid to St. Louis for it or what?" the thin one said.

"I'll be damned if I know what's taking the lad so long," O'Brien said. Suddenly he spied Thad as he entered the door and stopped at the table where O'Brien was standing. O'Brien took the full bottle from the boy, then fixed him in a cold stare. "And what may I ask took you so long?"

"Took me so long? I ran all the way there and back," the boy said, surprised at the question. "I don't think I was gone more than five minutes."

"Never mind that now. Get back to your chores," O'Brien told him.

He turned back to his two customers. "If there's anything else you need, let me know," he said, a smile once again on his face.

"A couple of glasses would be nice," the thin one said.

"Oh, yes. Yes, of course," O'Brien muttered, then walked away hoping his face wasn't too red. He returned in a few seconds with the glasses and then made sure to give the table a wide berth as he moved about the room. Something about the way the thin one looked at him made him uneasy. It reminded him of the sailors working the ship on which O'Brien had crossed the Atlantic. They'd as soon bash you over the head with a marlinspike as look at you. He'd learned to avoid such men.

Ledyard watched as his portly dining companion shoveled the stew into his mouth. "Take it easy, Ike. That food ain't going to run away. You eat like a pig at the trough."

"You got to try this stew, Ledyard. It's really good," Ike replied, paying no heed to the insult. Then he filled his mouth again.

Instead of trying the stew, Ledyard reached for the bottle and poured himself a double. Only after he had drained the glass and felt the raw liquid burn through his insides did he pick up his spoon.

"I like this town. What do you say we stay here awhile?"

Ike said between mouthfuls. "I'm tired of being on the move and sleeping on the ground. That hotel bed sure felt good last night."

"We've been here a day already. The horses are rested; we should be moving on."

"I don't think anyone's after us," Ike said. "The town where you shot that farmer probably didn't even have a lawman."

"Quiet, you fool!" Ledyard said, peering around the room to see if anyone was listening. "I swear, sometimes as much comes out of that mouth of yours as goes in."

After furtive glances to the left and right, Ike said, "Aw, nobody was listening. You're just jumpy, that's all."

"You'd be jumpy, too, if it was your neck the hangman was looking for," Ledyard replied, his voice almost a whisper.

"That may be, but like I said, I like this town; besides, I ain't even seen any wanted posters. You want to go out on the prairie and sleep with the snakes again, you go ahead and do it. As for me, I'm staying here a few more days."

Three feet to Ledyard's left a man with his young son stood at the counter paying their bill. The boy had his eye on a glass jar with peppermint sticks in it.

The father handed his tobacco pouch to O'Brien. "Better let me have some more tobacco, and some cigarette paper, too," he said.

The boy tugged at his father's coat sleeve with his left hand. "Daddy, can I have a piece of candy?"

"Naw, you don't need that stuff," the father replied pushing the boy's hand away.

The man and his son had their backs to Ledyard, but he heard them plainly. Interested, he turned around and watched the two as they stood there, only three feet away.

"What is it?" Ike asked.

Ledyard continued to watch the two, and without looking at Ike, waved his hand at him to keep quiet.

"Please, Daddy, can't I have some candy?" the boy asked as he once again tugged at his father's sleeve. He looked to be no more than four years old.

"I said no!" he replied, jerking his sleeve free from the tiny, clutching hand.

The boy looked down at the floor and began to whimper.

"Come on, O'Brien, hurry up with that tobacco," the man said. "I ain't got all day."

"I'm almost done. Keep your shirt on," O'Brien said.

The boy continued to whimper softly. Tears filled his eyes and ran down his cheeks, and he rubbed his eyes with his hands, choking back sobs and trying not to cry.

The father looked down at his son again; then he raised his right hand above his head with the palm up. "Damn it, I'll give you something to cry about!"

The boy saw the hand start down toward him and ducked his face behind his upraised arm and shoulder to fend off the blow.

It never landed.

The hand had only gone about six inches before Ledyard leapt from his seat and grabbed the man by the wrist. The father's startled eyes turned and looked into Ledyard's steeled, angry glare.

"What the hell?"

"You got money to buy tobacco for yourself, but you can't spare a penny so your boy can have some candy?"

"What business is it of yours what I give my son?"

"You're disturbing my lunch. That makes it my business," Ledyard said maintaining his vise-like grip on the wrist.

The father made his other hand into a fist and cocked it behind his ear. "I ought to—"

With lightning reflexes Ledyard let go of the wrist and

grabbed two handfuls of the man's shirt, pulling him closer and fixing him in a stare straight from Hell. "You ain't gonna do shit."

The boy grabbed Ledyard's leg. "Don't hurt my Daddy!"

His eyes still locked on the father and keeping a firm grip with his left hand, Ledyard reached down with his right hand and tousled the boy's hair. "Don't worry, son, I ain't gonna hurt your daddy." Then he paused and added, "Am I?"

"No, no, of course not," the man replied. Then he looked down and reached into his pocket with his left hand and brought out a penny.

"Put your money away!" Ledyard growled. "You had your chance." Then he released his grip on him and turned to O'Brien. "Give the boy whatever he wants and put it on my bill".

O'Brien leaned over the counter with the glass jar so the boy could reach in for himself. The boy took only one peppermint stick and looked sheepishly at his father.

"Go ahead, take some more," Ledyard said.

The boy took four more sticks and looked at his father once again for some sign of disapproval. The father did not look at the boy.

Ledyard put his hand on the boy's shoulder. "Why don't you go outside and have some of your candy. Your daddy will be out in a minute."

The boy looked up at his father again, stuck a peppermint stick into his mouth, then went outside and sat on the bench in front of the restaurant.

"I don't live around here," Ledyard said, "but I'm going to make it my business to come back in a day or two to check on that boy of yours. If I find out that you've laid a hand on him because of what happened here today I'm going to come looking for you." He fixed the man in a hateful stare. "And you don't want me looking for you," he said. Then he moved closer so that their noses were only inches apart. "Have I made myself clear?"

The man swallowed hard and nodded his head up and down.

Ledyard eyed him for a few more seconds, then moved a step back. "Go on, get the hell out of here," he said.

The man took his tobacco pouch and cigarette papers from O'Brien and stepped out of the restaurant.

Ledyard watched the man and his son walk away before he resumed his seat.

"What was that all about?" Ike asked. "Did you know that man from somewhere?"

Ledyard was quiet for a few seconds, his mind somewhere else. At last he said, "I know his son."

CHAPTER TWELVE

"You know his son?" Ike said. "What does that mean?"

Ledyard looked at Ike and wondered if his poor, dumb companion could understand what it was like to have a father who beat his defenseless son whenever he felt like it, usually for no reason.

No, Ike was like all the rest, like all the other people in the restaurant who just sat and watched as the man was about to hit his son. Like all the others had watched on those many occasions so many years ago when his own father used to beat him. Only once in his entire childhood did a stranger ever step in and help him.

Ledyard smiled at the memory. He was about eight at the time. He and Pa were on the way home from selling some cattle. Pa was angry because he didn't get the price he had hoped for, and when they stopped in a small town for lunch pa started in to drinking. Pa drank everyday, but even more so when he was angry about something.

The more Pa drank the more upset he got, and the more upset he got the louder he got. People were looking at them again. Why couldn't he have a good father like other kids did?

Why did he have to have such a mean old man for a father? Why?

Pa was cussing up a storm about how he got cheated, and who the hell did they think they were to cheat him, and on and on. Ledyard remembered trying to calm him down by suggesting maybe Pa ought to eat something so he wouldn't be hungry on the long trip home. Pa yelled that he didn't need no kid telling him when he should eat.

He knew then that his father would hit him. He tried not to cry, but the tears welled up in his eyes and then streamed down his face. He hoped Pa wouldn't see them, but, of course, he did. He was looking down at his plate when the blow landed—a hard slap that knocked him out of his chair and onto the floor.

How many people have experienced such pain and humiliation? Surely not Ike, and probably no one else in this restaurant since no one offered to help the boy.

But someone did help that long ago day when he'd been knocked out of his chair. A cavalry sergeant, outraged at Pa's behavior, picked Ledyard up and wiped a calloused hand across his reddened cheek; then he handed him to another soldier. Without a word, the sergeant whirled around and smashed a fist right in the middle of Pa's face. Pa did a backward flip out of his chair and landed face down on the floor. The sergeant told him he could get his son at the fort the next day—if he was sober.

Pa followed the soldiers all the way back to the fort, and while he himself went inside with the other soldiers, Pa went to the commandant's office and tried to get his son back then and there. There was a lot of yelling and cussing, and Pa had to spend the night in the guardhouse. Pa took him home the next day.

"Where do you know that boy from?" Ike asked.

What could he say to make Ike—or anyone for that

matter—understand what only he and that young boy knew? Would Ike understand if he told him that when the father raised his hand to strike the boy that he himself also felt the fear the boy felt: a fleeting yet very real fear that shot through him as it had so many times before? Would he understand if he told him of the constant beatings that scarred him so badly emotionally that he can't stand for a man to lay hands on him now? He knew that mere words could never convey the feelings he shared with the little boy. Oh, he knew that boy, all right.

Ledyard said, "My father used to beat me for no reason, like that man was going to do to his son. I couldn't allow that to happen; I can't stand someone hitting a kid."

"Didn't your ma do anything to help you?" Ike said.

"She died bringing me into this world. I don't think Pa ever forgave me for that. All the years I was growing up it was just me and him."

"So what finally happened?"

"You know how it is. He got older and I got bigger. One day he hit me and I decided to hit him back: laid him out in the front yard. Then I went inside, got my things and went off to fight in the war."

Ike sat up in surprise. "I didn't know you fought in the war." He paused for a few seconds before continuing. "Which side were you on?"

"Which side? WHAT DO YOU THINK I AM, A DAMN REB?"

Several diners turned to look at him.

"Hell, I was born and raised in Kansas. I joined the Eighth Kansas Infantry."

"All the time we've been together and you never said one word about fighting in the war," Ike said.

"I don't like to talk about it."

Ike finished the last of his stew and wiped the grease from

his scraggly moustache. His face was round and chubby under the worn, wide-brimmed brown hat plopped on his head. He took the bottle from Ledyard and poured himself a double. "You see any action?" he asked at last.

Ledyard shook his head in amazement. "Ike, you are one dumb son of a bitch, you know that? Of course I saw action. You ever hear of Chickamauga? How about Missionary Ridge?"

Ike bristled at the remark and pointed an angry finger at Ledyard. "Don't you ever call me dumb, you hear me? You ain't no smarter than I am. How the hell am I supposed to know what you did in the war?"

Ledyard scowled and looked away. "It's just that thinking about the war gets me all riled up."

"Yeah, well don't get riled at me," Ike said. Neither man spoke, and Ike took a drink of whiskey. Finally he said, "I heard of Chickamauga. I don't believe I ever heard of Missionary Ridge. You fought in those places?"

Ledyard nodded. "Yeah, seems like everybody's heard of Chickamauga, but my troubles started at Missionary Ridge." He took another spoonful of stew, then refilled his whiskey glass. He left the full glass on the table and returned his gaze to Ike. "Missionary Ridge was part of the Chattanooga Campaign."

Ike drew back in surprise. "Chattanooga? I thought that was a big Union victory. What trouble did you have there?"

Ledyard placed a finger on his own right cheek. "That's where I got this scar." He looked past Ike as his mind drifted back in time to a distant battlefield. "We were deployed at the bottom of a steep hill. The Rebs were up on the ridge shooting down at us. We were sitting ducks...."

... Rifle balls whistled all around. Some slammed into the hillside near Ledyard sending up a shower of dry dirt. Every once in awhile a ball found its mark and another Kansas boy's blood darkened the ground amid groans and screams. "Goddamn it, let's *do* something!" he said.

"Yeah, let's kill those sons of bitches!" another one replied. Then he shot off a round at the top of the hill.

"Hold your fire!" a captain on horseback commanded. "You can't hit anything from down here. Save your ammunition for when it can do some good."

Oddly enough, no one spoke of pulling back from their precarious position. It was as though they were waiting their chance to get even with the Rebs for all the men they shot up while they had to wait down at the bottom. Ledyard's own restlessness grew along with that of his fellow soldiers. Finally, one of the men started up the hill.

"Who gave the order to attack?" one man asked.

"The hell with orders," another replied. "Let's get 'em!"

The men surged forward, digging in with their boots and inching their way up the steep hill. Lead balls rained down all around, but still they kept going. Ledyard followed right behind the boots of the man above him, cursing as he doggedly continued up the hill.

Though men were getting shot and falling off the slope, more troops came behind them: the soldiers of the Eighth Kansas Infantry were not to be denied this day. Soon the first wave of Union soldiers crested the ridge and hand-to-hand combat commenced.

By the time Ledyard scaled the top, some of the Rebs were already in full flight; still, many stayed and fought. One charged him, bayonet fixed. Quickly he lowered his rifle and shot the man full in the chest while he was still fifteen feet away.

Another one came at him. He had no time to reload, but

fortunately his bayonet was in place. He parried the Reb's thrust, but the tip of the Reb's bayonet sliced his right cheek as it passed his face. Ledyard then buried his own bayonet deep in the man's chest. It stuck between his ribs and Ledyard struggled futilely to pull it free. All around guns were firing, and he looked up, still pulling desperately on the weapon—he had to get his rifle loose! He could barely see through the thick clouds of discharged gunpowder that assailed his nostrils. Suddenly, out of the corner of his left eye he saw a rifle barrel coming down on him. He tried to raise his left arm to fend off the blow. Too late. There was a heavy thud, then nothing.

It was late afternoon when he awoke. The air was deathly still. All around lay the bodies of Union and Confederate soldiers. He struggled to free his feet, fighting off the waves of nausea that came one after another. His head throbbed, and for a moment he did not know where he was. The right side of his face burned, and when he touched it his hand came away red and sticky.

Then he remembered the fighting and the Rebs running away. We must have won the battle today, he thought. Dazed, he began walking in the hope that he would stumble upon the victorious Union troops. Weak and dizzy, he plodded along the best he could, not knowing where he was headed. Things began to spin, and the ground rushed up to meet him. Landing on his right side, he rolled onto his back, eyes closed and mouth agape.

It was dark when he awoke to the crackling of a campfire and the smell of roasting meat. His mouth watered, and he rose up to look around. His heart sank. Everywhere were gray-clad soldiers.

"Look, he's awake," someone said.

"I still say we should kill him right now," another said.

"That's why you're neither an officer nor a gentleman," a

third voice said. Ledyard looked at the speaker, a captain in his mid-thirties. "Confederate troops don't murder unarmed prisoners," he said. "Now get this man something to eat and drink, then find him a place to sleep. Tomorrow we'll send him back with the other prisoners to wait out the war. . . ."

~

...Ledyard took a big gulp of whiskey before once again turning to Ike. "I spent the rest of the war in a prison camp."

"That must have been rough," he said. "Which one were you in?"

"Andersonville."

The glass fell from Ike's hand, shattering on the floor and drawing the stares of other diners. He paid no heed to the broken glass or the people looking at him. "You were at Andersonville?"

Ledyard nodded. "Over thirty thousand Union prisoners in a camp designed for no more than ten. Food was scarce. I went in weighing a hundred and seventy pounds and came out weighing one-fifteen. I've been able to put back some of the weight, but not much."

Ike stared at him like he was looking at a ghost.

"There was a stream running through the middle of the camp," Ledyard continued. "It was supposed to be for drinking water, but there weren't enough latrines and the water got fouled. We had to drink our own piss. Can you believe that? Ever since I got out I can't drink water without sniffing it first."

Ike screwed up his face and then took a long drink of whiskey straight from the bottle.

"Hey, take it easy, Ike. You're looking at one of the lucky ones; over ten thousand men didn't make it out of that hellhole."

CHAPTER THIRTEEN

"Think I'll head down to the Bald Eagle for awhile," Ledyard said as he and Ike emerged from O'Brien's. "You coming?"

"Naw, the liveryman said my horse is sick or something, so I got to go down there and see what's the matter. I got a couple of things to do after that. I'll see you later, maybe."

"I'll be around," came the reply.

On the other side of town, Billy was just riding into Rockford at the east end of Weymouth Street and kept a sharp eye in case Ledyard was about, but saw no one that even remotely resembled him. Still, he shivered slightly in anticipation. Would he see Ledyard today?

Up ahead, another street intersected with Weymouth. It came in from Billy's right, but dead-ended at Weymouth rather than crossing it, so that the two streets formed a "T". At the base of the "T" was the Town Marshal's Office. Billy stopped there and dismounted. He tethered his horse to a sturdy hitching rail that looked as though it hadn't seen its first winter yet. The wooden door to the marshal's office was also new and squeaked loudly as Billy pushed it open. A boy of about eleven looked up from his sweeping as Billy entered.

Billy nodded to the boy. "Is the marshal around?"

"No sir, he's out at his farm. He'll be back in a spell to see how things are going."

"Is he your father?"

"No, but since I live here in town I keep an eye on things for him and help out with the chores and taking messages. You can wait for him if you like, but it could be some time before he comes back."

Billy thought for a moment, then shook his head. "Maybe you can give him a message for me. I'm a Deputy U. S. Marshal and I'm looking for a killer named Ledyard. He's tall and thin, twenty-five to thirty years old and travels with a short, chubby fellow. You seen anybody like that in town?"

"No, but then I ain't looked, either," the boy replied.

The remark startled and offended Billy, but then he realized the boy was only speaking truthfully and not being rude. "I wanted to let your marshal know I was in town and why, so if he hears I'm snooping about he won't get upset. When he comes in just tell him I'm in town and what I'm doing. I'm going to have a look around and maybe I'll check back here later. Is there a place where a man can get a decent lunch?"

"Marshal Riddick says the best food in town is at O'Brien's. That's at the other end of the street that starts out in front of this office."

"I'm obliged for your help," Billy said, then he turned and walked up the street toward O'Brien's.

It occurred to him that just as he would have no trouble in recognizing Ledyard should he see him, it would be equally easy for Ledyard to recognize *him*. Billy pulled the brim of his hat down low over his forehead. No sense in giving him a good look at his face if he didn't have to.

His boots pounded loudly as he clomped along the woodwalk peering into shop windows as he passed. Normally he wouldn't even notice all the noise his boots were making, but the street was fairly quiet and he felt as though he was drawing attention to himself. His eyes flitted side-to-side rapidly in an attempt to watch both sides of the street at once. He felt that at any moment Ledyard would pop out, gun drawn and ready to fire without the slightest warning.

Just then the door to the general store slammed open and a man emerged right in front of Billy, his arms laden with packages. Startled by the sudden noise and the unexpected figure in front of him, Billy's hand flew to his gun. He had it drawn and pointed at the man, who jumped back in alarm dropping his packages and throwing his empty hands up in the air. "Don't shoot, mister," he cried out.

If Billy ever felt more foolish in his life he couldn't recall when it was. Sheepishly, he put his gun away and bent over to pick up the man's packages. "Sorry, I thought you were someone else," he said.

Angry now, the man turned on Billy. "You loco or something? You could have killed me! I ought to tell Marshal Ridd —". He stopped in mid-sentence when he saw the badge on Billy's shirt. "You'd think a lawman would be more careful with his gun," he said taking the packages from Billy.

Before Billy could say anything else, the man turned and stomped off in the opposite direction from where Billy was heading.

He had to get hold of himself, Billy thought, as he once again headed down the woodwalk toward O'Brien's. He passed in front of the Rattlesnake Saloon and stopped at the entrance. Without pushing the batwing doors, he stuck his head over the top of them and looked around. There were only four men and the bartender present. As he stood there peering into the saloon, all five men turned to look at him. He immediately pulled back out of the doorway.

This is no good, he thought; everybody saw him. He realized he had been too obvious and vowed to be more careful from then on. He decided to make a beeline for O'Brien's and see if could find out anything there.

He didn't look into any more of the shops and saloons as he made his way to the end of the street. He would check them out after lunch, and hopefully, after getting some help at O'Brien's.

The restaurant was still near capacity, as the lunchtime rush had not yet abated. A visual sweep of the room told him neither outlaw was present. Billy found a small table in a corner and was quickly greeted by Mrs. Finnegan.

He slid his vest aside displaying the badge. "I'm looking for a skinny fellow, about thirty years old with a dark moustache, tan hat, a buckskin vest and a dark blue shirt. Nasty scar on his right cheek. He may be traveling with a chubby fellow that's shorter than he is. You seen anyone like that around town?"

She shook her head. "I work in the kitchen," she said pointing a greasy thumb toward the door on the rear wall, "so I don't get to see the customers much. This is the first time I've been out front all day."

"Well, who usually waits on the customers?"

"The owner, Sean O'Brien. He stepped out a few minutes ago to get some more flour at the general store. He should be back in ten or fifteen minutes—if he don't stop at the Bald Eagle on the way. How about some stew while you're waiting?"

"What else you got?" Billy asked.

"I can't cook anything until Sean comes back. The stew is already made up and is simmering in the kitchen. If you want to wait I can make you a steak and potatoes when he returns."

WESTERN PURSUIT

"No, I'm in a hurry. Let me have the stew. That won't take long, will it?"

She shook her head. "Be right out with it."

He watched her waddle back into the kitchen. She was a mighty good cook judging by the size of her. Anyway, he'd eat real quick and if O'Brien wasn't back in ten minutes he'd go find him.

Billy looked around the room again. He was tempted to go from table to table and ask if anyone had seen his quarry, but if Ledyard had any friends in town he didn't want to show his hand without knowing it. No, he'd take his chances with this O'Brien fellow and with Marshal Riddick. He felt he could trust the lawman, and if this was the best restaurant in town, O'Brien was likely to see any strangers that came through.

He was still gazing around the room, lost in his thoughts when Mrs. Finnegan returned with a large bowl of her Irish stew. "I'd be careful if I were you, that stew is hot," she said.

He was going to make some kind of smart remark about her not being his mother, but she had already turned and left. Steam rose from the bowl of stew. It smelled delicious. He grabbed his spoon and ladled a heaping portion into his mouth—and burned his tongue, the roof of his mouth, his lower lip, and the lining of both cheeks. He grabbed his water glass and doused the fire with a large swallow. With a sigh of relief he looked up and saw Mrs. Finnegan looking at him and laughing softly to herself.

If she says "I told you so" he'd empty his .44 into her, he thought, only half-kidding. But she had already gone back to her other customers. He took another drink of water, then reached for his spoon again. Damn, but the stew was good.

Because the food was so hot, it took him a full ten minutes to finish it. He had the last spoonful in his mouth when Sean O'Brien returned, stooped at the waist with a large sack of flour on his right shoulder. He went directly into the kitchen and emerged a moment later without the sack. He was still stooped at the waist, Billy noted.

Billy was going to approach him right then, but he saw that Mrs. Finnegan was talking to him and gesturing in his direction. Sure enough, O'Brien came over to his table.

"I understand you want to ask me a few questions. I can only spare you a minute or two, mind you—I'm way behind with my customers already."

"I just want to know if you've seen either of the two men I'm after. One's real thin, thirty years old, maybe less. He had a dark moustache, a blue shirt, a tan hat and vest, a jagged scar on his right cheek, and wore a six-gun low on his right hip. He was with a chubby fellow that was shorter than him and had light hair. Last time I saw him he had on a plaid shirt. They killed a man in Wattersville, Kansas. You seen anyone like around?"

"For sure they were both in this restaurant not thirty minutes ago. Sat at that table right over there, they did. I knew there was something funny about them. The thin one had a coldness about him that you could feel just by being near him."

Suddenly, Billy had butterflies in his stomach. They're here, he thought, right here in this town. He leaned closer to O'Brien. "When did they leave, exactly?"

"Like I said, twenty to thirty minutes ago."

"Where'd they go from here?"

"I don't know. Look around you. Can't you see how busy I was?" He turned to go.

Billy grabbed his arm and pulled him closer. "Listen, I got to find those two. Do you think they left town?"

"I don't know. How would I know where they—no wait, I think I heard the fat one say he wanted to stay in town awhile, but I can't be sure. I can tell you this much: that thin one likes his whiskey. If he's still here he's probably in a saloon. That's where I'd look first if I were you." He pulled free of Billy's grasp. "I'll be taking my leave of you now, if you don't mind," he said, then walked away.

He'd find them, Billy thought. If Pa thought he was going to go running to him and hand those two over so that he could be the big hero he had another thing coming. Billy'd arrest them, put them in jail here and then go get him. Maybe then Pa would leave him and Zeke alone.

He stepped out onto the woodwalk and looked down both sides of the street again. There couldn't be too many saloons in a town this size. He'd already checked the Rattlesnake. He'd see what other saloons Ledyard could be holed up in. Billy crossed over to the other side of the street and started up the woodwalk. He hadn't gone but a hundred feet when he came to the Red Rooster Saloon. He walked through the batwing doors, his hand on the butt of his holstered .44.

He quickly scanned the room: two men playing checkers in the corner, another one standing at the bar, and an elderly bartender polishing glasses. No sign of the outlaws.

Back on the woodwalk again, he continued up the street. He passed a dry goods store where two elderly ladies where going in, and an assay office that had two pack mules tethered out front. Then he came to the Bald Eagle Saloon. Even this early in the day someone was playing the piano, and as Billy approached the entrance he could see three men standing at the bar. Putting his hand on the butt of his .44 again, he peered over the batwings.

This was the place. He knew it even before he saw Ledyard sitting alone in the corner. A cold shiver ran through him, then a bolt of fear pierced his innards as he laid eyes on the killer for the first time since that tragic night in Wattersville.

Ledyard hadn't seen him yet. For a fleeting second he thought of turning back and getting Henry after all, but then he was back in the cellar, pressed against the cool, damp earth paralyzed with fear as his mother fought the Indians alone.

He wasn't twelve years old anymore. He wasn't helpless, and he wasn't hiding in no hole. This time he would act.

CHAPTER FOURTEEN

Ike emerged from the gunsmith shop testing the hammer on his .44 Starr Double Action revolver. It was an old gun, but it had been a reliable weapon for him. He spun the cylinder listening with pleasure at the ratchety sound it made. Otherwise slovenly, Ike was always meticulous about his weapon. The gunsmith had cleaned and oiled the Starr and loaded the cylinders. Ike felt ready for anything.

He tipped his hat and smiled broadly as a young woman and her little boy passed by. He'd been afraid there was something seriously wrong with his horse, but when he got to the livery stable he was told his horse was just fine after all. That was a big relief. Ledyard wouldn't be too happy if Ike had to keep his horse at the stable where he couldn't get to it if it became necessary to leave in a hurry. But for the first time, Ike felt certain no one was after them.

Maybe he'd split from Ledyard; he was getting too ornery to be around and Ike was weary of his moods. Besides, if he was wrong and the law *was* after Ledyard, it wouldn't do to be with him during the capture—they might hang both of them.

That'd be a shame: after all, he wasn't even in the restaurant when Ledyard shot that farmer.

And what did he need Ledyard for anyway? He had plenty of money from those two jobs they pulled in Missouri. No one had seen them since they'd broke in after hours under the cover of darkness. The proof of that was the lack of wanted posters on either one of them.

Yeah, things would be a lot better if he stayed behind while Ledyard went on alone. He looked forward to relaxing in town for a few more days, playing some poker, meeting the ladies, and not looking over his shoulder every two minutes. Damn, but he felt good.

Ike unhitched his horse from the rail in front of the gunsmith shop and debated whether to visit the barber like he'd planned, or join Ledyard at the Bald Eagle instead. He took the reins in his hand and walked up the street toward the saloon. He was in too good a mood for a haircut; besides, it was too hot. Ledyard's horse stood in front of the Bald Eagle just a few hundred feet ahead. A cold beer would taste good on a day like this.

~

Marshal Riddick stepped out of his office and looked up the street. No sign of the deputy marshal Albert had told him about. Riddick didn't know why he'd come back early today—he certainly had plenty to do on the farm—but it was a good thing he had. If there were a couple of killers loose in town, that deputy might need some help.

Albert had said the deputy was going to O'Brien's for lunch, so Riddick decided to head in that direction and check the saloons along the way. Maybe he'd just get lucky. He'd try the Rattlesnake first, then the Bald Eagle, the Red Rooster, and finally O'Brien's.

He felt for his six-gun, an instinct he'd developed whenever he sensed trouble patrolling the streets of St. Louis. Things were quieter in Rockford than in the big city, and that's the way he liked it. Better for his family, too.

Riddick stepped into the street and walked toward the Rattlesnake Saloon. He tugged at the yellow bandana at his throat. Damn, it was hot today.

∼

Billy stood to one side of the doorway and continued to peer over the top of the batwings, his eyes sweeping the interior of the Bald Eagle Saloon. The three men standing at the bar were directly in front of him, fifteen feet away. To the right were two men in business suits, neither apparently armed. Ledyard sat in the corner to Billy's left next to the end of the bar. He had his back to the corner so that the entire room was in front of him. He was working on a bottle of whiskey and still hadn't noticed Billy.

Billy took a deep breath, then pushed through the doors. He wanted to draw his .44 Remington and confront Ledyard, but somehow he couldn't get his hand to take the gun. As quietly as possible, he moved to the far end of the bar keeping the three men between himself and Ledyard's table. He could see Ledyard if he leaned around the men.

Go on over there and arrest him! What are you waiting for? Still he couldn't move. His hand wouldn't draw his gun, and his feet were rooted to the floor where he stood. He thought of himself in the cellar as the Indians attacked his mother and burned their house. He wasn't a coward! He had only hid in the cellar because ma told him to. He'd *wanted* to help her, but she told him to stay in the cellar. *Go on, you're not afraid, go over there and arrest him.*

The bartender broke Billy's reverie. "What'll you have?"

"Beer," Billy said out of habit. He hadn't realized how dry his mouth had suddenly got until he spoke. "No, give me a whiskey—better make it a double."

He leaned over a little and saw Ledyard still sitting there, unmoving. Billy picked up the full glass and tossed it down, feeling the liquid courage burn his insides as it passed.

It made no difference. He couldn't find it in himself to approach Ledyard. If anything, he was more concerned that Ledyard might see *him*.

Pa was right, he thought: he *was* a coward. Billy never knew it till then, or maybe he knew it all along and wouldn't admit it to himself. He pushed the empty glass away, feeling a sick emptiness deep in his soul.

He placed a coin on the counter next to his glass and turned to leave, careful to hide his face from Ledyard. The scene from earlier in the day flashed through his mind as he moved toward the door. Pa was telling him to see if Ledyard was in town and to report back to him, and he had only mocked Pa and said maybe he'd arrest Ledyard by himself.

All talk, that's what he was, Billy thought. He was too ashamed to look at anybody, and kept his eyes on the floor in front of him as he walked. The fear consumed him completely, filling him with self-disgust. A yellow dog slinking away with his tail 'tween his legs: that was him, Billy McNichol.

Still lost in thought, he paid no attention to the man standing in the doorway. He looked up just as Ike's gun cleared its holster. For a split second time stopped as their eyes met. He thought of going for his gun, but he knew it was already too late.

Ike's gun roared and the slug slammed into Billy driving him backward. A white-hot searing pain burned through his right shoulder and he landed on the dirty floor of the saloon looking up at the ceiling. He slipped into the gray shadows of semi-consciousness, unable to move. Two figures loomed over him.

"Who is he?" Ledyard asked.

"Don't you recognize him?" Ike said.

"My memory ain't what it used to be."

"I ain't surprised, the way you put away the whiskey."

Ledyard jerked his head toward Ike, his eyes blazing. "You ain't my mother! What I drink or don't drink is no concern of yours." He glared at Ike for a long moment. "Now who is this fellow you just shot?"

"He's the one that gave us the hard time in Wattersville. As soon as I saw him I knew he was tracking us."

"What's that on his shirt?" Ledyard said. He bent over and pushed Billy's vest aside uncovering the rest of the badge.

"He's a deputy marshal!" Ike said.

Again aware of the other patrons in the saloon, Ledyard said to Ike, "Cover them." Then he saw Billy's gun. "I hope you don't mind," he said to Billy, "but you won't be needing this anyway."

Billy was too weak to protest. He struggled to keep his eyes open, but his strength was almost gone as he fought the terrible burning in his shoulder. He felt Ledyard unbuckling his gun belt, then a bolt of overwhelming pain as Ledyard grabbed him roughly by the injured shoulder and rolled him onto his side so he could jerk the holster and gun belt free. Billy moaned in agony.

"Come on, Ledyard, let's get out of here," Ike said.

"Don't look at me, watch them," Ledyard said.

Ike swung his gun in an arc around the room. "You men stay where you are and keep your hands up where I can see them."

Ledyard looped the gun belt around Billy's holster in his left hand, then drew his own six-gun with his right.

Ledyard straightened his right arm so that his .44 Army

Colt was pointed down at Billy's face. "Here's one lawman we won't have to worry about anymore."

"You can't just shoot him like a dog," the bartender said. "Why don't you just leave. He ain't going to follow you."

"You shut up," Ledyard said.

"Come on, let's go," Ike said. "The whole town heard the shot."

Billy looked up at the barrel pointed at his forehead, then past it to the steeled mask of hatred that was Ledyard's face. Then he saw a mock smile appear. He's going to do it, Billy thought. A sudden calmness came over him as he locked eyes with the killer, returning his contemptuous stare. The last thing his brain registered was the roar of the gun as it discharged two feet from his face.

CHAPTER FIFTEEN

Marshal Riddick was in the Rattlesnake Saloon when Ike's gun went off. He left the saloon and ran toward the sound of the shot. He stopped a young woman running in the other direction. "What is it? What happened?" he asked.

"I heard a shot. It sounded like it came from the Bald Eagle, but I ain't sure." Then she ran off. More people, mostly women dragging small children, passed the marshal as he ran toward the Bald Eagle.

He was only a hundred and fifty feet away when he heard the second shot. It definitely came from the Bald Eagle. Drawing his revolver, he moved closer to the saloon, wary of anyone who might emerge.

He'd closed to within fifty feet when Ledyard and Ike burst through the doorway. At the sight of the marshal both men opened fire. Riddick ducked behind a horse trough and returned their fire. Flying lead tore off a chunk of wood that whistled past the lawman's left ear. The air quickly filled with gun smoke making it difficult to shoot accurately.

The two outlaws jumped onto their waiting horses and rode west out of town as Marshal Riddick emptied his gun at them. Then Riddick went inside the Bald Eagle to see what happened.

He moved through the crowd of men gathered around the deputy who lay dead in a sticky pool of blood. Riddick pushed his way through to the body. He took one look and turned away in horror; the top of the deputy's head had been blown off. He forced himself to look again, but it was too much. He shoved the men aside in a desperate attempt to get out and broke for the street where he vomited up his lunch in front of the saloon. When he looked up, Albert, his helper at the office, was standing next to him.

"What's the matter, Marshal, you sick or something?" he asked.

Riddick walked a few steps to a horse trough and rinsed off his face, then dried it with his shirtsleeve. "Never mind that, Albert. Go over to the livery and tell Elroy to saddle my horse." The boy ran off. "And tell him to be quick about it," Riddick called after him.

Riddick went back inside, being careful not to look at the body anymore, and got the details of what happened from the bartender. The other witnesses present confirmed the story.

"Get Ned over here to take charge of the body and then get that mess cleaned up," Riddick told the bartender. In a moment he was back outside—and grateful for the fresh air.

He refilled the cylinder on his six-gun as he walked to the livery. By the time he got there his horse was saddled and ready to go. The outlaws had a head start of several minutes, but he knew the terrain and had the fastest horse in town. He left at a gallop.

The plains stretched out before him; there was no place for them to hide to lie in ambush. He urged his mount on, faster and faster. The horse lengthened its stride and flattened out as it swallowed up the prairie.

Riddick rode low in the saddle, ducking his head behind

that of his horse. Minutes went by and still the horse charged on, somehow sensing the urgency his master felt. As Riddick came over a low ridge he saw the two outlaws only a hundred yards ahead. Tiring, Riddick's horse began to flag, but he dug his spurs into the animal and it leapt forward, somehow finding the reserve that made the horse so special.

When he had closed to within thirty yards he drew his Colt and put Ike in his sights. He squeezed the trigger, but he was still too far away. The two men looked back at him, but still Riddick urged his mount on, closing the gap to twenty yards. He took aim again—it was difficult with the horse moving under him—and squeezed the trigger once more. Ike lurched forward, then rolled out of the saddle.

Riddick immediately shifted his sights to the other outlaw just as Ledyard turned in the saddle and fired. Riddick's left leg felt as if a hot branding iron had driven deep into his flesh. The force of the impact spun him out of the saddle, and, still clinging to his six-gun, he tumbled into the prairie grass several yards shy of where Ike lay.

Ledyard rode toward him, but Riddick got off another shot when the outlaw came into range. Realizing that the lawman was still capable of defending himself, Ledyard turned and galloped away. He didn't stop to check on his fallen friend.

Riddick's horse had continued to run and was nowhere in sight. The leg ached terribly, and blood poured out of his wound just above the kneecap on the side of his leg. He took his bandana off and wrapped it around the leg just above the wound. Still the blood gushed. He took his six-gun and knotted the bandana around the barrel. Then he twisted the barrel to cinch the bandana tightly around the leg as a tourniquet; the bleeding slowed to a trickle. Then he passed out.

The trail from Hendersonville to Rockford angled off in a southeasterly direction. Zeke and Henry had gone several miles when Zeke pointed off into the distance and said, "Hey, what's that?"

Henry squinted in the direction of Zeke's arm. "Appears to be a lone rider. Looks like he's heading northwest, but I can't be sure."

"Maybe he's headed toward Hendersonville," Zeke said, "and he sure seems in a hurry. Maybe it's Uncle Billy."

"No, he'd take the trail so he'd run into us. Billy ain't no tracker, but an old woman could follow this here path we're on."

Both men continued to stare at the rider. "Maybe it's one of the outlaws," Zeke said at last. "You think we should follow him?"

Henry shook his head. "We can't go chasing after every farmer or saddle tramp we seeing riding across the prairie. Billy and them outlaws ain't the only people traveling out here." He spurred his horse. "Come on, let's get moving."

A short time later Zeke and Henry sat astride their horses on the scraggly trail of flattened grass and worn earth between Hendersonville and Rockford. They had to be nearing Rockford and yet still hadn't seen Billy coming from the other direction.

Zeke looked ahead on the faint path and wondered where his uncle was. "He should have been here by now, don't you think?"

"Seems like it," Henry replied.

"Maybe something happened to him," Zeke said.

"Naw, he's probably in a card game and lost track of the time. You know how he gets."

Zeke didn't know how he got and didn't think his grandfather really thought Uncle Billy was playing cards, either. Maybe Uncle Billy found them and arrested them and that caused the delay. Or maybe Uncle Billy was somewhere between here and Rockford with a piece of lead in him. Zeke didn't want to think about that, let alone say it out loud. After all, he *was* with Uncle Billy's father.

"Come on," Henry said. "Let's go into Rockford. Don't make no sense to just sit here in the sun getting cooked."

They hadn't gone far when Zeke saw a man lying on the ground up ahead about a hundred feet to the right of the path. The breath went out of him and he strained to see if it was Uncle Billy or not. Just then Henry spurred his horse and rode past him. Henry got to the man and leapt off his horse for a closer look. "It ain't Billy," he called out. "Never seen this one before." A flood of relief washed over Zeke as he rode up and dismounted.

Henry pressed an ear to the man's chest, then looked up at Zeke. "This one's dead. Is he one of them outlaws we're after?"

"That's the fat one that was with Ledyard back in Wattersville," he said eyeing the dead outlaw. "You reckon Uncle Billy shot him?"

Henry flipped the body over, examining it closely. "One shot in the back. Maybe somebody was chasing him and shot him. Or maybe he had a fight with Ledyard and got shot in the back." Still kneeling, he examined the ground nearby. "Looks like fresh hoof prints."

"Where's his horse?" Zeke asked.

"Probably wandered off." He stood up. "Come on, let's have a look around."

Less than a minute later Zeke saw another figure lying in the tall grass. "What's that?" he called out to Henry, who was walking in another direction.

Zeke's belly knotted again as he and his grandfather approached. Was it Uncle Billy? He couldn't tell yet, and he was afraid to look.

A man lay still on the ground, his eyes closed. There was a bullet hole in his left thigh that oozed below a makeshift tourniquet. The pant leg was coated with dried blood.

There sure is a heap of maiming and killing you got to look at when you're a lawman, Zeke thought.

"Is this that Ledyard fellow?" Henry asked.

"No, I ain't seen this one before," Zeke said, breathing a sigh of relief.

Henry began examining him and his hand brushed under the vest exposing a gaudy star on the man's shirt. TOWN MARSHAL was stamped on it, and a metal strip inscribed ROCKFORD, KANSAS hung by two tiny chains from the bottom of the star.

"He's a lawman," Henry said. "Town marshal from Rockford."

"Is he dead?" Zeke asked as his grandfather pressed an ear to the man's chest.

"No, his heart's still beating. Get me a canteen." Zeke returned in a few moments and handed the canteen to Henry, who took his bandana off and poured water over it. Then he dabbed the damp cloth over the man's face. "Come on, Marshal, wake up," he said gently. Then he took the canteen and dribbled a little water into the wounded man's mouth. "Wake up, Marshal, wake up."

Slowly the man's eyes came open a bit, like a cowboy opening his eyes against the morning sun after an all night binge with cheap whiskey. Henry poured a little more water into his mouth and wiped his face again. The man came back to life.

"Who are you?" the wounded man asked in a weak, raspy voice.

"I'm United States Marshal Henry McNichol, and this here's my grandson Zeke—he's one of my deputies. What are you doing out here and who shot you?"

He reached for the canteen and took a long swallow before answering. "Name's Jess Riddick. I'm the town marshal in Rockford." Henry nodded at the remark. "I was chasing two men. I shot one of them, but the other got me in the leg and I fell off my horse."

"We found the one you shot," Zeke said. "He's dead."

"Why were you chasing them?" Henry asked.

"They shot a lawman in town," Riddick said.

Both Zeke and Henry froze at that remark. Henry pressed closer to Riddick. "Who was it? Was he one of your men?"

Oh, please, God, don't let it be Uncle Billy, Zeke thought. He didn't want to hear the answer.

Riddick shook his head weakly. "No, I never seen him before. His badge said he was a Deputy U.S. Marshal." His face got a peculiar look on it, as though he suddenly realized whom he was talking to. "Say, maybe it was one of your men. You got any more deputies working this area?"

Henry didn't bother to answer. He was already up and walking toward his horse. In a moment he was mounted, and then stopped to address Riddick one more time. "How badly was he hurt?"

"The top of his—" Riddick said; then he stopped and took a long look at Henry up on his horse. "This deputy, were you and him close?"

Henry nodded. "He's my son."

"I'm afraid your son is dead, Marshal."

"What were you saying about the top of something?" Henry asked.

"Your son is dead," Riddick repeated.

Henry sat stonily for a moment or two, then turned to Zeke. "Help the marshal onto your horse, Zeke, and we'll go back to town."

Uncle Billy's dead. Oh no, no, NO! Zeke rubbed a tear

away with his shirtsleeve, then jammed a forearm against his mouth to stifle a sob. He looked at Henry, who stared back at him. He tried to read the old man's face, but it was impassive. Didn't he care about Uncle Billy? Sure, they'd had their differences, but they were father and son. Zeke choked back his tears and bent down to help Riddick. In a few minutes they were riding double on Zeke's horse and the three of them headed for Rockford.

Uncle Billy had always tried to enjoy life. Whether he was winning at poker or joshing with some waitress over his morning coffee, Uncle Billy was someone to look up to, and to learn from. Who'd he have to spend time with now? Grandpa? Uncle Billy hadn't thought much of Grandpa as a man to look up to or learn from.

They didn't say much on the way: Riddick was in no shape to talk. The ride was an ordeal for Zeke. Uncle Billy was already dead. Zeke didn't care that Ledyard was past them riding in the other direction. All he could think about was that every step brought them closer to Uncle Billy's dead body.

> Alone with his thoughts, unable to ride fast because of the wounded marshal propped up in front of him, the trail stretched on interminably. He didn't want to see Uncle Billy laid out in a wooden box with a blank look on his face. Uncle Billy was usually smiling; that's how Zeke wanted to remember his uncle.

CHAPTER SIXTEEN

The carpenter, Ned Tull, had several coffins of various sizes made up already. He said his assistant was already out digging a grave, and Billy would be ready for burial in about an hour. Tull refused to show Henry or Zeke the body once he learned they were all related.

"How come he won't let us see Uncle Billy one last time?" Zeke said.

"Mr. Tull wants us to remember Billy the way he was, not the way he looks after getting shot."

Zeke's eyes filled with tears that spilled out and ran down his dusty face. He tried to stifle a sob, but couldn't. "I'll never see Uncle Billy again," he said, then cried openly.

Henry frowned, then turned away from Zeke. He took a deep breath and set his jaw, then turned back to his grandson. With a fatherly arm around Zeke's shoulders, Henry led him outside to a bench at the side of the building, away from foot traffic. "Sit here and rest a spell," he said. "I'll be back in little while."

Zeke nodded and buried his face in his hands.

While Tull did his work, Henry interviewed witnesses in

the Bald Eagle, all of whom were only too eager to provide graphic details.

They buried Billy an hour later. Tull and his assistant were there, of course, since they had brought the coffin, and would fill in the grave when the funeral was over. Besides Zeke and Henry, the only other people present were the preacher and his wife.

What a shame, Zeke thought, noting the tiny gathering. Had the service been in Wattersville half the town would have turned out.

They stocked up on supplies and water and left right after the funeral. Henry wanted to make the most of the remaining few hours of daylight; Ledyard was getting farther away by the minute. They took Billy's horse with them so that they had two spare horses. Since each horse would only carry a rider every other day, Henry said they could afford to ride them a little harder to make up time.

They rode west out of Rockford to the spot where they had found Marshal Riddick. Up ahead a ways they saw a fresh grave where someone from town had come out to bury Ike. Guess outlaws don't rate a plot in the town cemetery, Zeke thought as they passed.

They picked up the trail of a lone rider and followed it northwest for several miles. Henry said that that must have been Ledyard they'd seen racing across the prairie toward Hendersonville yesterday, but there was no way to know that at the time. The outlaw had made no attempt to cover his tracks, and they followed them easily.

Dusk was fast approaching, and since they were near a creek, Henry decided to make camp for the night. "I'd have liked to have made it back to Hendersonville—I know it's only a few miles up ahead—but the light's failing and I don't want us wandering around in the dark," Henry said. Then he sighed and said, "My bones sure don't fancy sleeping on this hard ground."

"Maybe we can sleep in a town tomorrow night."

"Maybe, but that don't help me none tonight."

They arose at sunrise and rode the last few miles back into Hendersonville following the trail Ledyard had left the day before. They arrived just as the town was coming to life.

Not wanting to waste time when they were there yesterday, Zeke and Henry had quickly looked around and, satisfied that Ledyard wasn't there, had left for Rockford.

Back in Hendersonville now, they stopped at the marshal's office, and at the livery stable, but neither was open yet. So they found a restaurant and had breakfast.

After that they found the marshal in his office, but he hadn't seen Ledyard and had no help to offer.

"Let's try the livery," Henry said when they were outside again. He set off with Zeke a few steps behind. Then Henry turned and said, "Come on up here and walk with me, Zeke." He waited as his grandson limped toward him. "Don't ever walk behind people you're with. It makes a man think less of himself than he ought to."

"It's hard for me to keep up, Grandpa; my knee bothers me."

"Zeke, all you've got is a little limp from a sore knee. It ain't like you got your leg shot off."

Zeke's gaze dropped to the ground, but he said nothing.

"You got two problems, Zeke. All your life you had your pa and your uncle telling you all the things you can't do."

"Yeah? What's the other problem?"

"You believe them."

The livery stable was a different story. The liveryman remembered Ledyard riding into town the day before demanding a fresh mount. His horse was lathered and its breathing was labored. "I could see it was played out," the liveryman said, "and I really didn't want it, and I told him so."

"What'd he do then, pull a gun on you?" Zeke asked.

The man jerked his head in surprise. "Why no, he just took ten dollars out of his pocket and offered it to me along with his horse for one of mine that was rested."

"Did you swap?" Henry asked.

"Sure I did. I looked his horse over. There was nothing wrong with it that a week's rest and feeding wouldn't cure."

"Did he leave right away?"

The man nodded. "He asked if the train stopped here. I told him he'd have to go fifteen miles east to Ellsworth, or twenty miles west to Russell if he wanted to catch it."

"Which way did he go?" Henry asked. "East?"

The man scratched his head. "No, he headed west. That surprised me. If a man wants to travel on a train, why not go to the nearest depot?"

"Did he say if he wanted to go east or west—on the train, I mean," Henry said.

"No, he just asked if the train stopped here. I told him it didn't."

"Do you think he caught the train yesterday?"

"No. It was too late in the day. He still had a twenty-mile ride to Russell and he couldn't have made it in time to catch the train. If he's taking the train, he's boarding it today at the earliest."

Henry thanked the man and they rode out of town heading west. They rode hard hoping to beat the train to Russell and catch Ledyard before he could board. After about ten miles they stopped to switch horses, saddling the two spare mounts.

They continued on, but after only a mile or so, the westbound train came up behind them. With a heavy heart, Zeke watched it pass by, its metal wheels clickety-clacking on the rails.

"What do we do now?" he asked.

"No telling how far we are from Russell, or how long the train will stop there. We might as well try to catch it," Henry said.

They rode on as hard as they dared without ruining the horses, but as the miles passed and no town came into view, Zeke knew it was a losing battle.

They followed the tracks right into the depot in Russell, but the train was long gone.

Henry questioned the ticket agent, who said that a man matching Ledyard's description bought a ticket to Denver and boarded the train.

"So he's going to Denver, then," Zeke said.

"Maybe. Maybe not. The agent said the train stops in Hays City, Trego, Buffalo Station, and Fort Wallace before crossing into Colorado. Ledyard could get off at any of those places."

Zeke and Henry spent the night in Russell, then boarded the train the next day. Zeke was amazed at how the train effortlessly ate up the miles. The plains seemed to fly past in gentle peaks and valleys, as the train roared through. Henry got off at every stop to question the station agents, but none had seen Ledyard.

The train was now at the depot in Fort Wallace, the last stop before Denver. Zeke watched Henry out the window as his grandfather spoke with the agent. Then he crossed the platform and reboarded the train.

"What did he say, Grandpa? Did he see Ledyard?" Zeke asked before Henry even had a chance to sit down.

Henry slid onto the seat and shook his head. "He ain't seen anybody that came close to looking like him."

Zeke shrugged and said, "Well, at least now we know he went to Denver."

"Maybe he did, and maybe he didn't," Henry replied. "He could easily have sat in the last passenger car, waited for the right time, then gone out onto the little platform behind the car—some men like to smoke out there or just get some fresh air and stretch their legs—and jumped off the train."

"Wouldn't he break a leg or something doing that with the train moving?"

Henry shook his head again. "Look how many times this train has slowed down since we've been on it. Every time it came into a depot it slowed to a halt, and then it was going slow again when it pulled out. Nobody would see him if he jumped off before or after the train reached the depot; Ledyard could walk to town and replace the horse and saddle he left in Russell, then go off in any direction. The train didn't stop long enough for me to check livery stables."

Zeke pondered this for a moment. "If he did that, he's already behind us and riding away. By the time we backtracked and picked up his trail again he'd be long gone."

"That's right. One thing we got going for us is that he's a big drinker and may not be thinking too straight. Another is that he's scared and may just want to run as far away as he can get. That's a natural instinct all people have."

"So he might take the train all the way to the end of the line in Denver, then go from there."

"That's what I'm hoping," Henry said.

It was late in the day when they crossed into Colorado. The gentle sweep of the plains gave way to a steady incline as the train climbed to higher elevations. Zeke's heart caught in his throat at the sight of giant mountains rising up above the horizon. Like jagged teeth they strained for the heavens, their peaks piercing the clouds.

"That's the most beautiful site I've ever seen," Zeke said at last.

Henry snorted. "It ain't so beautiful when you're riding through them mountains on a skittish horse with two feet of snow on the ground and an icy wind freezing your ears off."

As they approached Denver, the mountains grew larger and larger. The temperature dropped in the railroad car and the glass was cool to Zeke's face as he pressed against the window trying to see. Henry sat with his hat over his face and his arms folded

Finally, the train arrived at the depot in Denver. Henry headed straight for the station agent with Zeke in tow. The agent wasn't very busy as it was late in the day and no one was buying tickets.

"You seen a skinny fellow, twenty-five to thirty years old, tan hat and vest, and an ugly scar here?" Henry said running his right hand by his cheek. "He'd be traveling alone, most likely wearing dirty clothes, had a moustache, and wore a six-gun low on his hip."

"Sounds like the mangy feller that got off the train yesterday," the agent said through his wire cage window. "He wanted me to sell him a ticket on the train heading north to Cheyenne."

"You sell him one?"

"Couldn't. The track's out and no trains are running up that way until we fix it."

"Track's out? I thought this was a new line," Henry said.

"It is, but if some damn outlaws want to blow up the track to rob the train it don't matter how new the track is."

"When that happen?"

"What's your interest in all this, mister?"

Henry pushed his vest aside revealing the badge. "United States Marshal. We're tracking a killer—that fellow I asked about."

"Some outlaws blew the track two days ago. A rancher saw the missing track and rode up ahead to warn the engineer, but it was too late. He wasn't able to stop in time and the engine derailed. The rest of the cars are still on the track behind it." The agent pushed his glasses up on his nose with a finger. "What a mess. As it was, the bandits got away with the mail shipment and some greenbacks."

"How long you reckon before the trains are running again?"

The agent shrugged. "This is all new to us, but I'd guess a few weeks at least. We got to get some heavy equipment up there to move that engine, and the tracks are blocked in both directions."

"So what'd this skinny fellow do when you didn't sell him a ticket?"

"Well, he commenced to cussing me, that's what he did. That's why I remember him so well."

"What else he say?"

"He asked if there was a stagecoach heading north. I told him the line stopped running out of Denver when the railroad began service. I also told him there were some feeder lines up north, but nothing from here."

"What'd he do then?"

"He cussed me some more, then walked away."

"Obliged," Henry said, then turned and left the window.

"What do you think, Grandpa, is Ledyard still in Denver?" Zeke asked.

"No, I doubt it. A city this size has too much law for him to stay here. Besides, he knows we're after him now. Most likely he'll want to put some more distance between himself and us."

Zeke nodded in agreement. "Do you think he went north?"

"Yeah, I think so," Henry said. "Come on, they're unloading our horses from the train."

Ten minutes later they rode into Denver trailing the two spare mounts. The city had more streets than Zeke had thought one place could hold. Everywhere there were people, horses, noise, street filth, and buildings, buildings, and more buildings—mostly made of brick. "This must be the biggest city in the world," Zeke said.

"Shoot, this ain't nothing," Henry said. "You should see St. Louis. And if you think St. Louis is big, I'm told there are cities like Chicago and New York that are even bigger."

Bigger than this? Zeke thought, as they maneuvered their horses through the congested street passing several hotels and five times as many saloons. "Why would anybody want to live in a place like this?" Zeke asked. "People are packed together like cattle in a pen."

"It ain't for me, that's for sure," Henry replied. "All this open land and everyone here's crowded together. Just being here makes me feel like I can't breathe."

They stopped to let a man driving a buckboard pass by. "What do we do now?" Zeke asked.

Henry glanced up at the sun still high in the western sky. "We got several hours of daylight left, and this Ledyard fellow has already got a head start on us. Let's get these horses to a livery stable for feed and watering while we have an early supper."

Less than an hour later, their bellies full, Henry said, "I got to send a wire. You get our horses and find a well or a pump somewhere and fill our canteens. Then meet me at that general store we just passed. We'll get whatever supplies we need, and get after him again."

"You wiring for more deputies?"

Henry grimaced. "Hell, no. It's another matter."

CHAPTER SEVENTEEN

A day and a half out of Denver and they still hadn't caught Ledyard, but any doubts about the direction the outlaw was heading vanished when they came upon the remains of a day-old campfire. A single set of footprints marked the area, and a quick look around uncovered a whiskey bottle with a few drops still in the bottom.

"He's none too good at covering his tracks," Zeke said.

Henry surveyed the scene. "He could be drunk, or careless, or maybe he thinks he's in the clear. If he hadn't cussed the station agent we couldn't even be sure he arrived in Denver, let alone know he wanted to go north." Henry paused, still staring at the campsite. "Then again, he could be laying an ambush for us. We'll have to keep our eyes open; don't just look at the ground, Zeke, watch the trees and the hillsides, too."

They passed through a few tiny settlements and asked about Ledyard, but no one had seen anyone matching his description. Then they came to a trading post about thirty-five miles north of Denver. It was a solitary log building, dark and dirty inside, the air damp and ripe with mildew. The owner said someone fitting Ledyard's description bought two bottles of whiskey from him the day before and left heading north.

It was late afternoon when they approached another settlement. In stark contrast to the flat, grassy plains of Kansas, mountains loomed up in the distance beyond the town's rolling terrain. Ponderosa pines and cottonwoods dotted the landscape.

As they rode along, Zeke repeatedly looked at the badge on his shirt tucked behind his vest. He had not been tested yet. He wondered if he would make Grandpa proud when the time came, or if he'd lose his nerve at the last minute and turn tail. Maybe Ledyard was in the town just up ahead. The thought that a confrontation might occur that very day made Zeke's stomach churn and his mouth go dry. But it was for this purpose that they'd been on the trail, and that Uncle Billy had died. He mustn't chicken out now, when courage was needed more than anything. He tried to get his mind on something else.

Zeke thought of how much closer he'd grown to his grandfather in the days since they'd left Rockford. He'd listened to Henry's tales of his younger days when the land was even more unsettled and life was a daily battle for survival. Zeke admired him for his courage and the adventurous life he had led. He couldn't understand why there'd been so much friction between Grandpa and Uncle Billy.

Another ten minutes at an easy gait brought them to the edge of the settlement. Someone had stuck a board sign into the ground that said WELCOME TO EVANS in unevenly painted letters.

"Looks like a new town," Zeke said as they rode down the main street. The smell of sawdust hung in the air, and in the distance carpenters hammered away. Buildings were freshly painted and many had false fronts.

Zeke was amazed at the number of pool halls and saloons. They also passed a few establishments where young women sat out front in gaudy attire and full-face paint. They smiled at Zeke as he rode by. One or two even called out to him. Blushing, he turned away.

They stopped at the marshal's office, but there was a sign on the door saying he was having supper and would return at six.

Henry drew out his pocket watch and opened the cover with a practiced flip of his thumb. "It's just past five o'clock; let's get these horses to a livery stable and then go get some supper. Maybe the liveryman can recommend a decent restaurant."

"When are we going to look for him?" Zeke asked.

Henry turned to his grandson with a wry smile. "You're a deputy marshal; what would you do if you were tracking this killer by yourself—aside from checking with the town marshal?"

Zeke thought for a minute. "I'd have supper real quick and then start checking the hotels and saloons. I'd see if he was about and I'd ask people if they'd seen him." Zeke felt pretty good about his answer. It made sense and seemed to him to be the best course of action.

"What about your horse?"

Zeke was confused. "My horse? What about him?" Zeke asked.

"What would you do with your horse?"

"I'd leave him at the livery like we're going to do now." *What's the old man getting at?*

"So where's the first place you'd start looking for this Ledyard fellow?"

"Like I said, at the saloons and hotels. He'd have to go in some of those. Where else would he be?"

"How many saloons, hotels, pool halls, and bordellos you think this town has?"

Zeke shrugged. "I don't know. A lot I guess. We already passed quite a few."

Henry nodded in agreement. "If you started right after supper and kept at it you might finish in a couple days—if you were lucky and he didn't double back into a place after you'd already checked it. And after you got all done you still wouldn't know if he'd been here or not, would you?"

Zeke stared at Henry's smug face. What's he getting at? "What do you think I should do, stand in the center of town, call his name and see if he answers?"

The smile vanished from Henry's face. "Don't sass me, boy—I don't like it."

"Well, what do you expect me to say? I gave you my answer."

"I expect you to think! Any fool can go through the whole town asking questions, searching blindly and alerting any friends he might have here. I want you to learn to be smarter than the man you're chasing." He stared at Zeke for several seconds before continuing. "The graveyard's full of lawmen who couldn't think."

Anger welled up in Zeke. "So what should we do?"

"Just keep your eyes and ears open and see if you can't learn something about tracking outlaws." Then he started down the street with Zeke trailing behind.

After they'd gone a short distance, Henry stopped a man walking nearby and asked him for directions. Henry led the way again and turned at the corner and went only a short ways down another street and stopped in front of Johnson's Livery Stable. Following Henry's lead, Zeke dismounted and went inside. A heavyset man in his late forties was raking hay into a corner stall. He was blond at the temples and bald on top, and he wheezed with the exertion of working the rake.

He looked up at the sound of the two men entering the stable.

"Evenin'. Need to board some horses?"

"Maybe," Henry said. "You seen a tall, thin fellow around town, mid-to-late twenties? He's got a black moustache, tan hat and vest, and an ugly scar on his right cheek. Wears his gun low on his right hip."

The man stopped raking and leaned forward with his chin resting on the back of his hands as they covered the end of the handle, his eyes turning upward in thought. "No, I can't say that I have. Sorry."

"How many liveries in Evans?" Henry asked.

"Two. Mine, and Eli's down at the other end of the street."

Henry touched the brim of his hat. "Much obliged."

So that's it, Zeke thought as they rode toward the other stable. No matter how many hotels and saloons a town had, it only had one or two livery stables. Instead of finding out where Ledyard had been, find out where he took his horse. That way he'd know if he'd been in Evans or not.

"What if he hasn't been to the other stable, either?" Zeke asked.

"All right, suppose he hasn't. What would you conclude from that?"

"I'd figure he didn't come through Evans."

"Suppose he *is* here, but didn't take his horse to a livery," Henry said.

Zeke shook his head. "No, he wouldn't do that. If I was on the run I'd take every opportunity to see that my horse was well fed and groomed."

Henry nodded approvingly. "You reckon his horse is being kept at the stable?"

"No. If it was me, I'd want my horse close by where I could get to it right away."

"Now you're thinking like a lawman," Henry said.

Zeke hesitated for a moment, then blurted out, "I'm sorry, Grandpa. I'm sorry I smart-mouthed you back there." Zeke saw Henry turn toward him, but he was neither smiling nor scowling. Zeke couldn't read his face. Was he still angry? "It's just that I thought I had the right answer, and then you made me feel so stupid that I didn't know what to say."

"You're not stupid, Zeke, you're just ignorant. You don't know about being a lawman. That's why I'm teaching you—so you won't be ignorant anymore. I tried to teach Billy, but he wasn't one for listening to others, especially to me." He paused and looked at Zeke for a moment, then said, "I could teach you all there is to know about marshalling if you'll let me."

Not knowing what to say, Zeke remained silent.

"Tell you what, when we get to this other stable, you do the talking," Henry said.

Why not, Zeke thought? Anyone can ask questions. "All right, I'll take care of it," he said.

A few minutes later they stopped in front of a barn-like structure with ELI'S LIVERY STABLE crudely painted on a board sign over the large entranceway. The door was slid out of the way so that almost the entire front of the building was open.

Zeke dismounted and went inside. Henry waited outside, still on his horse. The stable was large, and almost every stall was occupied. Two burly men worked with pitchforks tossing hay into the stalls. The smell of horses was overwhelming, although not unpleasant to Zeke. Both men looked up when Zeke entered; neither one returned his smile.

"Howdy," Zeke said.

No response.

"I'm looking for a fellow who's about twenty-six, twenty-seven years old with—"

"Do you want your horse tended to?" one of the men asked.

"Well, I don't know, maybe," Zeke said.

"Maybe? Well, do you or don't you?"

Zeke swallowed hard and looked back at Henry, who sat calmly on his horse and gave no indication of intervening. "What I really need is some information. Have you seen—"

"If it's information you need, why don't you buy a newspaper?" Both liverymen laughed at that one.

"Look, all I want to do is ask you a simple question. Is that so much—"

This time the other one interrupted him. "No, you look! We've both been working in this filthy stable all day long, and we're hot and tired and hungry. And we ain't got time for any bullshit questions. So why don't you beat it, kid?"

"Yeah," the first one said. "We're both here minding our own business and you come in and bother us. Can't you see we got other things to do?"

What should he do now, Zeke thought? He didn't want to fail right in front of Grandpa, but these fellows weren't being very helpful. Maybe if he just asked it real quick they'd answer him and he could leave. "The man I'm looking for is a—"

The man to Zeke's left grabbed his pitchfork and lunged at Zeke, stopping inches from his throat. "I said beat it, kid."

Leaping back from the threat, Zeke bumped into Henry, who placed a hand on his shoulder to steady him. A flood of relief washed over Zeke; still, his heart was racing. He saw the two men back away, then saw the .44 in Henry's hand.

"It's been quite a while since I've seen two more unfriendly, ornery cusses than you two," Henry said. "I ought to shoot both of you just to teach you some manners,"

"Hey, old timer, you don't want to be shooting anybody," one of them remarked.

"Good. I see I have your attention now," Henry said. "You

two don't realize who this young man is you've been funning with. His name is—"

"Look, old man, it's late. Why don't you skip the introductions and state your business?"

Henry stepped forward in two rapid steps and swung his left hand up in a wide arc backhanding the man across the left side of his face. Startled, the man recoiled at the blow as a patch of crimson blossomed on his cheek.

"You interrupted me," Henry said. "When I talk, you listen. When I'm done talking, then *you* can talk."

Unable to hold Henry's gaze, the two men looked down at the hay-strewn ground. Neither man said a word. Henry watched them quietly for a few seconds, asserting his control. Finally, he began to speak again. "Now then, we've wasted enough time with you two. I've got something to say and I'm only going to say it once. Then I'm going to ask you a few questions and you're going to answer them. And you better tell me the truth 'cause I'll know if you're lying."

Henry stopped and studied their faces as they looked back at him. "I'm a United States Marshal and this is my deputy."

"Lawmen?" one of them said. "Why didn't you tell us who you was in the first place? Me and Orrin always help the law when we can. Ain't that right, Orrin?"

Orrin nodded in agreement, but said nothing. His cheek still flamed red where Henry had slapped him.

"I'm sure you are the two most law-abiding citizens in Evans. That's why we came here to talk to you," Henry said. "We're looking for a fellow twenty-five to thirty years old with a scar on his right cheek. He's thin, real thin, and wears a tan vest and hat. Seen anyone like that lately?"

The two men looked at each other, neither saying anything.

Henry eyed the man next to Orrin. "What's your name?"

"Jim."

"Well, Jim," Henry said, "have you seen this fellow?"

Jim hesitated for a second, then said, "He was here. Got in last night."

"His horse here now?"

"No, he left it for about an hour and told me to feed it and rub it down for him. I was going to tell him that I was too busy to get to it right away, but I could tell by the way he looked that he didn't like being disappointed."

"You think he left town?"

"He didn't say and I didn't ask."

Henry nodded, then he and Zeke remounted. Henry faced the two men again from atop his horse. "That wasn't so hard now, was it?"

Henry and Zeke rode up the street again. "What about our horses?" Zeke asked.

"I wouldn't let either one of them touch my horse. You want them tending yours?"

"No, I reckon not."

"You reckon not is right. We'll go back to Johnson's."

A few minutes later they were back in front of Johnson's Livery Stable. "Back so soon?" Johnson said.

"The fellows down at Eli's convinced us that this is a better place to board our horses," Henry said. "They'll need feeding and grooming."

"I'll take good care of them."

"What's a good hotel here that has a dining room?"

"That'd be the Anderson Hotel."

"What about saloons? Is there any one of them that's better than the rest?"

"That's easy. Outside of Denver, the Blue Saloon is the best saloon in the whole Colorado Territory by a country mile," Johnson said.

"Really," Henry said. "I'm surprised to hear that. This

looks like a new town, and none too big at that. How's it support such a grand saloon?"

"Four miles north of here is another new town, called Greeley. It's got almost three times as many people as Evans, but you won't find a single saloon or pool hall anywhere. Greeley's full of libraries and churches, but no gambling dens or bordellos."

"So the people of Greeley have to come here to do their drinking," Henry said.

Johnson shrugged. "And gambling, and whoring."

Henry nodded, then turned to his grandson. "Let's get us a hotel room and some supper and lay plans for catching this Ledyard fellow."

Henry reached into his pocket and pulled out a couple of coins. Handing them to Johnson he said, "If we have to leave in the middle of the night we'll just take the horses and go." Johnson accepted the payment with a nod of his head. "If you should see this fellow we're after, leave word for me at the hotel," Henry said. "Name's Marshal Henry McNichol."

"I'll keep an eyeball peeled," Johnson said.

CHAPTER EIGHTEEN

Obeying the neatly lettered sign at the entrance, Zeke and Henry wiped their boots on the mat before pushing through the batwing doors. It was the first time either had ever done such a thing before entering a saloon.

Zeke looked around the large room in awe. The Blue Saloon was doing a brisk business with the after-dinner trade. It was a grand saloon befitting a much larger town—maybe Denver or Kansas City, and was certainly the finest saloon Zeke had ever seen in his young life.

The hardwood floor had been scrubbed clean of the previous day's accumulation of mud and dirt as it was every morning before opening. Along the rear wall was a long, ornately carved bar made of fine oak by craftsmen in Chicago. The bar had been sanded smooth and varnished before shipment to Evans for installation. A brass rod traveled the length of the bar about ten inches off the floor and served as a footrest.

The bottom of the walls was covered with four feet of wood-paneled wainscoting. The upper part was medium-blue wallpaper with a large print pattern. The ceiling was painted a light blue. Kerosene lamps hung suspended from the ceiling every ten feet or so. Men shouting numbers as the wheel spun surrounded a roulette table in one corner. In the opposite corner a pot-bellied stove yawned widely displaying its empty interior. The remainder of the room was filled with tables and chairs, almost all of which were occupied.

Oil paintings depicting women in various stages of undress adorned the walls, and there was a large mirror behind the bar, its surface coated with a film of accumulated tobacco smoke. Mounted above the mirror was the stuffed head of a stag, its antlers pointing up at the ceiling. Brass spittoons were placed no more than eight feet apart, and signs on the walls read NO SPITTING ON THE FLOOR.

Some men were drinking with friends, others with saloon gals. At some of the tables poker games were in progress. The room was alive with activity, and a score of voices speaking at once assaulted Zeke's ears. A thick cloud of blue smoke engulfed the kerosene lamps choking off the meager yellow light they emitted.

"This is unbelievable," Zeke said. "Have you ever seen anything like this before?"

"Once," Henry said, "when I was in St. Louis. It's still impressive, though."

Both men stood gaping at the room, transfixed by the magnitude of it all. Zeke felt his breath catch in his throat when a young saloon gal walked past. She wore a dress that pushed her breasts up, fit tightly around her midsection, and then cascaded almost to the floor. When she walked Zeke spied her ankles, which were covered by a mesh-like stocking. The firm flatness of her stomach and the fullness of her breasts commanded his attention.

He stared at her, and his face flushed red when she turned and held his gaze. Before he could look away, she smiled at him and then continued on her way.

"He may come in here, and then maybe he won't," Henry said. "This is obviously the most popular saloon in Evans, but there are a lot of other places he could go—if he's still in town. Since you know him on sight, you stay here and keep an eye out for him. If you see him, stick with him. Maybe we can find out where he's staying. I'll check back with you later."

"Where are you going to be?"

"I'm going to look around town and see if I can't find him. No sense in both of us staying in the same place." Zeke nodded his agreement with that. "Remember now, if you see him don't approach him and don't let him know you're a lawman." Henry turned to leave, then turned back again. "Oh, and one more thing."

"I know. Stay away from them saloon gals," Zeke said.

Henry didn't return Zeke's smile, but gave a slight nod of his head, and then was gone.

Zeke surveyed the room again wondering what to do next. He couldn't stand in the doorway all night. That was too obvious and Ledyard might recognize him if he stumbled into him. He thought about standing at the bar, but it was too far from the door to see people coming in. He suddenly felt awkward and self-conscious standing in the room with no one to talk to and no place to sit down.

Zeke walked left past the large front window, then turned right and walked several steps along the wall and stopped to get his bearings. Three men sat at a nearby table drinking whisky. Fifteen feet straight ahead along the wall, a man pounded away on a piano, although no one seemed to be listening. Zeke thought that would be a good place for him since he could stand by the piano and see the entire room from there.

Just then one of the men at the table looked up at Zeke. "Hey, kid, you want to play some poker? We need a fourth to get a game going."

Zeke was caught by surprise. The men looked rough, not the kind of men he'd want to get in a disagreement with. "No, no thanks," Zeke said. "I'm waiting for someone."

"So play a few hands till he gets here."

"I'd better not," Zeke said feeling his mouth go dry.

"Come on, kid, without a fourth we can't play."

"Don't beg the kid," one of his companions said. "If he's afraid to play, leave him alone."

"I ain't afraid to play," Zeke said. "I just got other things to do, that's all."

"Yeah, sure, kid," came the reply.

Zeke started toward the piano without looking at them again. He'd only gone a few steps when the same saloon gal came back.

"Buy a girl a drink?" she asked.

Zeke was at a loss for words. She was a few years older than he, and had beautiful auburn hair that fell richly to her shoulders. Her breasts were swollen and strained against the fabric covering them. Her hourglass figure was accentuated by the cut of her dress, and Zeke could sense the taut, young legs moving under the folds of the material.

He was attracted to her, but he didn't know what to do; he had no experience whatsoever with women. It reminded him of the time he went to a church social in Wattersville and stared across the room for two hours at Molly Bennett, working up the courage to ask her for a dance. When he finally asked and she accepted, his inept dancing embarrassed both of them so much that she got mad at him. And he and Molly were only fourteen at the time—this woman was surely used to men who knew what to do with a woman. He didn't know what to say: he could do nothing but stare in reply to her question.

She smiled again. He knew she could read his mind. "Don't you want to have a drink with me?" she said.

He wouldn't be made a fool of again. And certainly not now when he needed to keep his mind on what he was there for.

"Well, I'd like to ma'am, but I really hadn't planned on drinking tonight," he said. If Ledyard came in the last thing Zeke would need was a bellyful of alcohol.

She drew back in surprise, giving Zeke a second look. "No?" she said, her anger rising. "You mean you don't want to have a drink with me?"

He wanted to reply, but he couldn't think of anything to say.

"You're not gambling, you don't want a drink, and you obviously don't want a woman; then what'd you come in here for in the first place?" she said almost shouting.

"I didn't mean anything—", he said, but she turned and walked away before he could finish.

Zeke saw that people were looking at him. He felt the self-consciousness that comes with public ridicule. She's right, he thought. He wasn't drinking, gambling, or looking for a woman. A man like that would stick out in a place like this. He didn't want to draw attention to himself, and he sure didn't like the awkwardness he felt.

Still, he didn't want to drink, and he didn't want to be distracted by a woman. That left gambling. He had a pocketful of money, and he could afford to risk a little bit of it in a poker game if it would allow him to blend in with the crowd and keep an eye on the door. Sure, that's what he'd do. That would be easy—he'd already been asked to play in a game. He walked toward the table where the three men still sat drinking whiskey.

"Well, look who's back."

"That invite still good?" Zeke asked.

"Pull up a chair. We've been saving it for you," came the smiling reply.

CHAPTER NINETEEN

Fortunately, the empty chair provided a good view of the entrance. Zeke sat down and ran his eye over the three men at the table. They were all smiling—not at Zeke, but at each other. They smiled the way a man smiles when he pays twenty dollars for a fifty-dollar horse.

Zeke reached into his pocket and took out two coins, holding them under the table. Four five-dollar half-eagles. He put them on the table. "So, what are the stakes?"

The man across from Zeke, a heavyset fellow with greasy blond hair trailing down in long tangles from under his brown hat said, "Is that all the money you got?"

"No, I got more," Zeke said, then immediately regretted it.

To Zeke's right sat a burly fellow with a week-old growth of thick black whiskers who was staring at the coins in front of Zeke. He stared the way a man who hasn't had water in three days stares at a full canteen. "Dollar ante, three dollar limit on raises," he said.

Zeke sucked in his breath. "Kind of a rich game, ain't it?" he said.

"If we're going to play, we might as well make it interesting," the burly one said. "Here, let me change that half eagle for you." He reached over and took one of Zeke's coins, and gave him five silver dollars

The man to Zeke's left spoke next. He was thin, with pock-marked skin and narrow eyes. "I believe you said you had to leave when a friend of yours came in?"

"That's right, I'm waiting for someone," Zeke said.

"I bet you won't be so eager to leave if you win a few hands," the thin one said. He was talking to Zeke, but looking at his two companions when he said it.

The man across from Zeke, a heavyset fellow with greasy blond hair trailing down in long tangles from under his brown hat, pulled out a deck of worn pasteboards. "Since I'm holding the cards, supposing I deal the first hand," he said smiling as he began to shuffle the deck. Although he had big, meaty hands he was adept at handling the cards.

Everyone threw in a dollar. "Five-card draw, need a pair to open," the dealer said.

Zeke waited until the deal was finished before he picked up his cards. He saw a pair of tens, a two of spades, a four of diamonds and a seven of spades.

"It's to you, Josh," the dealer said to the burly one to Zeke's right.

"Can't do it," Josh said.

Zeke felt the dealer's eyes shift to him. "What do you say, kid?"

Zeke looked at his cards and swallowed hard. "Open for two dollars," he said placing two silver dollars into the pot.

"Oh, boy, here we go," the thin one to Zeke's left said. "I knew it the minute we asked this kid to sit down. Alvin, I said to myself, this here's a wolf in sheep's clothing."

Zeke puffed up at that remark. They thought he knew

what he was doing! If they only knew that he'd never played poker for money before. Zeke suppressed an urge to smile.

"Come on, Alvin, you in or not?" the dealer said.

"Well, I'd like to stay in, but I can't play with this mess you dealt me," he said throwing his cards down in disgust.

Zeke felt the dealer's eyes on him again. Zeke could almost see the wheels turning in his brain as the dealer studied him.

"Call you," he said at last. "Back to you, Josh."

"I agree with Alvin," he said throwing his cards down. "These are mighty sorrowful cards you dealt."

The dealer ignored the remark and looked at Zeke. "How many, kid?"

"Three."

"And dealer takes two." He put the new cards into his hand and studied it for a moment. Then he looked at Zeke. "It's to you, kid."

Zeke still only had a pair of tens. He didn't want to put any more money into the pot behind such a weak hand, but he remembered a similar situation a few years back when he was playing for matches with Uncle Billy. Zeke had opened and then didn't raise his bet when he failed to strengthen his hand. "Don't ever do that," Uncle Billy had said. "You tell everyone in the game that you didn't improve your hand when you don't raise after getting new cards. You can always drop out later if other players raise you again." It made sense then and it still made sense. "Two more," Zeke said.

"What'd I tell you, Tom?" Alvin said to the dealer. "We got us a regular card shark in this here game."

Tom ignored the remark. His eyes shifted from his cards to Zeke, then back to his cards. "Call," he said, throwing coins into the pot. "What you got, kid?"

A losing hand, that's what he had, Zeke thought. "Pair of

tens," he said. He waited for Tom to reach in and scoop up the coins in his big paw.

"Beats me," Tom said, throwing his cards face down onto the table. Then he guffawed. "You boys is right. Them's mighty poor cards I dealt." Then he laughed again. "See if you can do any better, Josh."

Zeke watched Josh shuffle the cards. He was surprised at how well he and Tom handled them. He looked down at the new pile of coins he had in front of him. It was the first money he'd ever won playing poker! He wanted to count it, but he knew he couldn't do that in front of them. He made a quick calculation of the last game and figured he'd won a ten-dollar pot, five dollars of which was his own money. So he'd won five dollars!

The three men continued to drink, reaching for the bottle and filling their glasses as soon as they were emptied. Zeke was glad they didn't offer to share their whiskey with him.

Zeke won a twelve-dollar pot with three fours in the next hand.

Zeke kept an eye on the entrance throughout the game: no sign of Ledyard. On his deal Zeke called for a game of five-card stud. He lost five dollars before dropping out after his third card. Alvin had a pair of queens showing, and the highest card Zeke had was an eight of hearts. Alvin won the pot and called for another bottle.

It was Alvin's turn to deal, and he decided they'd play five-card draw again. Zeke won a fifteen-dollar pot with a diamond flush.

The three men continued to drink.

On Tom's deal, Zeke had three fives before the discard. Alvin and Tom couldn't open, but Josh opened for three dollars. Zeke called, took two cards and drew the fourth five. Alvin and Tom also called.

Josh bet another three dollars, and Zeke raised him three

more. Alvin, Tom and Josh all stared at Zeke in disbelief. Alvin and Tom then dropped out, and Josh raised the bet three more. Zeke raised the bet again.

Josh looked at Tom. Zeke thought he saw Tom give Josh an almost imperceptible shrug in reply. "Three more," Josh said.

Zeke threw some bills onto the pile in the middle of the table. They were looking at the largest pot of the night. "Call," Zeke said.

"Full house, kings over tens," Josh said. He leaned forward as though to draw in the bills and coins in the center of the table.

"Four fives," Zeke said.

Suddenly the three men stopped as though frozen in time: Alvin with his glass in the air, Tom with his hand around the bottle, and Josh with his hand near the pot. None of them moved.

What's going on? Zeke thought. Why are they acting so strangely? He'd been getting good cards all night. Suddenly, Zeke jumped as Alvin slammed his glass onto the table.

"What I want to know is where'd that other five come from?" Alvin said.

"Yeah! Did you give him that other five, Tom?" Josh asked.

Did they think he was cheating, Zeke wondered?

"Quiet, you fools! You drink too much!" Tom said to Alvin and Josh, giving them each a hard stare. Then he pushed the cards over to Josh. "Go on, it's your deal."

Josh muttered something under his breath that Zeke couldn't make out. The pile of money still sat in the middle of the table.

"It's your pot, kid, go ahead and take it," Tom said.

Zeke would just as soon have the left the pot for them if they'd let him out of the game. That would never do, though, and he knew it. He pulled the bills and coins toward himself, not looking up at any of the three men. He now had an impressive pile of money in front of him.

Zeke lost four dollars in the next hand. He drew a pair of threes, but dropped out when Tom began raising his bets.

It was Zeke's turn to deal again, and he still felt the glare of their eyes on him. As the dealer, he'd be even more of a target if they called him a cheater. What if they pulled a gun on him?

He dealt the hands and then looked at his cards. His heart sank when he saw that he had dealt himself three eights. They'd think he was cheating for sure now!

Alvin and Tom couldn't do it, but Josh opened for three dollars. Zeke breathed a sigh of relief. He called the bet, as did Alvin and Tom.

"How many?" Zeke asked.

"Three," said Alvin.

"Two," said Tom.

"Two," said Josh.

Zeke looked at his cards again: three eights, a four of hearts and a jack of diamonds. He pulled two of the eights out of his hand and threw them face down onto the table. "Dealer takes two," he said.

After sliding two more cards off the top, Zeke was almost afraid to look at them. He turned up the corners on a queen of hearts and a six of clubs. Trying not to smile, Zeke picked up the two cards and added them to his hand.

"Raise two," Josh said.

"I'm out," Zeke said throwing his cards face down onto the table.

"What's the matter, you don't want to stay in unless you got four of a kind?" Josh said leaning toward Zeke and spewing whiskey breath in Zeke's face.

What's going on, Zeke thought? They got mad when he won, and they got mad when he dropped out. Zeke looked at the three men, each one glaring back at him. How could a friendly game turn ugly so fast? Subconsciously he ran his hand down to the butt of his Colt for reassurance.

"Keep your hand away from that gun!" Josh roared, reaching for his own gun.

"I wasn't doing anything," Zeke said thoroughly shaken.

"Just the same, you keep your hands where we can see them!" Alvin said.

Zeke put his hands on the table, his money lying in a loose pile between them. He watched quietly as Tom went on to call Josh's bluff and win the pot.

It was now or never, Zeke thought. Quickly, he stuffed the bills and coins in his pocket, then stood up. He looked down at the three surprised faces. "I got to be going," he said.

"Sit down! You ain't going nowhere!" Alvin said.

"Thought you said you could stay until your friend showed up," Tom said. "I don't see nobody."

"That's just it, I got to go look for him. He must have misunderstood where we were supposed to meet," Zeke said. He watched the entrance again, hoping Henry would walk through the door. Zeke backed away from the table.

He felt Josh grab his right wrist in a powerful hand that came halfway to his elbow. "You ain't leaving with our money!" Josh said tugging on Zeke's arm.

Let me go! Let me go! Zeke thought as he panicked at the grip on his arm. He used his free left hand to pull his vest aside displaying the badge. "I'm a Deputy United States Marshal!" he announced. Caught by surprise, Josh relaxed his grip and Zeke pulled his arm away.

There, that got them, Zeke thought, his fear abating now that his arm was free.

The men began to laugh.

"That's a good one. Deputy U. S. Marshal," Tom said. Then he slapped his thigh. "And I'm President Grant!"

"Laugh all you want, but I *am* a deputy marshal," Zeke said. Then he backed away from the table a few more steps. The men stopped laughing.

Josh got up and reached for him again. "Get your ass back here! You ain't going nowhere with that money!"

Suddenly the same saloon gal Zeke had been talking with before appeared and stepped between Zeke and Josh. "What's all the ruckus about?" she asked.

"This kid sat down to play poker with us and after winning a few hands he wants to leave without giving us a chance to win our money back," Josh said.

"Yeah, and we ain't hardly played more than a half hour," Alvin said.

Zeke continued to back away from the table in the direction of the entrance. As he reached the door he saw Josh raise his fist toward him and try to get past the girl. She planted both hands firmly on his chest and continued to talk to him and the other two men. Zeke turned and pushed through the batwings into the street. Never before had the night air felt so good to him.

The relief he felt quickly gave way to shame. He looked down at the badge on his shirt, a cold piece of dull metal unable to produce any light of its own: it only reflected light from an outside source. In the semi-darkness of the street, it hung lifelessly on Zeke's shirt with nary a glimmer.

Zeke thought of his grandfather taking on two big men in the middle of the street and taking them both to jail in front of the whole town. And how he dealt with the two roughnecks in the livery stable. Then he thought of his own behavior just now: how he ran off, hiding behind a woman's skirt.

He pulled the badge off his shirt and stared at it in his hand. Stupid badge! He never wanted it in the first place. He didn't ask for this job. Who did Grandpa think he was ordering him and Uncle Billy around and forcing them to do something they didn't want to do?

Zeke looked at the badge one last time, then flung it to the ground. The hell with this job and the hell with Grandpa! He'd start for home in the morning, and get back to doing what he knew best—farming.

CHAPTER TWENTY

Zeke began to walk up the street.

"Wait," a woman's voice called.

He turned to see the saloon gal walking toward him. "I suppose I should thank you for helping me in there," he said.

"No thanks necessary. I did it for them, not you."

Zeke flashed a puzzled look at her.

"The way them boys was acting you might have killed all three of them. I mean, here you are, a professional lawman against three drunk ranch hands."

She moved closer to him. He could smell the cheap perfume she had splashed all over herself. To Zeke it smelled like the finest perfume that ever came out of France. She flashed a smile. Her teeth were yellow, but she was only missing one front tooth. She slipped her right hand onto the bare part of his chest where the top of his shirt was unbuttoned.

He felt a wave of heat rush from his head down into his feet, and suddenly all of his nerve endings came alive.

"Come on, let's get out of the street," she said.

Her left hand went around his waist and gently pulled him

along with her as she walked toward the stairway at the side of the saloon.

"Where we going?" he asked.

"I got a room upstairs. We'll use the outside stairway; no sense using the one inside and running into those three again."

He had to agree with that. Actually, he'd have agreed with anything she said. He placed his right arm around her waist as they climbed the stairs.

She looked up at him and giggled like a schoolgirl. "We're almost there."

Two more steps and they were on the landing at the top of the stairs. "Be a dear and light the lamp for me, won't you?" she said. "I so hate going into a dark room. There's matches on the table just inside the door."

He took his arm off her and pushed the door open. It was too dark to see anything, so he leaned in and used his left hand to grope for the table. He never saw the gun come down.

~

He awoke with his head feeling like it had a tomahawk buried in it. It hurt to open his eyes, and at first, everything was a fuzzy yellow. After a few seconds his eyes focused and he saw Grandpa, the girl, and another man in the room. A single kerosene lamp glowed on the table next to the door.

"What happened? What's going on?" Zeke asked. His eyes grew accustomed to the dimly lit room, and he saw that he was lying on a bed.

"That's what we'd like to know," Henry said. "What are you doing in her room, and how'd you get that bump on your head?"

Zeke ran his hand to the lump on his head and winced.

His fingers came away sticky with drying blood. He tried to sit up, but a wave of nausea hit him and he lay back down. He just wanted to close his eyes and sleep. He stared at the shadows dancing on the ceiling as the flame in the lamp flickered. His eyes began to close when he heard a man's voice and turned his head to the left.

"Zeke, I'm Sheriff Drummond. According to Carla, you and her was just coming into her room here when someone hit you over the head. She said whoever hit you then slammed the door on her and she couldn't see what happened next. Afraid to come in herself, she came and got me. I ran into your grandfather on the way over here. Does that sound about right to you?"

Zeke eyed the heavyset man standing before him. He had a bushy moustache, and from the creases in his face and the tired look in his eyes Zeke figured he was only a few years younger than Grandpa.

Zeke tried to remember, but it hurt to think. "Yeah, I guess that's what happened. I mean, I got hit over the head when I opened the door and leaned in to find the matches on the table. I don't know what happened after that."

"What in tarnation are you doing here in the first place?" Henry demanded. "I told you to stay in the saloon and wait for me if Ledyard didn't show up."

Zeke didn't answer that. What could he say, anyway?

"I invited him up here," Carla said. "He looked like he could use some cheering up after he had that argument with them cowboys and left the saloon."

"What argument? What cowboys?" Drummond asked.

"He was playing poker with three cowboys and quit after only playing a few hands. They were mad because he wouldn't give them a chance to win their money back. It looked like there was going to be trouble so I went over to see if I could smooth things out. That's part of my job, you know, keeping things friendly."

"So where's that money now?" Drummond asked.

Zeke ran his hand over his left pocket. He didn't feel anything. His stomach flip-flopped as panic set in. He shoved his hand deep into the pocket. Nothing there!

"It's empty," Drummond said. "All your pockets are empty. How much did you win?"

Zeke fought hard against the fog in his head to remember. "Fifty, maybe sixty dollars."

"How much did you have all together? You know, counting the money you had with you when the game started?" Drummond asked.

"A hundred dollars, I think. Maybe a little more."

Drummond let out a low whistle and shook his head slowly from side to side.

"Where's that Colt I gave you?" Henry asked.

Zeke struggled to sit up, wincing at the pain that shot through his head as he did so. The six-gun, holster and gun belt were gone. He turned a blank face to the two lawmen.

"Took that, too, did they?" Drummond said.

Henry leaned over and pulled Zeke's vest aside. "They even took his badge."

"He's lucky they didn't take his boots," Drummond said.

"What I don't understand is how'd this whole thing happen?" Henry said. Both he and Drummond turned and looked at Carla.

"What are you looking at me for? How the hell am I supposed to know? I told you the door was slammed in my face before I could see anything!"

Henry and Drummond continued to stare at her, neither man saying anything. She scowled uncomfortably under their scrutiny, then turned away, unable to face them. The silence continued.

"They must have followed us," she said at last.

"If they followed you, how'd they get in room ahead of you without you seeing them?" Drummond asked.

"I don't know. Maybe they used the stairway inside the saloon to get to my room."

"If they did that they couldn't have followed you, could they?" Drummond said. "How did they know you two were together and that you'd be going up to this room?"

"HOW THE HELL DO I KNOW?" she screamed. "I'm the innocent party here! What are you accusing me for? I came and got you as soon as it happened."

"You sure you didn't wait five minutes to give them cowboys time to get away down that inside stairway?" Henry said.

"Now why would I do that? I didn't even see who did it. All I know is I haven't got his money or his gun. So what are you treating me like a criminal for?"

"Oh, I wouldn't be surprised if some of that money finds its way back to you before too long," Henry said.

"YOU AIN'T GOT A DAMN THING ON ME!" she screamed. "NO WITNESS, NO EVIDENCE, NO NOTHING! Go on, get out of my room! And take him with you!" she said, waving her arm in Zeke's direction. "He's bleeding all over my damn sheets!"

Henry and Drummond leaned over and helped Zeke up by each arm. Maintaining a firm hold on him, they led him through the door to the landing outside at the top of the stairs. The door slammed behind them.

Zeke could see the steps clearly enough, but his feet had trouble hitting them squarely; he stumbled twice and would have fallen if the two men hadn't been there. Reaching the ground, Zeke leaned against the railing for support.

"Anything else I can do for you, Marshal?" Drummond asked.

"No, I'll take it from here. Thanks for your help, Sheriff."

Drummond nodded, then walked off down the street.

"Look at you! You got a bump on your head, your money's gone, your gun is gone..." Henry said. "They even took your badge." He glared at Zeke. "Ten years I had that Colt, and it took you only a week or so to let some saddle bums take it away from you."

Zeke studied his boots, then shifted his feet, still leaning against the railing for support. He looked up at Grandpa, but found it difficult to face him, and returned his gaze to his boots. What could he say?

"All you had to do was stay in the saloon and watch for Ledyard. That's all. But you couldn't do that, could you? No, you had to play poker. And then you had to have a woman. How many times have I told you to stay away from saloon gals?" Henry shook his head in disgust. "All you had to do was watch for Ledyard—not play cards, not drink whiskey, not talk to cowboys or saloon gals—just watch for Ledyard." He shook his head again.

"I didn't drink any whiskey," Zeke said. Immediately he was sorry he said it.

Henry shot him a look that would wither the Devil himself. "Don't get smart with me, boy," he said. His face got all red and he looked as if he might explode. Then, as if calling on some inner resolve, he regained control of himself. "I was hoping to show you and Billy a few things before I died. I wanted to make men out of you, but I never had a chance in the first place."

Henry shook his head slowly as he looked down at the ground as though he was talking to himself. "I don't know how I could have the two of you in my family. One was a coward, and the other's a fool." He looked up and saw Zeke watching him. "Neither one of you'd have lasted two days out here if you didn't have me to look after you," Henry said.

Who said they wanted to come out here in the first place, Zeke thought? Anger rose up within him and he stared hard at his grandfather. Because of Grandpa, Uncle Billy was dead. Because of Grandpa, Zeke's money was gone and his head was killing him. Grandpa had dragged them out here against their will, and now he was mad because they didn't measure up to his standards. Well, the hell with him then!

"Better go on up to the room and get cleaned up. Then get some sleep. I'll see you in the morning," Henry said. "It's still early; I'm going to see if I can't find this Ledyard fellow myself."

Zeke pushed himself away from the railing and walked slowly past Henry without a word. His head hurt with each footfall as he made his way up the street. When he got to the hotel, he turned to see if Henry was watching him; he was nowhere in sight. Zeke kept going past the hotel and walked over to Johnson's Livery Stable.

Sure enough, the door was unlocked. He pushed the door open just far enough to squeeze through and squinted into the darkness. In a few moments he could see well enough to find an empty stall. He scooped some hay together and made a bed for himself. Then he went back and closed the door all the way. He groped his way through the darkness back to the empty stall. In a few minutes he was asleep.

TuesdayZeke awoke just before dawn as he had done for as long as he could remember. He pushed the door open to let what little light there was into the stable. Quickly, he saddled his horse and led it out of the barn, closing the door behind him. Then he rode out of Evans heading east. With any luck he'd catch a train and be back in Wattersville in a few days.

Although the sun was still below the horizon, he could see the first rays of dawn fanning out in the distance before him.

He pointed his horse toward the light and moved past the edge of town at a lope.

He pushed thoughts of Grandpa out of his mind. He didn't let his mind dwell on Billy, either. Thinking of Billy only filled him with grief, and he wanted to feel good for a change. He thought about the farm back home, but that would never be the same with pa and Uncle Billy gone. Still, he could adjust—he'd have to. So he thought about how much he wanted to be back in Wattersville, to see his friends again, and to get on with his life. He pushed all unhappy thoughts out of his mind, and vowed to begin a new life starting today.

His head felt much better, although it still ached some. The nausea was gone and his vision was clear.

He would be all right.

CHAPTER TWENTY-ONE

The sun rose up before him causing Zeke to keep his eyes on the ground to avoid the blinding light. He didn't mind though; for the first time since he left Wattersville he had a care-free sense of freedom. He thought of the events that had occurred in just the past week or so: Pa getting killed, his becoming a lawman, Uncle Billy getting killed, and then traveling with Grandpa by himself. Until now he hadn't realized how much of a strain he'd been under. His thoughts drifted back to Wattersville, and how much he looked forward to getting home.

Soon the sun rose a little higher above the horizon, and Zeke dipped the brim of his hat to shield his eyes. The foothills of the Rockies were behind him and the open range lay ahead as he rode up and down hills on a decline into the flatlands.

Still, he had a long way to go. The pain in his head had subsided to a dull ache, but he was battling fatigue already as he had not slept well in the stable. What he really needed was to rest in bed, and the thought of a mattress and clean sheets tormented him. He knew he should have stayed in Evans until he felt better, but he couldn't abide Grandpa anymore. No, he'd have to carry on the best he could.

After a couple of hours his stomach began to growl, and he realized how hungry he was. Zeke rarely skipped breakfast since it was the most important meal of the day on a farm, and now his belly was telling him how it didn't appreciate his not feeding it that morning. He felt weak and dizzy.

Still, his spirits were high. And why not? The morning sun was shining on him, the open range beckoned him forward, and he was heading home. No more being a lawman, no more contending with Grandpa, no more thoughts of facing down a killer, and no more hanging around saloons with strangers. Just day after glorious day of peaceful work on the farm—<u>his</u> farm.

His stomach growled again, interrupting his thoughts. Maybe he'd come across a little town where he could get something to eat. No, wait, he didn't have any money!

Maybe he could kill a rabbit or something. He looked around hopefully. His mouth began to water at the thought of a rabbit turning on a spit, its juices dripping into the fire. He was so hungry he could almost picture one scampering into view. But he didn't have a gun! The Colt was gone, and his rifle was back at the hotel in Evans.

Suddenly the gravity of the situation hit him; his empty stomach lurched, and Zeke fought the panic welling up inside and threatening to boil over. He was out on the open range, four hundred miles from home, with no gun and no money. He didn't even have knife to skin a rabbit if he could somehow kill one. Then he remembered his grandfather's words the night before: "Neither one of you'd have lasted two days out here if you didn't have me to look after you."

He'd show him. He'd make it back to Wattersville without

Grandpa's help. Grandpa never did think much of him and Uncle Billy, but he was wrong—about both of them. Zeke set his jaw tightly in resolve.

But then the fear came back. What did he know about surviving out in the open? Not much, he had to admit. And, of course, he didn't have a gun for hunting or protection, and no money to get one or to buy food. Maybe Grandpa was right after all. It pained him to admit it.

Though the sun was no longer in his eyes, he dropped his gaze to the ground just in front of his horse. His whole posture slumped and his head dropped forward as he pondered his predicament. Maybe he should go back to Evans and make it up with Grandpa.

No! He could never do that. Not after the things Grandpa said. It was Grandpa's fault he was in this mess in the first place. If it wasn't for him he'd still be in Wattersville working the farm with Uncle Billy. Except for Pa's death, everything that had happened was because of Grandpa. No, he couldn't go back.

The horse moved steadily through the tall grass at a comfortable gait, and the rhythmic strides of the animal had a hypnotic effect on Zeke. Mile after mile of unchanging landscape further added to the monotony. There was no one to talk to, either, and it was getting hard to keep his eyes open.

Finally, sleep overtook him and he rode along with his chin almost touching his chest. The reins fell from his hands, and he sat precariously in the saddle.

Suddenly the horse reared up violently, startled at something. Roused from sleep, Zeke found himself tumbling backward off the animal; he grabbed frantically for the saddle horn, but it slipped from his grasp. Jerking his boots out of the stirrups so the horse wouldn't drag him, he rolled backward off the panicked roan.

Fortunately, he landed on his backside instead of on his already-injured head. He lay looking up at the clear blue sky and heard the pounding of hooves as the horse raced off. Zeke got to his feet. His backside was only a little sore, but his head ached again.

That's just great, he thought, watching the horse disappear in the distance. There went his water, his bedroll, and his way back home. He didn't even have money to take a stage if he made it to a town or relay station.

The land stretched out in front of him so pristine that Zeke feared he was miles from any help. Oh well, the horse would calm down in a few minutes anyway and Zeke would find him grazing a mile or so up ahead. He began to walk, continuing eastward, the same direction the horse had run off. Stiff at first, his back loosened up after a few minutes, but he was still sore and his head was throbbing again.

Endless waves of knee-high blue grama grass and buffalo grass lay before him ensnaring his legs with each step and draining his energy. After wading through the thick, tall grass for only an hour his legs were tired and heavy, and his left knee hurt. The sun bore down on him further sapping his strength.

He remembered refilling his canteen at a creek about an hour out of Evans. Maybe there was more water up ahead. He sure hoped so.

Hours passed and the sun crossed its zenith and dropped in the sky behind him. His left knee throbbing now, Zeke limped along mile after mile, but saw only grass and a few scattered trees.

Stopping for only a moment, he removed his hat and wiped the sweat from his brow as he scanned the horizon. No sign of his horse. Where was it? Why had it run so far away?

Averting his eyes from the blazing sun, he glanced at the

cloudless blue sky. No chance of rain. Boy, he sure could use a drink of water.

Zeke set off again across the empty Plains that stretched before him, trudging through the high grass. Hour after hour he continued across the unchanging landscape. Taking an occasional break helped some, but his strength continued to ebb. Although he was still sweating somewhat, which was a good sign, his mouth was dry and his meager urine had turned dark yellow.

It was barely dusk when Zeke stopped for the day, thoroughly spent. Pulling up some long grass, he made a mat for himself, and fell asleep in a few minutes.

The next morning he awoke hopeful of finding water, and maybe something to eat. Despite the grass mat, his back was even stiffer than it was when he fell off his horse the day before. With great difficulty, he rose to his feet and headed toward the sun just above the eastern horizon.

He trudged on all day with no sign of his horse, water, or food. He saw nothing and no one. Just more of the same: endless acres of grass shimmering in the hot sun.

With the sun at the horizon behind him and darkness setting in, he stopped for the day. Once again he made a grass mat for himself and tried to get comfortable. Unaccustomed to walking long distances, his leather boots had rubbed his feet raw. Zeke dared not remove them to sleep—as swollen as his feet were he might never get his boots back on.

He awoke an hour past dawn. The night's rest did little for his head, which hurt so much he barely noticed the pangs of his empty stomach. Pulling his hat brim low against the rising sun, he once again fought his way through the tall grass.

It was much slower going than the day before as he tired rapidly and took frequent breaks. Doggedly he pressed on, though his head ached, his legs were leaden, and his weak left knee throbbed protesting every step on that foot. The knee hadn't hurt like this since the day that darn young colt kicked him when he was seven.

The sun continued toward its apex in a cloudless blue sky, baking Zeke. His only relief from its rays came during breaks under the dwindling cottonwoods scattered along the way. Still, he saw nothing and no one save the vast Plains that stretched before him. Nauseating fear pierced his stomach: what if he never found water or crossed paths with anyone?

Dizzy and weak, he pressed on, stumbling and falling more repeatedly. His empty stomach cried out for food, and his headache worsened as the afternoon wore on; he banged the heels of his hands on the sides of his head against the pain.

The sun was well behind him now in the western sky. He shuffled along, dragging his legs through the tall grass, his mouth as dry as the ground he trod upon. After a couple more hours, his legs cramped up and he had to stop for the day, although the sun hadn't set yet.

It wasn't until after Zeke took his hat off and placed it over his face to sleep that he realized he wasn't sweating anymore. His body had almost run out of water. He knew he had one more day, at most, to find his horse or get help. Tomorrow was his last chance.

Zeke awoke the next morning with the sun just above the eastern horizon. How long had he slept? Eight, ten hours? Recoiling at the massive throbbing in his head, he sat up and looked around, but nothing had changed from the night before: endless terrain with no hint of people or water.

Zeke struggled to his feet, pulled his hat brim low and headed toward the rising sun. As time passed, his headache got even worse, and the base of his skull throbbed mercilessly. In fact, it was so bad he had to stop a few times as the pain overwhelmed him.

Zeke remembered a time on the farm when he forgot his

canteen but kept working instead of going back for it. As dehydration worsened he had developed a headache like the one he had now, at the back of his head, only not nearly as severe.

Despite the pain, Zeke pressed on the best he could in the scorching summer sun. His tongue was swollen and his mouth as dry as a bucket of sand. Thoughts of cool water playing across his parched tongue tormented him until he thought he'd go mad.

Later in the morning, his foot caught in a prairie dog hole and he tumbled forward onto his face. He lay there, too tired and weak to move. It would be so easy to just stay here, to fall back to sleep and hope someone found him. But he was in the middle of nowhere and he knew if he didn't get up he'd die where he lay.

His stomach growled. Funny, he wasn't as hungry as he was yesterday, but he knew he had to eat to regain some strength. One thing he had plenty of was grass—it was everywhere. Cattle ate it; maybe there was nutrition in it for people, too. How bad could it taste?

Zeke pulled up a clump of little bluestem grass and bit off a mouthful. It didn't taste too bad, maybe a little bitter, but not bad. He chewed and chewed, but no saliva came and he couldn't swallow. If only he had some water to wash it down. He needed to eat.

He chewed a little longer hoping to get some of it into his stomach, but finally he knew it was hopeless and tried to spit it out. Only it wouldn't come out because his mouth was drier than a creek bed in a drought. The grass just lay there on his tongue; Zeke had to reach in with his fingers to pull out the mashed up pulp.

What was he to do? He thought of giving up, of just lying there until death took him and relieved him of his suffering. But once again he remembered Henry's words: "Neither one of you'd have lasted two days out here if you didn't have me to look after you."

Wearily, he struggled to his feet and set off eastward again.

He wouldn't give up. Not now, not ever.

CHAPTER TWENTY-TWO

He'd walked an hour or so and was approaching a small rise when suddenly a blood-curdling scream came from the other side. The hair on Zeke's neck stood up at the sound of it. Fueled by an adrenaline rush, Zeke covered the remaining fifty feet to the crest of the slope as fast as he could, crouching all the way.

He dropped to his belly and crawled forward a few feet until he could see over the rise. Grandpa was on the ground with an arrow sticking out of his side as an Indian bent over him, his left knee firmly planted on Henry's back. The knife in his right hand sliced the hair and skin free as his left hand peeled the scalp back. Blood poured over Grandpa's forehead and cascaded down onto his face. More screams.

That filthy savage. Doesn't even have the decency to wait until he's dead before scalping him. The anger welled up in Zeke, boiling over into rage. He stood up.

"Hey, you son of a bitch!" Zeke yelled, but it came out as a loud croak. He ran down the slope toward them limping badly on his left leg and waving his arms and screaming. The

Indian looked up and Zeke saw that he had a blue hand painted over his left breast.

Jerking the scalp free with a vicious tug, the savage held his dripping trophy up triumphantly for Zeke to see. Then he let out a whoop, jumped astride Henry's horse and grabbed the reins to the two spare mounts. In a moment he was gone.

Zeke got to Henry, pulled his grandfather's bandana off and pressed it firmly on top of his head to staunch the bleeding. Then he grasped the arrow with his other hand.

Henry's eyes opened. "Leave it," he said. "No point taking it out now."

"You came after me," Zeke said hoarsely through parched, cracked lips.

"Gall darn Indian," Henry said, then paused for breath. "Never even saw him."

"I never should have run away; this wouldn't have happened," Zeke said.

"Johnson told me he saw Ledyard leave town heading east that morning you ran off. I was tracking him, not you."

Relieved to hear that this was not his fault, Zeke nevertheless felt resentment, too. Grandpa cared more about catching an outlaw than he did about his own grandson's safety.

"You know I'm dying, don't you?"

Zeke nodded. "I wish I had some water to give you, but my horse threw me a ways back and ran off with the canteen," Zeke said.

"Never mind that now." He coughed up some blood and spat it out. "I ain't got much time, and got some things that need to be said, so listen good.

"Ledyard must know I'm after him 'cause he's led me around in big circles for the past four days. Maybe he likes it here or has kin in these parts—I don't know, but he may stay

JOHN ALEXANDER

in this area for awhile yet. Don't stray too far away unless you find his trail and you know for sure it's his."

Henry had trouble breathing, so Zeke eased him onto his back and then lifted his head so that it rested in the crook of Zeke's arm as Zeke sat cross-legged on the ground. Henry's blood still flowed freely from his scalp and the arrow wound, covering Zeke's arms and soaking his shirt.

Henry peered at Zeke with half-open eyes as the life drained out of him. Blood collected at the corners of Henry's mouth and he struggled for breath. "Maybe I was too hard on you boys," he said. "Especially Billy—he wasn't cut out for marshalling. But you, you could be a top lawman if you'd give it a try." He stopped to catch his breath, then continued. "Take my gun, my money, my badge, and anything else you want."

"Don't talk, Grandpa, save your strength," Zeke said struggling to keep his composure.

Henry ignored the advice. "I was young once, too. Reckon it was so long ago that I plumb forgot what it's like. I regret that Billy and me weren't closer, but he was still my son and it hurts me to know someone killed him." He stopped again, and his eyes grew suddenly intense as they bore into Zeke. "Don't let that dirty skunk get away with killing my boy and your pa. The four us is kin and no outsider can do us like he done and get away with it while one of us still lives. It's up to you now, Zeke."

Henry paused to catch his breath. "You need a fresh start, not to go back to Wattersville and try to work that farm by yourself. Even if you could, that's no kind of life for a young man. You need to meet new people and put the past behind you."

"What should I do, sell the farm and join the army?"

"They wouldn't take you on account of your knee. I get something better for you, anyway. Send a wire to Senator John

M. Worthington in Washington and tell him that I died. Then sell the farm and save the money. Don't spend it all."

"I don't know. I like farming, and I hate to give up the place where I grew up."

"You're almost nineteen years old, Zeke. You ever thought about getting married?"

Zeke was taken aback. "No, no I ain't. I never met a girl in Wattersville that I liked that way."

The old man closed his eyes and Zeke thought he had passed on, but then he heard him struggle for air. Henry's eyes opened partway, as if the weight of the lids was too much for him. "Well, you ought to think about it. You want to be like your Uncle Billy and chase skirts till your whiskers turn gray, and sleep alone every night? Wash your own clothes and cook your own meals, nothing but a book and four walls for company?"

"How's some senator in Washington going to help me?"

"You need a fresh start. Promise me you'll send the wire. Tell him that I'm dead."

Zeke hesitated, then said, "I promise", but his grandfather never heard him.

Zeke looked down at two vacant eyes and knew he was alone. He closed the lids and gently laid him on the ground.

He had no shovel to bury him, and no cloth to cover him. A great sadness came over Zeke: a gloomy sense of loss coupled with a feeling that the weight of the world was on his shoulders. He sobbed openly, not just for his mutilated grandfather, but for the violent deaths of all three of his relatives. No tears came, and his headache only got worse, but he cried anyway, fueled by the emotional strain of his own predicament. Finally, thoroughly spent, he struggled to his feet.

He took Henry's hat and covered his face with it. Then he removed the holster and gun belt and put them on. He hefted the .44 Remington getting the feel of it before he returned it to its holster.

He found seventy-eight dollars in Henry's pants. Zeke felt like a thief going through his pockets the way he did. Then he stared at the tarnished star and shied away from it, as though it was alive. But the old man had told him to take it, and he wanted to honor his last wishes; he dropped the badge into his shirt pocket.

"I'll be back as soon as I can and you'll get a proper burial," Zeke said as though his grandfather could still hear him. He checked for landmarks to aid in finding this spot again, and saw two trees standing about twenty feet apart, one dead, split by a lightning strike. Hopefully he could find this spot again.

CHAPTER TWENTY-THREE

Zeke had no horse, but at least he was armed in case the savage came back. The land stretched out in front of him as empty and untouched as it had been for the past two days. Would he ever find help, or would he die a slow, agonizing, obscure death? Would Ledyard succeed in not only killing Zeke's father, but the whole family as well?

Pushing these thoughts aside, Zeke continued as the sun rose steadily in the eastern sky before him. The adrenaline rush had abated and every step was a challenge. His left knee ached more and more as the day wore on. Zeke fell several times and half-crawled his way until he gathered the strength to get up again...and again...and again.

Weak and badly dehydrated, he stumbled once more and crashed to the ground. He was only out a minute or two, but when he awoke his head throbbed mercilessly.

He crawled to his hat and then, by an act of will, dragged himself to his feet. Stubbornly he pressed on despite his throbbing head and aching left knee, not willing to lay down and die.

Water... he must have water.

Semi-conscious, he barely kept his eyes open, just putting one foot down in front of the other, stumbling, falling, getting up, pressing forward.

On and on he went.

A brown spot appeared in the distance. What was it, a grazing buffalo? Maybe it could lead him to water. Zeke walked a little faster, but the effort was too much and he fell once again. As before, he crawled and walked the best he could, moving ever forward.

When he got closer he saw that it wasn't a buffalo, but a ranch house. Summoning the last of his strength he struggled forward.

Water... water... there had to be water....

A few chickens scratched at the dirt at the side of the house. At least the place wasn't abandoned, he thought.

As he entered the yard a young woman came out onto the porch and watched his approach. She was about eighteen years old, the same as Zeke.

He tipped his hat to her and gave her a weak smile. She did not smile back.

"Water," he said, his voice raspy and weak.

She remained on the porch, keeping her distance. "Where's your horse?" she asked.

"Water," he whispered just before he fell to the ground.

It was hard to open his eyes, as heavy as they were. He could feel the sheets and covers, the softness of the mattress under him. Where was he? Then he saw the young woman and remembered seeing her on the porch.

"How are you feeling?" she asked.

"Water," he whispered. "Water."

She filled a glass from a chair-side pitcher, cradled his head in her left hand and held the glass to his cracked lips. "Slowly," she said. "Take a little at a time."

Spent, he leaned back against the pillow. "I'll get Pa," she said.

She returned in less than a minute with a middle-aged man wearing bib overalls and a straw hat. "My name's Charles Drake," he said. "I can see you're in a bad way, so don't try to talk."

Zeke nodded his head, then suddenly realized he wasn't wearing his shirt. He peeked under the covers and saw his pants were gone and he was in his underwear.

Drake must have seen the panicked look on Zeke's face because he said, "Don't worry. I took your clothes off, washed you from the waist up and put you in bed." He looked at the young woman and said, "This is my daughter, Betsy. She wanted to wash your clothes for you. They're hanging on the line right now."

Zeke was too weak to respond.

"Well, again, I'll let you rest. We'll talk when you're up to it. I'm real interested in hearing about the U. S. Marshal's badge I found in your pocket, and why you showed up here covered in blood and near dead." He patted Zeke on the shoulder before he left. "Betsy will take good care of you. I'll be right outside."

After her father left, Betsy brought more water to Zeke. He sipped at the glass as water trickled down his chin onto the sheet while Betsy again supported his head in her left hand.

Over the next few hours, Zeke drifted in and out of sleep. Betsy was never far away and was able to get more water and some chicken broth into him.

Although young and strong, Zeke did not recover quickly. When he awoke again late in the afternoon, Betsy rose from her chair in the corner and came toward him. "Feeling better?" she asked smiling.

"Some."

"I bet you'd like to sit up awhile." She helped him up in the bed and propped a couple pillows behind him. Then brought over a glass of water and handed it to him. "Go slowly, but drink as much as you can."

He took a few sips from the glass; the water felt so good flowing over his tongue and down his throat, but he could only take a little at a time.

"You walked in off the Plains on foot," she said. "Where's your horse?"

"It threw me. I was hoping to catch up to it, but I never saw it again."

"When's the last time you ate?"

Zeke thought for a moment. "What's today, Thursday?"

She shook her head. "Friday."

"Friday?" Zeke paused to think. "Let's see, I left Evans at dawn on Tuesday, so the last time I ate was at supper on Monday night. I hadn't had any water since Tuesday morning."

Betsy shook her head again. "So where'd all the blood come from? I figured you killed a deer or something." Before he could reply she said, "You spent three nights and almost four days on foot on the Plains with no food or water." She shook her head. "You're lucky to be alive."

Zeke ignored her remark. "Like I was saying, my horse threw me. I was hoping to catch up to it but I never saw it again."

"Well, it didn't come by here."

"Listen, my grandfather was killed by an Indian this morning, and I'd like to bury him."

"Could have been the same Indian that came here yesterday. He was after our horses, but Pa saw him and drove him off with some rifle fire." Her features softening, she took another long look at Zeke, sizing him up. "That's too bad about your grandfather. Was that his blood on you?" Zeke nodded. "How come the Indian didn't get you, too?"

"Grandpa and me had a quarrel in Evans, and I left him Tuesday morning to go home to Wattersville. Grandpa continued on after an outlaw who led him circles for the past three days."

"Why was he trailing an outlaw?"

"He was a United States Marshal. The man he was after killed my father and my uncle, who was my grandfather's son."

"You're getting me confused," she said.

Suddenly, Zeke was angry. He was weak and tired, emotionally spent, and as if that wasn't enough, sitting up made his head hurt even worse. "Look, Grandpa and me had a fight, so I was going home alone. My horse threw me. I had no food or water. After three days I came upon Grandpa and the Indian. I was still a ways off, but I could see the arrow sticking out of Grandpa's side and hear his screams. The Indian scalped him, then rode off on Grandpa's horse. Before he died, Grandpa told me to take his gun and his money. I wanted to bury him, but I didn't have a shovel. So I started out walking again and here I am. Now do you understand?" He choked back a sob and ran his shirtsleeve over his eyes.

"I'm sorry," she said putting her hand on his. Despite his anger her touch felt good on his hand. "I didn't mean to get you upset," she said. "I just wanted to understand what happened to you, that's all." She rose to her feet. "I have to get Pa."

She returned with her father a few minutes later, having told him what had happened to Zeke, and about his grandfather.

"I better get out there and bury him before it gets dark," Mr. Drake said.

"I was planning on doing that myself."

"Your grandfather needs burying, Zeke, and I mean today. Digging a proper grave in this hot sun is hard work, even for a young man like you. You need a few more days to get your strength back."

Grudgingly, Zeke agreed. He was in no shape to bury Grandpa today or tomorrow, and he didn't want to leave his grandfather's body rotting in the hot sun while birds and animals fed off of him. He told Mr. Drake the body was located several miles west of the ranch near two trees—one split by lightning—at the bottom of a small hill.

Mr. Drake said he thought he knew where that was. He set off at once.

Betsy moved the pillows and helped Zeke to lie flat in the bed again so he could rest. In a few minutes, Zeke was asleep. Betsy left the door open so she could hear him if he called.

Despite his youth and strong constitution, Zeke was slow to recover. The ordeal on the Plains had taken a tremendous toll on his body: it was five days before he was fit to leave.

Despite enjoying Betsy's company more and more, Zeke was anxious to go.

"You sure you're well enough to travel?" Betsy asked. "You're still limping on your left leg."

"Oh, that didn't just happen," Zeke said. "When I was seven a young colt kicked me. Lucky for me my father saw it coming and pulled me out of the way; it was just a glancing blow, not a direct hit. Still, it never got strong like the other one." He forced a smile. "It's not so bad. I'm always the first one to know when it's going to rain."

Instead of returning his smile, concern covered Betsy's face. "But are you sure you're well enough to go?"

Zeke nodded. "I've been laid up long enough; I need to get moving. I sure do appreciate all you both have done for me."

"Glad to help," Mr. Drake said. "The relay station is only

seven miles west of here, and the stage is due to pass through later this afternoon. I got work to do, so Betsy will take you there. Once you get to a sizeable town you can buy a horse and provisions and continue on your way."

"I've been such a burden already," Zeke said. "I sure hate to be a bother again."

Mr. Drake shrugged. "It's a tough life out here. Helping each other is the only way to survive."

Later that morning Mr. Drake had a horse hitched up and the wagon ready to go with a rifle and a canteen on the seat. After thanking him again, Zeke shook the reins and the wagon lurched forward.

The wagon seat rolled and swayed with each dip in the undulating ground. When asked about her mother, Betsy told him that typhoid fever had taken her and Betsy's older sister five years ago. "It was surely Providence that me and Pa didn't get it, too," she said.

She looked off into the distance for only a moment, then turned to him. "It's been rough for me and Pa, but it's made us closer."

Now that he was feeling well again, he saw her in a new light. He had gotten to know her over the past five days; she was a hard worker, and easy to be with. He looked at her again, and Grandpa's words came to mind: *stay away from them saloon gals.*

Now he knew what Grandpa was talking about. Zeke thought of the saloon gal in Evans, and then of Betsy. He had been attracted to both of them, but the saloon gal was cheap, appealing to his urges. She wore makeup caked on her face, and she reeked of alcohol, sweat, and cheap perfume. In the end, she had helped those men steal from him. He didn't believe it when Grandpa accused her, but he believed it now.

On the other hand, Betsy had taken time from her own chores to help a stranger. She wore no makeup that Zeke could see, and yet she had a natural beauty about her: tall, with clear skin darkened by the sun, light brown hair pulled back in a ponytail, her body lean and strong. Whereas the saloon gal had taken from him, Betsy gave freely, expecting nothing in return.

Zeke eyed Betsy's left hand on the seat between them. Suddenly he took the reins in one hand and put his right hand over hers.

She turned to him and said, "I'm glad you came to our place."

So am I, Zeke thought. So am I.

∼

"Not what you expected, is it?" she said when the Helstrom's place came into view.

Zeke shook his head. "It sure ain't. The only relay stations I've seen were broken down shacks with some old-timer tending a few horses and keeping a bottle for company. But this, this is something else. Look at those crops out back, and how large the house is, and the new corral on the side. This doesn't look like any relay station I've ever seen."

She laughed at that. "It isn't. Mr. Helstrom and his wife started the farm out here a few years ago. Shortly after that the stage company asked them if they wanted to make some extra money serving as a relay station. The stage line built the corral and added a large room at the other side of the house as a dining room for the stage passengers. So, in addition to their farm chores, they keep a few horses for the stage, and feed the passengers when they come through. It works out well for everyone. By the way, Mrs. Helstrom is a great cook."

Zeke remembered that he had Henry's money in his pocket. "You've been so kind to help me all week," he said to

Betsy. "There's not much I can do to repay you, but could I at least buy you lunch here?"

She looked him in the eyes and said, "I'd like that."

Zeke jumped off and tethered the horse, then he and Betsy walked to the door, which was wide open. Zeke rapped on the wooden doorframe with his knuckles.

"Come on in, folks," came a male voice from within.

They stepped inside. It was a large room, clearly made after the rest of the house had been finished. It was joined to the house by a door in the back that led to the kitchen. Two round tables about five feet apart sat in the middle of the room with five chairs around each. There was a makeshift counter against the far wall where several whiskey bottles were lined up. The floor was clean, and the room smelled of fresh-cut timber. Zeke took a deep breath, reveling in the pleasant odor, then hung his hat on one of the pegs in a row along one wall.

"Hello, Mr. Helstrom," Betsy called into the house.

A man of about forty came out of the kitchen wiping his hands on his pants. "Oh, hello, Betsy. I thought the stage came in. Didn't expect to see you today. What brings you out this way?"

She introduced Zeke to Mr. Helstrom, and without going into detail briefly told him about Zeke stumbling upon their ranch.

"So you lost your horse, huh?" Helstrom said. "A horse wandered in here several days ago. I figured its owner would show up sooner or later—they always do—and kept it here. It's in the barn right now."

"That's probably my horse!" Zeke said. "I can describe it for you."

"No need," Helstrom said smiling broadly. "I saw your name carved into the underside of the saddle."

"Maybe your luck is changing," Betsy said to Zeke.

"I was just thinking that same thing myself," Zeke said. He turned to Helstrom. "By the way, are you serving lunch today?"

"We sure are. The stage is due in a few minutes, so we got it ready now. Go ahead and have a seat, I'll be right with you."

They chose the table nearer to the entrance and had no sooner settled in when Mr. Helstrom brought out two steaming bowls of stew and two large glasses of water. Mrs. Helstrom came out with him to greet Betsy and her friend, then went back to the kitchen.

Zeke rubbed his hand gingerly over the lump on the back of his head. Despite a week's passing, it was still prominent.

"Head hurt?" Betsy asked.

Zeke nodded. "That bumpy ride in didn't do it much good."

"I meant to ask you about that. Did you get it when you fell off your horse?"

"No. I had a run-in with some fellows after a poker game in Evans and a woman that worked at the saloon broke it up and was taking me up to her room. I reached in to light—"

Betsy drew back in anger and surprise. "What were you going up to her room for?"

Zeke's head spun. Suddenly, he was confused. "I...I don't remember."

"You don't remember? What do you mean you don't remember!"

Before he could say anything else, she turned and looked away. Her back now to him, she said, "I wish I hadn't come in, but I don't want to explain my leaving to the Helstroms. I'm just going to eat my lunch and then go."

"But I didn't do anything," he pleaded. She kept her back to him refusing to discuss it further.

A few minutes later Zeke heard the pounding hooves and creaking wheels of the stage pulling up out front.

CHAPTER TWENTY-FOUR

Ledyard rode along at a lope thinking back to the saloon where Ike shot the deputy marshal, and then how that other lawman chased them and shot Ike.

So the law *had* tracked them for that killing in Wattersville. But were the two lawmen together, or was the second one just a town marshal rushing toward the sound of shots? No matter, he'd put them both out of commission. But what if there were more than two of them? Or if the first one was traveling with other federal marshals?

He didn't know if he was still being tracked, but he sure couldn't take any chances. The layover in Evans had helped him regroup. He'd eaten well and had a good night's sleep in a regular bed. Likewise, his horse was rested and fed.

He figured that since he had been running west ever since Wattersville, the law would assume he was still going that way, but he couldn't be sure. One thing he *was* sure of was that they'd assume he'd get as far away as possible.

It would be better to lay low for a few days and hope whoever might be on his trail would move on. There might not be any other lawmen looking for him who could even identify him.

Slowing his horse, he rode for a couple hours seeing nothing but the long grass ripple in the wind, and an occasional bird fly overhead. He'd check behind him every couple of minutes, but saw no one.

Spurring his horse to the top of a hill, he turned the horse back around and peered into the distance he came from. Movement caught his eye and he stared at a lone rider coming his direction from a long way off. Ledyard couldn't see the rider at this distance, but he did see him looking at the ground as he rode, obviously following Ledyard's track.

What should he do now? He rode down the crest of the hill to the far side, out of view. He could lay in ambush; after all, there was only one rider. But Ledyard didn't have a rifle, and he wasn't much of a shot at long distance. He sure didn't want to get in a gunfight against a rifle with his Army Colt.

He could try to outrun him heading east, but Ledyard didn't cotton to the notion of looking over his shoulder every few minutes for several days, and having to sleep with one eye open.

The last place that rider would look for him would be back where he came from. Not in Evans, though, people had seen him there, like those two bumpkins at the stable. He'd go to Greeley instead and lay low for several days—no one knew him there—while the lawman got further and further away. Then Ledyard could make his escape.

He liked that idea. Instead of being on the run, sleeping on the ground and grubbing for food, he could stay in a hotel until it was safe to leave. But first he had to lose the rider tracking him. Ledyard didn't want to get too far away from Greeley, but he didn't want to lead his pursuer back there, either.

So for the next two days, Ledyard rode in big circles,

always trying to shake the lawman, always checking behind him. When he no longer saw the lawman following, he dismounted at the top of a hill with his horse out of sight on the far side and laid on his belly watching for any sign of the lone rider. After an hour, he figured he'd shaken his pursuer and rode west to Greeley, arriving under the cover of darkness.

Registering under the name of Tom Smith from Denver, he told the clerk, a fellow named Miller, that he was dodging a lawman his rich wife had set on his trail after he left her. He leaned closer, and in a conspiratorial whisper, slipped a five-dollar half eagle to Miller and said some lawmen were skunks and would lie about a man just to get people to talk.

With a wink, Miller said his lips were sealed and that he'd take care of everything. After giving him a room key, he took Ledyard's horse to the livery. Taking all his meals in his hotel room, Ledyard didn't show his face except for sneaking out the back door to use the privy.

Ledyard didn't take kindly to the fact that no whiskey was sold in Greeley. He thought of pulling out, but he had a good setup and figured he could do without it for a few days if it meant avoiding a necktie party. The thought of having Miller send a boy to Evans for a few bottles crossed his mind, but he didn't want to draw attention to himself.

He had an early breakfast five days later and had Miller bring his horse around. After paying for everything and settling his hotel bill, Ledyard left another half eagle with the clerk and told him he'd probably be back soon and would like to use the clerk's discretion again—if he kept his mouth shut. "I'm your man," Miller had said.

Heading east about an hour out of Greeley, Ledyard saw nothing but the long grass ripple in the wind, and an occasional bird fly overhead. He'd check behind him every couple of minutes, but saw no one.

The ground dropped away about a hundred yards up ahead, and he could just see the tops of some cottonwoods above the ridge. More than likely there was water down below, he thought. Ledyard slowed his horse as he approached the edge.

Instinctively, he ducked just as an Indian let fly with an arrow. It passed so closely to his face that he felt the rush of air as the arrow flew by. The Indian reached back into his quiver for another arrow. He was about thirty yards away at the bottom of a broad, flat plain where he'd set up camp on the other side of a creek.

Drawing his gun, Ledyard spurred his horse and came down the slope with his .44 Army Colt blazing away. His second shot hit the mark and the savage fell before he could loose another arrow.

Ledyard jumped from the saddle and kept his Colt on the Indian as he cautiously approached. The Indian lay dead, shot through the chest. Ledyard put his Colt away and was then startled by an angry shriek from behind him.

He turned just as his attacker leapt at him driving a knife toward his throat. He reached up and grabbed the knife hand by the wrist and then tumbled backward as his attacker fell on him. He squeezed the wrist as hard as he could, but she kept her grip on the knife. Then she grabbed him around the neck in a headlock as they rolled about on the ground.

Ledyard kept his left hand firmly on her right wrist and struggled to keep her from driving the knife home. Her left arm had his head pinned tightly against her and he couldn't move. She rolled again and he felt the knife slice through the sleeve of his shirt and break the skin. Damn, she was strong!

Their legs intertwined as they continued to struggle on the ground. His nose was pressed against her sweat-slicked skin and he took in her odor with every breath. He felt her firm breasts pressing against his chest as he remained locked tightly against her.

He reached up behind her with his right arm and grabbed a handful of her hair; then he pulled down with constant pressure so that her neck arched back and her face tilted away. She relaxed her grip on him slightly, and he slammed her knife hand down on the ground with as much force as he could muster. The knife dropped free and then she rolled him over again, still maintaining the grip around his neck. She straddled him as he lay beneath her on his back, no longer pulling her hair. Her knee was on his left arm pinning it to the ground.

Then she released her grip on his neck and raised her left hand high in the air. She brought it down with an open palm slapping him hard on the face. She did it again two more times in rapid succession until she was able to pull her right arm free of his grip. Then she alternated each hand as she slapped him repeatedly and screamed hysterically. His cheeks glowed crimson with the force of her slaps.

In desperation he balled up his right hand and drove his fist into her side. Then he flipped her off of him and jumped atop her as she fell to the ground. As he stretched for the knife lying nearby, she reached up and dragged the fingernails of her right hand across his cheek, opening four oozing tracks.

He let out a cry of pain and then his fingers closed on her throat. "Now I've got you, you bitch!"

They stared contemptuously at each other for several seconds. She wasn't bad looking for an Indian. She looked to be only twenty or so, and her face lacked the broad, flat features most Indians have. Maybe she's a half-breed, he thought.

Still holding the knife against her throat, he pulled up on her dress so that she'd know what he wanted. A terrified look came into her eyes, and she shook her head. He pressed on the knife and a trickle of blood appeared on her neck. He looked at her again, and saw her reach for the hem of her dress... .

He stood up a few minutes later, but she continued to lie on the ground. She stared at him with empty eyes, as though she didn't see him.

Ledyard picked up his hat, then straightened his shirt and pants as he surveyed the scene around him. The brave lay dead about ten feet away, and the two ponies grazed nearby. Obviously there weren't any other Indians around, or they would have come when the shots were fired. He drew his six-gun and aimed it point-blank at the girl's head: still no reaction. Just two vacant eyes looking, but not seeing. He cocked the hammer and held the gun on her for a few seconds. "Aw, the hell with it," he said and put the Colt back in its holster.

He debated what to do next. Should he take their horses with him so she couldn't get back to her people too soon? He pondered that, but then decided it wouldn't be a good idea for him to be seen by other Indians trailing two of their ponies across open land.

He could run off the two ponies, but if they were found by her people, they'd surely come looking for her and the dead brave.

So he tied her up and left the horses alone. She'd get free eventually, but all he needed was a head start. He bound her ankles with some rawhide strips that he found among their things. She didn't resist; in fact, she just stared at him with vacant eyes. He rolled her onto her right side and tied her hands behind her back.

Ledyard mounted up and took one last look back. She was still lying on her side where he'd left her; the same lifeless eyes trained on him, seeing right through him.

He should go back and kill her, he thought, but the way

she stared at him unnerved him, and he couldn't bring himself to turn around.

After he'd ridden awhile and put the girl out of his mind, he realized how hungry he was. Damn, why didn't he have Miller fill his saddlebags with provisions before leaving Greeley? He just wasn't thinking clearly anymore. All he had was some jerky and hardtack.

He kept his eyes open for any kind of game he could kill, but after a few hours he hadn't seen a thing. He was just about resolved to another meal of jerky and stale biscuits when he saw something off in the distance. He couldn't make out what it was right away, but after he got closer he saw that it appeared to be a farm.

He continued toward it and saw that out front was a stage, a small wagon, and a lone horse tethered to a hitching rail. Maybe this was a relay station for the stage line, he thought. If so, he just might be in time for lunch.

CHAPTER TWENTY-FIVE

Zeke couldn't see the stage, but he heard it from a ways off as it rumbled into the station with wheels creaking and the driver calling to his horses as he came to a halt out front. Then he heard a few people milling about as they got out of the coach and stretched their legs.

Two women in their thirties came in first. Zeke could see from their faces and the way that they shuffled in that they were tired from their journey. They brushed the dust off their clothes, and, to Zeke's surprise, stopped at his table instead of taking the empty one. Remembering his manners, he rose to his feet.

The blonde one smiled at Zeke, then turned to her dark-haired companion. "Let's sit here, Anne."

"Whatever you say, Elizabeth."

Zeke remained standing until both women were seated. Elizabeth plopped her things on the remaining empty chair. "I hope you don't mind, but I simply have to get away from that man, if only for a short time," she said in a low voice with a nod of her head toward the man coming in behind them.

Zeke saw that she was referring to a man of about forty who ran his fingers through his bushy moustache in a futile attempt to clean the dust out of it. He had removed his hat and seemed to be uncertain of what he should do next. As the man moved closer, Zeke saw the only clean-looking thing he wore: a highly polished belt buckle with the bold letters "CSA" clearly visible. He carried no weapon that Zeke could see.

"It's not that he's a bad sort, you understand," Elizabeth said, her blue eyes darting back and forth between Zeke and Betsy. "It's just his incessant talking! I need to give my ears a rest." She smiled at them. "I hope you don't mind," she said again.

He should have known it was too good to last, Zeke thought. He looked at the doorway again as the driver came in behind the Reb. Mr. Helstrom went over and shook hands with the driver.

"Excuse me, gents," the Reb said to them. Then he looked at Mr. Helstrom. "Privy out back?"

"Yes, just go out the door here and follow the path around the side of the house and you'll see it."

The Reb nodded and went back outside.

The stage driver went over to the empty table and sat down. Helstrom brought him a whiskey, then went back into the kitchen.

Zeke turned to the door again at the sound of footsteps. Boy, that was quick, he thought, expecting to see the Reb coming through the door again. Suddenly, Zeke's blood froze and the stew caught in his throat. Ledyard walked past Zeke's table and stopped in front of the stage driver, who had four empty chairs at his table.

"Looks like I'm just in time for lunch," Ledyard said.

"That you are; have a seat," the driver said. "We haven't started yet."

JOHN ALEXANDER

Ledyard nodded and sat down. He eyed the empty whiskey glass in the driver's hand. "Who do I see about getting a drink?"

"Nils will be back in a minute. He's in the kitchen getting lunch." The bloodied tracks on Ledyard's cheek caught his eye. "You have a run-in with a polecat?" he asked.

Ledyard glared at him for a few seconds. Then he said, "So where's that fellow with the whiskey?"

"Like I said, he's getting lunch. Keep your shirt on."

No sooner had the driver said that than Helstrom came out carrying a tray with four glasses of water and four bowls of stew trailing steam. He served Anne and Elizabeth first, then moved quickly to the other table. A confused look came over his face upon seeing Ledyard.

"You got another guest for lunch, Nils," the driver said.

"I see," Helstrom replied. "No matter, the other gentleman hasn't returned so I'll leave these here and bring out another serving for him." He placed the two glasses of water and two bowls of stew on the table before the two men.

"How about some whiskey?" Ledyard said.

Helstrom's eyes went to Ledyard and settled on the damaged left cheek. He looked like he was about to say something, but then thought better of it. He went to the corner and returned with a bottle and another whiskey glass. He set the glass in front of Ledyard and then filled both his glass and the driver's. He moved to return the bottle to the counter when he felt Ledyard's hand on his arm. "Something else?"

"Leave the bottle," Ledyard growled.

Helstrom hesitated, then placed the nearly full bottle on the table. "That'll be two dollars for the whiskey, and two bits for the stew."

Without looking at Helstrom, Ledyard reached into his pocket and withdrew some coins. He sifted through them, then flipped a few onto the table.

Helstrom scooped them up and, hearing footsteps, turned toward the door as the Reb came back into the room. "Ah, here you are. I'll bring your lunch right out to you." He went back into the kitchen.

Ledyard had the bottle in his hand pouring a second drink when he saw the belt buckle. He glared at the man as he approached the table. "That's an interesting buckle you're wearing," he said.

The man smiled. "It keeps my pants up."

Ledyard didn't return the smile. "There's worse things can happen to a fellow than losing his pants."

The man stood by the table, returning Ledyard's stare. "I wear it to remember my fellow soldiers who died fighting for the Confederacy." He pulled out a chair.

"Don't sit down. I ain't eating with no Johnny Reb!"

The driver spoke up. "There's no need for this. The war's been over for years. Everyone's been hurt by it. It's time to forget about it and move on together."

Ledyard said, "You want to forget the war, this fellow here wants to remember Confederate soldiers, and I see them every night in my dreams. So where does that leave us?"

Zeke's heart raced as he witnessed the confrontation. He desperately wanted to do something, but he was frozen with fear and struggled to break free from its grip.

"Somebody should do something about this," Anne said. "There's no call for that man's behavior. We're all just trying to enjoy a quiet lunch."

Elizabeth called over to the Reb, who was still standing and facing Ledyard. "Why don't you sit with us? We have an extra chair."

Before the man could move or say anything, Ledyard spoke up. "You don't understand, ma'am. When I said I didn't want to eat with him, I meant I don't even want him in the same room with me."

"Well, where am I supposed to eat, then?" the man demanded.

"I don't care if you have to eat outside on the ground as long as I don't have to look at you—or smell you."

The scene tormented Zeke. He wanted to act, but was afraid. But if he didn't do something, then he really was a coward just as he feared he might be.

"This is crazy," Elizabeth said to Zeke. "You're wearing a gun. Can't you help that man?"

Filled with shame, Zeke looked down, avoiding her eyes. If he got out of this he was going back to the farm in Wattersville and never leave again.

"Oh, I wish I was a man!" Elizabeth said thoroughly frustrated. She shifted in her chair and her napkin fell from her lap onto the floor. Zeke bent over to pick it up and Henry's badge fell out of his shirt pocket and clanged to the floor landing face up at her feet. "You're a U. S. Marshal!" she said.

"No, he isn't," Betsy said as Zeke scooped up the badge and put it back into his pocket. "Keep your voice down."

"I will not!" Elizabeth said. Outraged now, she shifted her attention back to Zeke and spoke in a loud voice of indignation. "You're a U. S. Marshal! Why don't you do something?"

Zeke was suddenly aware that everyone was looking at him, including Ledyard. Time seemed to stop as he locked eyes with the killer for a long moment.

Ledyard went for his gun.

Zeke came up off his chair, drew his .44 Remington and thumbed back the hammer as Ledyard's Colt just cleared leather. Zeke squeezed the trigger as Ledyard's gun came up. Just then the Reb grabbed the table and slammed it into Ledyard knocking him off balance.

Zeke's shot ripped through Ledyard's right arm causing him to drop his gun before he could pull the trigger.

The driver and the Reb were on him then, grabbing him and kicking the gun away.

Ledyard looked at Zeke with contempt. "Who said he was a U. S. Marshal? He's just a boy."

"He has the badge," Elizabeth replied.

Zeke bent over to pick up Ledyard's .44 Army Colt off the floor. "It's not my badge," he said. "It belonged to my grandfather who was killed several days ago. Before he died, he told me to keep it."

"Well, no matter," the driver said clapping him on the back. "You did just fine."

"I'll say," the Reb added. "You sure were fast with that gun. If it weren't for you, who knows what would have happened?"

"So what do we do with him now?" the driver asked.

"He killed my Pa back home in Wattersville, Kansas. I'd like to take him there to stand trial," Zeke said.

"We better bandage his arm first or he may bleed to death before you get him there," Betsy said.

"Would that be such a bad thing?" the driver said.

"Here now, let's have none of that kind of talk," Anne said.

"Have you got anything we can use for a bandage?" Betsy asked Mrs. Helstrom, who had come out of the kitchen after the shooting.

"I'll see what I can dig up."

Zeke watched the blood drip from Ledyard's wound, and the gravity of what just happened sunk in. His stomach flipped, and the room began to spin. That could be him bleeding instead of Ledyard; or worse, he could be dead on the floor from a bullet in the face...or in the chest. He pictured himself on the floor with Ledyard's bullet in his chest, but then the image changed to that of his father on the floor at Chadwick's with two of Ledyard's bullets in his chest, trying to breathe through blood-filled lungs.

Zeke began to shake all over, and he sat down before the others could see his condition. It had all happened so fast. He didn't want to confront Ledyard, but once Elizabeth announced that he was a U. S. Marshal—even though he wasn't—he knew Ledyard would go for his gun. Zeke's reaction had been purely instinctive, as he hadn't had time to think about it. Now that it was over, the fear set in and he struggled to get a grip on himself. Oh, how he wished he was back on the farm in Wattersville. What was he doing out here, anyway?

The driver set a glass of whiskey in front of Zeke. "Drink this, you'll feel better," he said.

Without looking up, Zeke drained the shot glass. It burned going down and he coughed, but it did steady him.

"Go ahead, have another," the driver said, refilling the glass.

Zeke quickly downed that one, too, and his body stopped shaking. Zeke looked up at the driver standing next to him, ashamed for the way he'd just reacted.

The driver seemed to read his thoughts and gave him a reassuring nod of the head. "You'll be all right now," he said. Then he went back to where the others were standing by Ledyard, who was sitting down. At the same time, Mrs. Helstrom returned with an old shirt and handed it to Betsy.

Zeke got up and joined them as Betsy tore the shirt into strips and tightly wrapped Ledyard's wound. Still, blood oozed through the cloth. "I don't like the look of that bleeding," she said.

"Where's the nearest doctor?" Zeke asked.

"Evans," Mr. Helstrom replied. "About ten miles west of here."

"I'm going the other direction," Zeke said. "How close is the nearest doctor heading east?"

"Not for another thirty miles," the stage driver said. "He'd never make it."

Zeke pondered what to do. He wanted Ledyard to pay for his crimes, but he wanted the law to handle it. If he didn't take Ledyard to the doctor in Evans and he bled to death that'd be the same as murder. No court in the land would convict him, of course, but he wondered if he could live with himself. He had enough things he was trying to forget without adding something else. He hesitated only another moment. "Evans it is, then," Zeke said.

"How are you going to get him to Evans?" Betsy asked. "He looks too weak for a ten-mile ride."

"Which way are you heading?" Zeke asked the stage driver.

"South. We just came from Greeley."

No help there, Zeke thought. What could he do?

"We could take him in the wagon," Betsy said.

"How far is it from your place to Evans?"

"About eight miles," Betsy said.

"We could take him in your wagon," Zeke said, "and we could tie my horse and Ledyard's horse to it and take them with us to Evans. Then you could take the wagon back home. There's still plenty of light."

Betsy looked disappointed, then said, "I've already spent seven miles in that wagon getting here. Now you want me to go ten miles into Evans, then turn around and go eight more miles to get back home. That's twenty-five miles for me to sit in the wagon going in a big circle around the countryside."

"I don't see any other option, do you?" Zeke said.

"My father's brother and his wife own the Peaks Hotel in Evans. I could stay the night there and then come home tomorrow morning. Pa wouldn't mind since I'll be staying with family."

"How's he going to know where you're at?" Zeke said.

"I could go out to her place and tell her father what's going on," Mr. Helstrom said. "I wouldn't mind going for ride out in the country, and my horse could use the exercise."

Betsy smiled. "It's settled then. I'll go with you to Evans and come home tomorrow."

"What would your father say?"

"Just what he told you: people need to help each other out here to survive. My father wouldn't like it if I cut and run on someone who needed help. He trained me to shoot, to ride, and to stand on my own two feet. Not to run from trouble."

Zeke pondered this for a few moments. "I still don't like it," he said. "I'll be heading east from Evans with Ledyard and will pass near your place, but he won't be able to travel for a few days, and I don't like you traveling home alone tomorrow with Indians around."

"She's right, you know," Mr. Helstrom said. "Her father didn't raise her to be a shrinking violet—Betsy's one tough cookie. Under the circumstances, I think he'd expect her to help you."

"No, I can't let her go back alone," Zeke said. "Here's what we'll do. The three of us will go to Evans and get Ledyard to a doctor. The sheriff can keep him in a cell until the doctor says he can travel. That would leave me free to go back with Betsy tomorrow. I'll take my horse along and then ride him back to Evans."

"Then it's settled," Betsy said.

Mr. Helstrom produced a length of rope, and the Reb tied Ledyard's hands together in front of him, then passed a loop through Ledyard's belt securing his hands to his waist. They led him outside and helped him onto the back of the wagon.

The Reb then tied Ledyard's ankles together. "That ought to hold him," he said.

Betsy put a blanket under Ledyard's head as he stretched out on the back of the wagon. Mr. Helstrom brought up Zeke's horse and Ledyard's horse and tethered them to the back of the wagon, one on each side while Zeke went to the pump in the front yard and filled the canteen to the brim. Then he and Betsy climbed onto the wagon seat and waved farewell as Zeke took the reins. The rifle was between them, leaning against the seat.

They rode in silence for a few miles. Ledyard slept deeply on the wagon bed, and snored only occasionally. Once again the Rockies loomed ahead in the distance as Zeke headed west.

"How's he going to feel about you going off with a stranger and spending the night in a hotel?"

"It won't bother him at all. I won't be spending the night with you, and my aunt and uncle will be right there in the hotel."

"Well, let's get going then," Zeke said, unable to suppress a grin.

CHAPTER TWENTY-SIX

Except for occasional small talk, they made the rest of the trip in relative silence. Although Ledyard had lost blood and was noticeably pale and weak, Zeke stopped in front of Sheriff Drummond's office instead of looking for the doctor. Zeke cut the rope binding Ledyard's ankles, but left his hands tied, and helped him off the back of the wagon. Betsy then took the wagon and the spare horses to the livery stable.

Zeke found Drummond sitting at a tiny desk talking to an elderly man who sat on a bench across from him. "Well, what have we here?" Drummond said coming up from behind his desk. "I thought you and your grandfather left town."

"We did. You remember that fellow my Grandpa said we were looking for?"

Drummond nodded. "Your grandfather told me what he did to your pa and your uncle."

"Well, this is him."

"Oh, yeah?" the sheriff said stepping forward and eyeing Ledyard up and down, the distaste evident on his face. "Looks like he needs to see Doc Tatum." Drummond then glanced at the elderly man on the bench. "Excuse me," he said. "Judge, this is Zeke Halstead. His grandfather's a federal marshal and they've been tracking this here fellow." He turned to Zeke. "Zeke, this is Judge Winston McGrath. Judge McGrath is with the U. S. District Court in Denver."

Zeke shook hands with the judge, who remained seated. "Denver?"

The judge smiled. "Court's in recess for two weeks, so I went up to Fort Collins to see my son. He's a lieutenant in the cavalry. I stopped here on the way back to see my old friend Sheriff Drummond. I was lucky enough to get a train north to Fort Collins before they stopped running, but now I'm left with a long ride back." He turned to Drummond. "I need to send a wire. Which way's the telegraph office?"

"Out the door and to the left. You'll see the sign."

"Nice to meet you, Zeke," the judge said getting up. Then he said to the sheriff, "I'll see you later for supper. Shall we say five o'clock at the Paradise Hotel? If I eat too late I can't sleep."

"See you then, Judge," Drummond said.

Zeke nodded to the judge as the old man left. Then he said to Drummond, "I came here first because I wondered if you could come with me. I'd hate for this fellow to cause any more trouble or hurt your doctor."

"Good idea."

On the way over to the doctor's office, Zeke filled in the sheriff on what had happened to his grandfather, and how Ledyard killed Billy even though Billy was helpless after Ledyard's friend had shot him. Then Zeke told how he himself came upon Ledyard at a relay station and had to shoot him.

"Sorry to hear about your grandfather, Zeke. I only spent a short time with him, but I could tell he was a good lawman and I liked him right off. I didn't know Indians were causing trouble again in these parts, especially this close to town. I appreciate that bit of information and will pass the word around."

"I only saw the one," Zeke said.

"If you saw one, then there's bound to be more of them roaming about."

They came to the doctor's office and Drummond pushed through the door. A young man in a business suit looked up. "Oh, hello, Sheriff," Dr. Tatum said. "You caught me just in time. I was on the way out to check on Mrs. Simber and her new baby." He looked at Ledyard, then back to Drummond. "Outlaw?"

Drummond nodded, then cut Ledyard's hands loose.

"Well, let's have a look at him. He's obviously lost a lot of blood judging by his skin color and the way the bandage is soaked through." He removed the bandage and saw the shredded tissue on the upper arm. "Look, it's still oozing."

Zeke watched as the doctor examined Ledyard. He was the youngest doctor Zeke had ever seen. He looked to be about Uncle Billy's age.

The doctor turned to Zeke. "Are you the one that shot him?"

"Yes, sir."

"Your bullet nicked a vein; that's why he's still bleeding. It could have been worse, though: if you'd hit an artery he'd be dead already."

Zeke nodded in agreement, as if he knew what the doctor was talking about.

"I'll have to stitch him up to stop the bleeding. It won't take long; I can see the vein plain as day."

"Hold still," Dr. Tatum said to Ledyard. "This is going to hurt." He dabbed at the wound with a clean cloth to clear the blood away, then picked up a needle and thread and a pair of forceps. He went to work on the damaged vein.

"Ow!" Ledyard screamed. "What the hell are you doing, Sawbones?"

"Just hold still," the doctor said.

Despite the interesting scene before him, Zeke's mind was elsewhere. Meeting the judge had reminded him of his promise to Grandpa that he'd send a wire to Washington. But what was the point? It made no sense to Zeke and he considered forgetting the whole thing. After all, his grandfather was dead and it surely made no difference to him now.

Still, he *had* promised, and Zeke wasn't one for going back on his word. Whether or not it made sense, he'd send the wire; it was important enough to Grandpa that he used his last breath to remind Zeke of it.

"Sheriff, do you think it'd be all right if I went over to the telegraph office? I need to send a wire before it gets too late in Washington."

Drummond stood with his hands in his pockets chuckling at Ledyard's squirming. The sheriff was thoroughly enjoying himself. "Sure, it's all right. If Old Nate's sleeping just rap on the counter a few times and he'll wake up."

Zeke looked at Ledyard and hesitated.

"Go ahead, son, I got things under control here," Drummond said. "I'll take him over to the jail when Doc's done."

"Obliged, Sheriff."

Five minutes later he was at the Western Union office. Old Nate was leaning forward on his desk with his head resting on folded arms. His wrinkled scalp was flecked with age spots, and was bare except for a few wisps of thin, silvery hair. His breathing was labored, wheezing when he exhaled. The floor around the old man was littered with cigarette butts.

Zeke rapped on the counter with his knuckles and said in a loud voice, "Excuse me, sir, I'd like to send a wire."

The old man jerked his head up with a start. "What's that? What'd you say?"

"I said I'd like to send a wire."

"I must have dozed off," Nate said, rubbing his eyes. "All right, who's the wire going to?"

"Senator John M. Worthington, in Washington."

The old man pulled a pencil from behind his ear and repeated each word aloud as he wrote on the pad in front of him. He looked up at Zeke when he'd finished writing, and waited a few seconds before he said, "Well, what's the message?"

"I don't know how to word a telegram," Zeke said.

"Just tell me what you want to say and I'll take it down proper-like."

Zeke hesitated, then blurted out, "Just tell him that Marshal Henry McNichol was killed this morning."

Without looking up the old man asked, "Anything else?"

"No, I reckon that's all."

"How do you want to sign it?"

"What do you mean?"

The old man sighed and looked up. "What's your name, kid?"

"Zeke...Zeke Halstead."

"Where'll you be if there's a reply?"

"I doubt that there'll be a reply," Zeke said.

"Look, kid, I don't aim to go chasing all over town if that there telegraph key taps out a message with your name on it."

"You can leave a message for me either at the Peaks Hotel or at the sheriff's office."

The old man nodded. "That'll be four bits."

"Yes, sir," Zeke said as he handed over the money.

He went back to the sheriff's office, but no one was there. So he walked over to the Peaks Hotel and met Betsy's Aunt Sarah at the front desk. She informed him that a nice upstairs room overlooking the street had been reserved for him. "Betsy's in room seven. She said to knock on her door when you're ready to have supper," Sarah said.

"I thought she'd be having supper with you and your husband."

"We're working through the dinner hour, but we'll have breakfast with her tomorrow morning." Sarah smiled and said, "Besides, I have the feeling she'd rather have supper with you."

Zeke blushed and looked at the wall clock behind her. It was almost four o'clock. He'd just have time to get to the barbershop for a haircut, shave and a bath. He'd get a change of clothes out of his saddlebags then head over there. "Okay, thank you." He turned to leave.

"Excuse me, Zeke," Sarah said.

He turned back. "Yes?"

"Betsy said you'd pay for her room, too. That'll be a dollar-fifty for the two rooms."

Zeke blushed again and fumbled in his pocket. He found two silver dollars and slid them across the counter to her. He just wanted to get out of there. He turned to leave again.

"Uh, Zeke?" she said.

Now what? He turned back to her yet again. "Yes?"

"Here's your change and room key. You're in room five."

Zeke felt the heat rush to his face as he blushed even brighter. He took the coins and the key. "Thank you," he said already turning away from her.

An hour later he emerged from the barbershop all spiffed up and sweet-smelling. He took his dirty clothes to the livery stable and packed them in his saddlebags. If Ledyard wasn't fit to travel tomorrow he'd drop them off at the laundry.

He went to the sheriff's office and found Drummond behind his desk and was introduced to his deputy, Otis. "You missed it, son," Drummond said. "Your tough outlaw howled like a hungry coyote when Doc sewed him up."

"Yeah?" Ledyard said. "Well, you'd a howled, too, if that horse doctor was doing you like he done me," He was sitting on a cot in his cell, his right arm in a sling. "Damn quack!"

Drummond's temper flared. "That damn quack just saved your worthless life, you ungrateful son of a bitch!"

"So when do I get something to eat?" Ledyard asked. "That boy there ruined my lunch today."

"You'll eat when I say so," Drummond said. "I put some water in your cell for you. Doc says you should drink lots of water."

"The hell with the water! How about some whiskey? My arm hurts something fierce."

"Now ain't that just too bad," Drummond said. Then he turned to his deputy. "Otis, go on down to the café and bring back some supper for our prisoner. We wouldn't want folks to think we were mistreating him just because he murdered an unarmed man and later killed one of our fellow lawmen who happened to be helpless at the time."

"And don't forget the whiskey," Ledyard said.

"You ain't getting no whiskey!" Drummond said. "If you don't want the water I'll take it out right now."

Ledyard slumped back on the cot muttering under his breath.

Drummond turned to Zeke. "Doc said your prisoner will be able to travel tomorrow. Doc was able to patch him up pretty good so he won't bleed anymore. He said a good night's sleep and a couple of hot meals should make a big difference."

"It's too bad the trains are out," Zeke said. "I was hoping to catch one to Denver, then another one going east."

"Yeah, that's a tough break." Drummond looked at his pocket watch. "Well, I got to meet the judge for supper."

"I sure do appreciate your help, Sheriff."

"We lawmen stick together, son. We're the only thing between decent folks and outlaws like that one there."

"Yes, sir. I'll remember that."

"You do that." Drummond got up to leave. "Have a good evening, Zeke. Your prisoner will be here when you need him."

After a quiet supper with Betsy, Zeke returned to his hotel room. He entered the dark room and lit the single candle on the table by the door. He pulled his boots off, and slipped off his shirt and pants before lying down. Not sleepy at all, he watched the candle burning low in its dish in the center of the table. The flame flickered in the darkened room sending a soft glow for a few paltry feet before giving way to the blackness at the perimeter of the table and beyond.

Zeke thought of Pa being gunned down, and a wave of horror and fear swept over him. He thought of Uncle Billy inside the wood coffin, and recalled how reluctant his uncle had been to make the trip, and how he himself had accused his uncle of being yellow.

Then he thought of Grandpa screaming as an Indian held him down with his knee and sliced his scalp away. Oh sure, Zeke thought, he had run toward the Indian, but what would he have done if the Indian had come at him instead of riding away? He was too weak and sick to fight then, of course, but what if he wasn't? What if he was healthy and strong, like he was now?

Would Zeke have fought him, or would he have run from a fight again, the same way he'd backed down from the three men at the poker game? And what if he and the Indian *had* fought? Suppose the Indian got him on the ground and scalped him the same way he did Grandpa. Zeke shuddered as an icy shiver ran down his spine and into his legs.

No! He couldn't allow himself to think that way; he must

not be afraid like Uncle Billy was. Being the only one left, it was up to him to make Ledyard pay for what he'd done.

The hotel was quiet, and the air in the room was still. The flame had ceased flickering and stood straight up, motionless. Zeke lay calmly, staring into the flame, mesmerized by its steady glow even as his mind raced with turmoil. He thought again about Pa, Uncle Billy, Grandpa, and, of course, about Ledyard and the trip they would start in the morning.

He thought about all of them, but mostly he thought about how very much he wanted to be brave...and wondered if he would be.

CHAPTER TWENTY-SEVEN

Zeke arose early the next morning and went down to the lobby. He was hoping to see Betsy and her aunt and uncle, but they were nowhere in sight. He introduced himself to the young woman behind the desk—she said her name was Mary—and asked about Betsy and her relatives, but Mary hadn't seen them. Disappointed, Zeke went into the dining room for breakfast and grabbed a small table by a window.

His thoughts ran back to supper with Betsy the previous evening. Just as Zeke had done, she'd bathed and changed clothes. She was beautiful in a pale blue dress. Her skin was fresh-scrubbed, and she wore just a touch of make-up, borrowed from her aunt, no doubt. She talked of how much she liked working on a farm, but mentioned again how it did get lonely with just her father for company. She missed the female companionship of her mother and sister, dead these past five years.

Zeke wondered if he wouldn't feel the same way, too. He'd lost his three living relatives in the past couple of weeks, and was now alone in the world himself. Things had been so hectic he hadn't had a chance to think about loneliness, but what would it be like for him back in Wattersville once all this was behind him and he worked the farm by himself and lived alone?

He was just finishing breakfast when he saw the desk clerk pointing him out to a young boy who was standing next to her. Mary caught Zeke's eye, smiled, and then returned to the lobby.

The boy approached Zeke. "Are you Zeke Halstead?" he asked.

"Yes, I am. Who are you?"

"Name's Thad. I work for Mr. Boyd."

"Who's Mr. Boyd?"

"You know, the telegraph operator."

"Well, what does he want with me?"

"Got a telegram for you." He produced a pencil and paper. "Sign here, please."

Numb, Zeke signed the paper and took the telegram. Before he could say anything else, the boy turned and left. He opened the telegram, read it, and almost fell off his chair.

What was he to do? He decided to ask Sheriff Drummond's advice. Would he be at the jail this early? He shoveled the last of the eggs into his mouth and got up from the table.

Sheriff Drummond was bent over making up the cot in his office when Zeke arrived. "Do you live here, Sheriff?" Zeke asked.

Drummond laughed. "No, although sometimes it seems that way. I keep a cot here for me or Otis whenever we got a prisoner overnight. Fortunately, that doesn't happen too often and I usually get to sleep at home in my own bed." He smoothed the blanket and stood up straight. "You pulling out already?"

"Not yet. I want to talk to you about something."

"Sure thing. Have a seat. Your prisoner's not what I'd call a sound sleeper. Kept me up most of the night with his moaning and crying out. He finally quieted down about six this morning. I think he's still asleep."

"I'm sorry to put you through that. Was he having a bad dream?"

Drummond nodded. "Hard drinkers like him get mighty powerful nightmares on a regular basis—especially if they don't get their whiskey. The way some of them holler you'd think they saw the Devil himself." He glanced toward the cells in back. "I reckon this one will soon enough." He looked back at Zeke sitting on the bench across from the desk. "You said there was something you wanted to see me about?"

"I need your advice." He handed the telegram to Drummond. "What do you make of this?"

Drummond took the telegram and went over to his desk for his reading glasses. As he read the message, his jaw dropped and his eyes grew larger. He finished the telegram, looked at Zeke, then read it again. He thought for a few seconds, then said, "Come on, Zeke, let's go."

"Where are we going?"

"To the Paradise Hotel. Hopefully, Judge McGrath is an early riser."

They found the judge in the hotel dining room having breakfast. Drummond handed him the telegram, then he and Zeke sat down when the judge indicated the chairs with a sweep of his left hand.

After he read the message, he looked at Zeke and said, "You're the young man I met yesterday. Are you the Zeke Halstead mentioned in this telegram? Eighteen years old?"

"Yes, sir."

"I don't understand this at all," the judge said shaking his head.

"I don't, either, Judge," Zeke said.

"Well, who is Senator John M. Worthington? Do you know him?"

"My grandfather did. He told me to contact the senator if he died. Right after I met you yesterday I sent a wire to Senator Worthington telling him of my grandfather's death."

The judge nodded. "Now it's beginning to make a little more sense. Apparently your grandfather had an arrangement with this senator; your grandfather wanted you to take his place after he died. That's why Senator Worthington asked President Grant to nominate you as U. S. Marshal out of Cheyenne, Wyoming Territory. At least, that's the way it looks to me."

"Makes sense to me, Judge," Drummond said.

"And since I'm a federal judge, you want me to swear you in," McGrath said to Zeke.

"I didn't say that," Zeke stammered.

Judge McGrath looked away, lost in thought and thinking aloud. "It seems to me I recall reading somewhere that there was a minimum age requirement for federal marshals; I thought it was twenty-one, but I could be mistaken. You'll have to be approved by the Senate, of course, but apparently President Grant feels that's a formality. At any rate, if Ulysses S. Grant wants you to be a U. S. Marshal, I'm not about to argue with him." He turned his attention back to Zeke. "Now raise your right hand so I can swear you in."

"But I don't want to be a marshal," Zeke said. "I wouldn't know what to do." Fear consumed him, turning his legs to jelly and his insides to water. He was glad to be sitting down.

"Let's have none of that now. It's all been settled, and I've got a long trip ahead of me," the judge said. "Now raise your right hand. Sheriff Drummond is our witness."

Reluctantly, Zeke put his hand in the air.

"Do you promise to uphold the Constitution and the laws of these United States of America to the best of your abilities, even with your life?"

Zeke hesitated.

"Say, 'I do', son."

"I do."

"Then by the authority vested in me as a judge of the United States District Court, and by appointment of President Ulysses S. Grant, I hereby declare that you are a United States Marshal." He shook Zeke's hand. "Congratulations, my boy. Your pay will be sent to you in Cheyenne once a month. Now, if only we had a badge for you."

Zeke took the star out of his shirt pocket. "I have my grandfather's badge." Now he knew why Grandpa had told him to take it before he died.

"Excellent," the judge said. "Allow me to pin it on for you." He took the badge and began to pin it on Zeke's vest.

"If you don't mind, Judge, I prefer to wear it on my shirt under the vest."

"As you wish, Marshal."

Zeke felt a cold shiver run through him when the judge called him "Marshal". That's going to take some getting used to, he thought.

"Better keep this telegram with you," Judge McGrath said handing over the directive from Senator Worthington. "It'll serve as written confirmation of your appointment. As young as you are, people may not believe you're a federal marshal just because you're wearing a badge."

Sheriff Drummond nodded in agreement. "It was thoughtful of the senator to have the Director of the Marshals Service inform every U.S. Marshal of your appointment, giving them your name and that you're eighteen years old. If anyone questions you just show him this telegram and tell him to contact any U.S. Marshal and he'll confirm that you are the genuine article."

Zeke took the folded telegram and slipped it into his hip pocket. He felt like he was in a dream he couldn't wake up from. "Is there anything else?" he asked.

"No, that's all," Judge McGrath said. "Good luck."

"Thanks," was all Zeke could think of to say, although he had no idea what he was thankful for.

He and Drummond walked back to the sheriff's office. Drummond went to the pot-bellied stove and poured two cups of coffee. He handed one to Zeke then sat behind his corner desk propping his chair against the wall on its back legs and said, "You're looking mighty glum, Zeke. What's the problem?"

Zeke almost jumped off the bench. "What's the problem? The problem is I don't want to be a marshal!"

"I don't understand," Drummond said calmly. "You were already a deputy, now you're the marshal. More power, more money. What's wrong with that?"

"I didn't even want to be a deputy. Grandpa bullied me and Uncle Billy into it so we could help him catch Ledyard."

"Didn't you want to help catch your father's killer?" Drummond asked. "If I was your age and someone shot my pa I'd go after him no matter what."

Zeke could feel the whole matter getting confused in his mind, and he regretted even coming back with the sheriff to his office. "I wanted to go with Grandpa, but Uncle Billy said I was a fool, and that he wished he didn't have to go along."

"Maybe your uncle wasn't cut out to be a lawman."

"And maybe I'm not, either."

"I hardly knew your grandfather," Drummond said, "but I got the feeling right off that me and him was cut from the same stretch of rawhide. I've been a lawman almost ten years. Before that I spent twenty years in the cavalry—got all the way to first sergeant when I retired. I suspect your grandfather had a similar background. He looked like an old Indian fighter to me, and I've seen more than a few of those. Anyway, I doubt he'd push you into taking his place if he hadn't seen something in you that told him you were right for it."

"But what if I'm not?" Zeke asked, exasperated. How could he tell Drummond of the fear he felt at the relay station? How could he tell him he wouldn't have done anything if that lady from the stagecoach hadn't forced his hand? How could he tell him that the thought of wearing a badge without Grandpa to back him up just scared him to death? He looked at Drummond, unable to speak his mind.

"Seems to me you're getting all worked up over nothing," Drummond said. "You're trying to map out the rest of your life when you should be concerned with the job of getting Ledyard back to stand trial."

The sheriff rocked his chair forward onto all four legs and opened a desk drawer. He produced cigarette paper and a pouch of tobacco. In a few seconds he had rolled a cigarette and twisted the ends tight without spilling a shred of tobacco.

"I'm always amazed at how easy men make that look," Zeke said. "I tried it once; took me five minutes and I spilled tobacco all over the place."

"I've had a lot of practice," Drummond replied. He took a match out of his vest pocket and thumbed it to life. After a few puffs he leaned forward with his elbows on the desk and studied Zeke. "You do intend to take him back for trial, don't you?"

"Yes, of course," Zeke said without hesitation.

"All right, then let's think about that. If you weren't a lawman, how could you take him anywhere against his will?"

"I don't follow you, Sheriff."

"There aren't any wanted posters out on him, are there?"

"No."

"So what's to keep Ledyard from yelling his head off the first time you hit a town or pass a lawman? He'd claim you were abducting him and you couldn't prove otherwise." He took a long drag on the cigarette and looked hard at Zeke. "You got to understand how that would look to people. He's a grown man, while you're just getting there. It would be your word against his. Even if you were finally able to sort it out, it could take a heap of doing. And you might have to repeat the whole process every time you go through a town or pass near a group of men." He stopped to let his words sink in.

"But with the badge all I'd have to do is say he's my prisoner and that would be the end of it," Zeke said.

Drummond smiled. "Now you're getting the idea. Even if a local lawman wanted to he couldn't make much trouble for you."

"Why's that, Sheriff?"

"You're the highest ranking lawman there is. You see, Zeke, a town marshal is usually appointed by the mayor; a sheriff like myself is elected by the people of the county; but a U. S. Marshal is appointed directly by the President of the United States. No other lawman can make that claim.

"Town marshals and county sheriffs get run out of town or even gunned down. But anyone who tries that with a federal marshal knows he's going to have to deal with other federal marshals, or maybe even the U. S. Cavalry." He took a final drag on the cigarette before grinding it out under his heel. He looked back at Zeke and held his gaze. "Son, I don't think you realize how much authority your grandfather had."

Zeke shook his head. "I had no idea," he muttered.

"Zeke, it seems to me your grandfather went to a bit of trouble and involved some mighty big people to pass that power on to you. Maybe you oughtn't be in such a hurry to get rid of it."

"I don't know," Zeke said. "I'm just not sure I can handle that kind of responsibility."

"There you go again, looking at the long view instead of

thinking of what needs to be done now. You need that badge to get Ledyard back for trial, right?"

Zeke nodded in agreement.

"All right, so don't worry about it—or even think about it—until you get him to trial. Then, if you still don't want the job, you can quit and go back to doing whatever you were doing before this whole thing started."

"That makes sense to me."

"Good. Now that that's settled, there's some things I want to go over with you before you take him out of here. I wish I could go with you to help you out, but I can't; besides, sooner or later every lawman has to depend on himself. First of all, just because Ledyard is injured don't mean he can't make trouble for you. His kind is always dangerous, so don't take your eye off him unless you got him tied up good. Now once you get out on the open range...."

Zeke spent the better part of hour listening to Sheriff Drummond school him in being a lawman. Most of the time the sheriff drove home the lessons by recalling some incident from his own experience. To his surprise, Zeke found the stories fascinating. He would have stayed even longer, but he needed to get on the road. He told Drummond he'd see him again when he came for his prisoner, and headed for his hotel room.

He threw his saddlebags on the bed and opened them up seeing the two guns in their holsters with the gun belts wrapped around each. Zeke had too many guns. He was wearing Grandpa's .44 Remington New Model Army, and the saddlebags contained Ledyard's .44 Army Colt and the .44 Remington that Ledyard had taken from Uncle Billy.

Zeke knew he couldn't sell Ledyard's property, but he could sell Billy's gun and holster. It would fetch a fair price here in Evans, and besides, what did Zeke need with three guns?

JOHN ALEXANDER

He took Billy's gun, holster, and gun belt down to the local gunsmith and offered them for sale. The gunsmith, a portly man with oil-blackened hands, a bald pate, long straight hair that swept down on each side from the temples, and wire-rimmed glasses that kept sliding down his sweaty nose, was unable to hide his delight.

Zeke demanded five dollars more than the gunsmith offered, but was pleased when he immediately agreed and handed over the money.

Then Zeke went to the general store and stocked up on provisions for the long trip to Wattersville, then returned to his hotel room and packed for the trip.

Betsy was ready to go as well, having changed back into the riding clothes she'd worn on the trip yesterday. She accompanied Zeke to the livery stable. Halfway there she slipped her hand into his and said, "I'm sorry to see this trip end."

Her hand felt so good and so natural in his that he didn't want to let go of it. "I know what you mean," he said.

"Do you think you'll get back this way again?" she asked smiling.

He shrugged, still holding her hand. "I don't know. Wattersville is a long way from here. And so is Cheyenne, for that matter."

The smile left her face.

They arrived at the livery stable where they got her wagon and horses as well as Zeke and Ledyard's horses. He threw his things in the back and they rode over to the sheriff's office to get Ledyard.

Sheriff Drummond tipped his hat to Betsy, then helped her onto the wagon in the street outside his office. Zeke and Ledyard's horses were again tethered at the back, one on each side. Drummond then spoke to Zeke, but his eyes never left Ledyard, who was lying in the back of the wagon. "Remember what I said, Zeke: if he tries to run don't chase him, just shoot him in the back."

Zeke nodded. "Thanks for everything, Sheriff."

Ledyard smiled at Drummond, who was still staring at him. "See you around, Sheriff," Ledyard said.

"I don't think so," Drummond replied.

Ledyard returned his stare for a few seconds, then grinned and shook his head as the wagon lurched forward.

Drummond watched the wagon roll east past the edge of town and continue until it was out of sight. "Good luck, kid," he said. "Don't turn your back on him."

CHAPTER TWENTY-EIGHT

As the sheriff had instructed him, Zeke kept his six-gun and the rifle on the floor in front of his feet where Ledyard couldn't get at them should he work free of his bonds. If he got his hands free, it would be child's play for Ledyard to reach from behind Zeke and Betsy and grab a rifle leaning against the wagon seat, or pull Zeke's .44 from its holster.

Zeke knew he wouldn't have thought of that himself, and that's what scared him the most: there were so many little things he didn't know about being a lawman, and it only took one mistake to get himself killed.

Betsy was strangely quiet, even more so than usual. Several times already Ledyard had tried to start up a conversation, but Zeke ignored him. He knew that Ledyard would try to distract him, and he had enough on his mind as it was.

"Come on, kid, when are we going to take a break?" Ledyard said. "We've been riding for hours. How about we stop under one of these cottonwoods and get out of the damn sun."

"It's barely over an hour since we left Evans. Quit your belly-aching," Zeke said.

"I need a break; you know, get down and stretch my legs a bit—I'm all cramped up back here—and my arm hurts likes hell." He paused and gave Zeke an imploring look before he spoke again. "Got me a bottle in my saddlebag that I need to get out."

"We'll stop at Betsy's ranch, not before," Zeke said.

"You think you're something special, don't you?" Ledyard sneered. "You figure you're a big man now that you outdrew me. Well, don't get to feeling too high and mighty, boy. If that Reb hadn't pushed that table into me I'd have gunned you for sure." He spat contemptuously over the side of the wagon. "Hell, you didn't even have the nerve to kill me—you only shot me in the arm. You're yellow, boy; that's what you are. You hear me? Yellow!"

Zeke turned around and saw Ledyard leering at him, the same way he did back in Wattersville before he threw the glass that started the fight with Pa. Zeke could contain himself no more. All the fear, grief, worry and anger he'd experienced since the outset of the trip came together and raged out of control within him, as boiling water spews over the sides of a pot. "Don't talk to me about being yellow. You got your nerve after the way you shot my pa when he wasn't even carrying a gun. IF ANYONE'S A COWARD, YOU ARE, YOU YELLOW DOG!" Zeke shouted at him.

Betsy patted Zeke on his left forearm. "Take it easy, Zeke. No sense in getting all worked up. He's just baiting you."

Just as Zeke's temper flared, Ledyard calmed down. He answered Zeke in a matter-of-fact voice. "Your pa shouldn't have put his hands on me. I don't let no man lay hands on me."

"I suppose that justifies shooting an unarmed man!"

Betsy patted him on the arm again. "Calm down, Zeke. Calm down," she said.

Ledyard shrugged his shoulders. "Like I said, kid, he shouldn't have put his hands on me." He held Zeke's stare, then turned away as if the matter was closed.

Zeke shook with rage, but there was nothing more to be said. He might as well be talking to the man in the moon for all the good it'd do.

Heading east out of Evans, about forty miles north of Denver, they crossed the terrain in silence neither seeing any houses nor encountering anyone. Ledyard had become morose, and Zeke wondered if he was still thinking about the bottle in his saddlebag.

It must be terrible to be enslaved to alcohol like that. He looked at Ledyard again, for the first time seeing what the ravages of alcohol had done to him: the withered flesh of a malnourished body and the pickled skin that made him look years older than he was. The man's pathetic, Zeke thought. Maybe he shouldn't be so hard on Ledyard; after all, he'd be dead soon enough.

Zeke pulled over near a large red maple tree and announced they'd take a break for a few minutes so everyone could stretch their legs.

"It's about time," Ledyard muttered.

Zeke helped him out of the wagon and untied the rope binding Ledyard's hands to his belt so he could move his arms, but left his hands bound. Back in Evans, Drummond had tied Ledyard's ankles together about two feet apart so he could shuffle along but not run away. That way Zeke wouldn't have to untie his feet every time they stopped—that was another lesson Sheriff Drummond explained to him.

Zeke looked up and saw Betsy walking deeper into the woods. "Where are you going?" he asked.

"Someplace where I can have some privacy for a few minutes."

Zeke blushed. "Oh, okay. Don't wander too far off."

Betsy just shook her head and disappeared behind some bushes.

Zeke went to Ledyard's horse and unfastened the strap on the saddlebag as Ledyard watched him. He reached inside and pulled out a long-necked bottle nearly full of whiskey.

"Hey! What are you doing?" Ledyard said. "Get away from my whiskey!"

"Thought you said you wanted a drink," Zeke said bringing the bottle over. Ledyard's eyes shifted from the whiskey to Zeke. As he reached for the bottle, Zeke pulled it away. "Just don't drink too much of it—I don't want you drunk."

"Yeah, fine, just give me the bottle," Ledyard said taking it from him. He uncorked it and tilted his head back, taking a long pull.

Zeke watched his Adam's apple bob as Ledyard nursed on the bottle. He shook his head and turned to walk away when suddenly he realized his mistake and whirled around just as Ledyard brought the bottle down on him with both hands still bound together.

Zeke ducked his head and threw his right arm up to protect himself. The bottle slammed down on his shoulder and Zeke's right arm went numb. Ledyard threw the bottle down and made a grab for Zeke's revolver. Unable to move his right arm, Zeke reached across his body with his left hand and held the six-gun down in its holster as Ledyard frantically clawed at the gun.

Zeke hooked his right leg behind Ledyard and threw him off balance. Both men tumbled to the ground still grabbing for the .44. Zeke wanted to take a swing at Ledyard to drive him away, but he dared not let go of the gun. They rolled over a few times and Ledyard cursed him as his frustration grew.

Suddenly, Ledyard had the six-gun out of its holster. Before he could position the gun to fire it, Zeke grabbed the barrel and jerked it out of his hand. Unable to turn the gun around to use with only one hand, Zeke threw it several feet away.

"Hey!" Betsy yelled running toward them from the woods.

Ledyard pulled free and dove to the ground stretching for the six-gun with both hands. Zeke grabbed Ledyard's left foot and pulled him back away from the gun, which lay only a foot or so beyond his reach.

Ledyard kicked at Zeke's hand with his right boot and managed to break free. Just as he reached for the .44, Betsy jumped on his back and an arrow whistled into the ground near the gun, missing Ledyard's hand by inches.

All three turned to see three braves on horseback watching them. Only one had a bow, and he had another arrow nocked ready to shoot again. Zeke, Betsy, and Ledyard sat up and faced them as one of the other braves got down and walked toward them. He picked up the .44 and motioned with it for them to get up. As they did so, he pulled the arrow out of the ground and returned it to its owner. Then he took the rifle from the wagon and remounted his horse.

The Indian with the bow swung it in a wide arc indicating he wanted them to get into the wagon. It was then that Zeke saw the blue hand painted on the left side of his chest. It was the same Indian who had killed Grandpa and took his scalp. But why didn't they just kill them now?

One brave led the way while the other two flanked the wagon. Zeke had never been so close to Indians before. He could smell the rancid grease coating their bodies. They wore pants and boots made from buffalo hide, and were naked from the waist up. Each brave had several strings of beads cascading onto his chest from around his neck. Their hair was adorned with a feather or two, and Zeke noted that each one carried a knife in his waistband.

Zeke's heart pounded and his mouth was dry. "What do you want with us?" he asked the brave next to him.

No answer.

"Well, where are you taking us, then?" Zeke asked.

Still no answer.

"Save your breath, kid," Ledyard said from the back of the wagon. "These savages probably don't even speak English."

"What's going on?" Zeke asked Ledyard. "Why didn't they kill us?"

"They want us alive."

"Why? What do they want from us?"

"A little fun, I reckon. I stumbled upon a Cheyenne and his squaw not too far from here. They attacked me and I killed the brave and had a fight with the squaw." He shook his head ruefully, then spat. "I knew I should have killed her, too."

"So what happens now?" Zeke asked.

"You don't want to know, kid, believe me." He looked off into the distance, then repeated in a low voice, as if to himself. "You really don't want to know."

CHAPTER TWENTY-NINE

There were several tepees erected in a clearing near a small creek. As they drew closer to the camp Zeke saw women working at various chores. A few children played near their mothers, some braves sat on the ground talking and laughing, and an elderly man sat cross-legged in front of his tepee smoking a pipe. His black hair was streaked with gray, and he seemed oblivious to the activities around him. Was he the chief? Zeke wondered.

At the sound of the approaching horses, the entire camp turned its attention to the incoming riders. Everyone gathered near the old man to await the riders.

The horses and the wagon stopped near some cottonwoods by the creek and the three braves quickly dismounted. Each dragged one of the captives from the wagon.

Zeke's right arm was no longer numb, but his shoulder ached where the bottle had landed. He was relieved that he could move his arm, and that no bones were broken.

Zeke noticed that the brave with the blue hand on his chest was now wearing Ledyard's six-gun in his waistband. The other brave still had the rifle and Zeke's .44. They didn't waste any time going through the saddlebags, Zeke thought. Now two of the three braves had guns. He was glad he'd sold the third revolver in Evans.

Grabbing them firmly by the arms, two braves led Zeke and Ledyard to the chief. They lined up four abreast facing the old man in front of his tepee.

The brave with the blue hand on his chest took Betsy into one of the other tepees. Zeke struggled to break free, but his captors held fast. "What's he doing with her?" Zeke yelled.

No reply.

Betsy screamed from inside the tepee.

"WHAT'S HE DOING TO HER?" Zeke yelled. "TELL HIM TO LEAVE HER ALONE!"

"Save your breath, kid," Ledyard said. "It's already too late."

"This is all your fault," Zeke said.

"Yeah, I know, kid. Everything is my fault."

Then a young woman stepped forward for a closer look at the captives. Zeke saw that she didn't look so much like an Indian as the other women did.

She only looked at Zeke for a second, then moved directly in front of Ledyard. Her arm came straight up and pointed at him. Holding eye contact with Ledyard, she said something in the Cheyenne tongue. Ledyard squirmed as the braves tightened their grips on his arms.

The chief looked at Zeke and said something to the woman. Nervous beads of cold sweat broke out on Zeke's forehead as he faced his captors and wished he could communicate with them.

As though in answer to his plea, the woman spoke to Zeke. "White Eagle wants to know why you were with that man. Is he your friend?"

"You speak English," Zeke said.

She nodded. "My father was white. He only spoke to me

in that language even though he knew our tongue. My mother was Cheyenne and I grew up living with both parents in a Cheyenne village." She paused and looked at the ground, then back at Zeke. "I am called Pony Woman."

She was only two or three years older than Zeke. Her skin was smooth and about the same color as Zeke's tanned arms. Her hair was black and straight, but her eyes were light brown, and she lacked the high cheekbones and broad features of an Indian woman. Her body was firm and strong, and she was two or three inches shorter than Zeke. The left side of her face was swollen and covered with a large, purple bruise.

"My name is Zeke." He remembered her question about Ledyard. "No, he's not a friend of mine. I was taking him back to Wattersville, Kansas to stand trial for killing my father."

Her eyebrows arched in surprise, and she studied Zeke for a long moment. "I will speak with White Eagle about you and ask him to let you leave."

"You mean I'm not going to be killed?" Zeke said.

"The other one wronged me, not you."

"Do you think White Eagle will listen to you?"

"I think so," she said. "He is my grandfather."

"What about Betsy—the woman that was with us?"

"Is she your wife?"

Zeke shook his head.

"Sister?"

He shook his head again.

"It's just as well. She belongs to Two Horses now."

"Who is Two Horses?"

"The Cheyenne with the blue hand on his chest."

The chief made a gesture with his hand, and the two braves dragged Ledyard away as he cursed them and struggled vainly to break free. Everyone followed after except for Zeke, Pony Woman, and White Eagle.

Zeke placed a hand on Pony Woman's arm. "He really should go back with me to stand trial."

Her eyes grew cold and empty. "I think you'll find that the Cheyenne know how to deal with men such as him."

Suddenly, there was a male scream of horror from the tepee where Two Horses and Betsy were. The flap flew open and Two Horses stormed out yelling at one of the old women nearby.

The old woman went inside, then emerged with Betsy a moment later. Betsy's pants were ripped and she held them together at the waist with her hand while the old woman tugged at that arm; Betsy covered her face with her other hand. Zeke heard her sobbing as the old woman led her out of camp in the opposite direction.

Two Horses came back to the group and stood next to the chief, his body stiff, muscles taut, arms folded across his chest as he glared at Zeke.

"What in the world is going on?" Zeke asked Pony Woman.

But she turned away from Zeke and spoke with White Eagle in Cheyenne again. The chief looked at Zeke, then answered her.

She translated for Zeke. "White Eagle says you must stay here tonight, but you can leave in the morning. The other two must remain."

Two Horses said something angrily to White Eagle. The old man shook his head. Two Horses grew angrier and shouted at the chief. White Eagle made a sweeping motion in front of his body with his right hand as if to say he'd heard enough. Then he turned and ducked into his tepee.

Zeke was totally confused, but then remembered the issue

at hand. "If your people won't release the man and the woman, then I'm not going, either," he said.

"You must go. Two Horses is very angry that White Eagle is releasing you. Two Horses says you are a white man and demands you be treated the same as the other one."

"But White Eagle is chief," Zeke said. His stomach roiled.

"A chief is not like one of your leaders. He has influence, but he cannot tell a full-grown Cheyenne warrior what to do. No Cheyenne can order another one to do something, or not do something."

"So am I safe or not?"

Pony Woman shrugged. "I don't know. I don't think Two Horses will defy White Eagle, but I can't be sure. You must not leave the camp until White Eagle says you can go."

"Aren't they going to tie me up?"

"No. You are free to roam the camp. If you leave the camp before White Eagle releases you the men will hunt you down. Two Horses would like you to do that. I know him. He would not only own you as his prisoner, but he would also enjoy the sport of the hunt."

Pony Woman and Two Horses walked away and Zeke followed them to an area just beyond some tepees where Ledyard was now staked out spread-eagle on the ground, bound tightly by his wrists and ankles. The crowd made a circle around him watching as he lay helplessly struggling against the rawhide restraints.

Pony Woman stepped into the center of the circle, and all eyes went to her as she approached Ledyard. She would have the honor of inflicting the first wounds. The crowd pressed closer, tightening the circle.

Zeke jumped as Ledyard's scream broke the silence. He didn't see what she'd done, but rather than look closer, he turned away. The hair on the back of his neck stood on end. The crowd roared its approval, urging Pony Woman on.

Another long, tormented scream. Zeke's stomach roiled and he swallowed hard, the bitter taste of bile in his mouth. He thought he might be sick, but though his stomach continued to churn, he did not vomit.

His eyes scanned the camp for Betsy. Looking across the circle of enthusiastic onlookers, Zeke saw her and the old woman off in the distance at the other end of the campsite. Why were they so far away?

As he walked closer to them he saw the rope around Betsy's wrists that ran along the ground and looped around a tree. They've got her like a dog on a leash, he thought. The old woman stood nearby with a thin, four-foot branch.

Just as Zeke got to the old woman she yelled and swung at him viciously in a wide arc. He didn't understand her, but he understood the flexible branch that cut through the air like a quirt inches from his nose. He jumped back as she continued to yell at him, shooing him away with her left hand.

Zeke stepped back a few paces and said to Betsy, "Are you all right? What happened back there?"

Betsy stifled a sob. "That Indian was forcing himself on me." She sobbed again. "After he ripped my pants off he saw that it was that time of the month for me and he screamed and ran out."

"That time of the month? What does that mean?" Zeke said.

The old woman took three quick steps toward Betsy and quirted her across her bare arm. Betsy screamed. The old woman raised the branch above Betsy again and looked back at Zeke.

"Don't hit her anymore," he said, his hands in front of his chest palms out as he backed away. "I'm leaving."

He walked past the boisterous Cheyenne surrounding Ledyard. Two Horses looked up and glared at him. Zeke continued to the other end of camp and sat on the ground.

He could hear Ledyard sobbing between screams, even from this distance. Zeke had never heard such agony in his entire life, and wondered what Pony Woman was doing to him—but he really didn't want to find out.

Was Ledyard only getting what he deserved—what he had in fact brought upon himself by his own foul deeds—or was this more than any man should endure? What would Grandpa say if he saw this? Or Uncle Billy? Or Pa?

After awhile Zeke saw Pony Woman emerge from the center of the circle, her face slick with sweat and her hands spattered with blood. As he watched her walk away, Zeke saw Two Horses glaring at him again. Zeke looked away.

Other women joined in the torture, taking turns. They were relentless. Not actively participating, the men and children only watched. Always the pattern was the same: Ledyard would scream out in pain, then he'd moan or whimper as the torment abated, only to start up again a few seconds later. It was as if the Indians felt that the contrast between inflicting pain and then allowing a few seconds of rest actually caused more anguish than constant pain.

Indeed, the intermittent screams wore Zeke down, as he nervously anticipated each one, not knowing when exactly they would come. What he couldn't imagine is what it must be like for Ledyard. After all this time, Zeke hadn't moved from his spot on the ground.

The deep fear that consumed Zeke, that made his stomach roil and his body shake, gave way to an even more intense emotion, closer to panic. What if he was next? What if they came and dragged him away, and staked him out like a buffalo hide drying in the sun? And then the Cheyenne would close in, one after the other, torturing him fiendishly over and over until he was dead.

Zeke shuddered convulsively. He wanted to run. To get away from here. To go as far and as fast as he could. But what about Betsy? He couldn't just leave her here. And how far would he get anyway? The way Two Horses kept looking over at him it wouldn't be long before he discovered Zeke was missing. If Zeke ran away, the Cheyenne would surely hunt him down and drag him back here, or just kill him slowly out on the prairie.

Zeke's only hope was to wait until morning and hope that Two Horses didn't come for him before then. If White Eagle let him go, he could get safely away. But what about Betsy? Zeke didn't know what to do. He listened to Ledyard's agony with his stomach churning and his mind in utter turmoil. He jammed his hands against his ears and shut his eyes for a few minutes providing a temporary respite.

A long time passed—it seemed like hours to Zeke as he sat worrying about Betsy, listening to Ledyard and wondering if he would be next.

Not far from the circled Cheyenne a fire crackled as the fat from a skewered hunk of buffalo meat dripped into the flames of a campfire. The smoke drifted over the village, and the aroma of roasting meat filled the air.

At last the screams stopped and the crowd drifted away. Pony Woman approached Zeke with something in her hands. She sat down next to him with a bowl of buffalo meat.

"Is he dead?" Zeke asked.

"No, we have stopped for supper. Also, he needs to rest before we begin again." She pushed the bowl closer to him. "I brought some for you, too."

The very thought of food nauseated him. He shook his head in refusal of the meat. She took a knife from her belt and cut off a large piece for herself, eating with her hands and leaving the rest in the bowl.

Ledyard's moaning carried throughout the camp, and Zeke wondered how these people could suddenly go on about the business of their daily routine as though nothing had happened.

He watched Pony Woman as she chewed large chunks of meat, sucking the buffalo grease from her fingers with every mouthful.

"You're sure you don't want any meat?" she asked. "You've got a long ride tomorrow."

"No, I'm not hungry. Thank you, anyway."

"I don't understand you," she said. "That man killed your father, and yet you don't even watch his punishment." She wiped her hands on her dress and put a greasy hand on his arm. "Come, I will show him to you now."

"No, I'm staying right here." He looked off in Ledyard's direction, then back at her. "So when are they going to kill him? How will they do it?"

"Kill him? We do not want to kill him. We want to keep him alive as long as possible."

Zeke shivered, as though someone had poured icy water down his back. What kind of people were these? "If that's the case, then I hope Ledyard dies soon. He shouldn't have to suffer like this."

"You should hope that he lives, not that he dies."

"Why?"

"Because if he dies before you leave tomorrow morning Two Horses will almost certainly come for you to take his place." She stood up. "I'll leave some meat here in case you change your mind." Then she walked away.

Zeke shivered again. The thought of taking Ledyard's place, of being staked out and tortured while a circle of angry Cheyenne encouraged his tormentor was too much to bear. Would Pony Woman join in, he wondered?

He watched her as she walked away. Why was Pony Woman so friendly to him? Was it because both of them had suffered at Ledyard's hands? Was it because she was half white? No one else in the camp even paid any attention to him except for Two Horses.

He crossed the camp to see how Betsy was doing, but as soon as the old woman saw him she raised the quirt again menacingly at Betsy, so he returned to where he'd been sitting.

He lay back with his hands behind his head and studied the fleecy cumulus clouds floating lazily in the early evening sky. There was still a few hours of daylight left. His mind drifted back to the farm in Wattersville. Was it really only two weeks ago that he was there with Pa and Uncle Billy, working hard and enjoying every minute of it, content in his own little world that barely extended beyond the area bounded by the farm and the nearby town?

He longed to return, and yet, he knew it could never be the same.

He lay there for several minutes mesmerized by the fluffy white clouds drifting past against a pale blue sky that extended deeper than his eyes could see. If he ignored the background noises and smells of the encampment he could almost pretend he was home. He'd spent many a lazy summer evening after supper just like this, lying under the elm tree on the hill next to the house, watching the clouds go by and letting his mind wander to wherever it wanted to go.

Suddenly a long, tortured scream of agony pierced the air, and Zeke bolted upright to a sitting position. His heart pounded and his mouth went dry. He could hear Ledyard moaning now; then another long cry of pain that made Zeke's skin crawl. More moans followed by more screams as the pattern repeated itself over and over again until Zeke thought he was going mad.

Another long scream, and then, instead of moaning, Ledyard began to cry. He sobbed openly. "Please, please, no more. I can't take no more of this. Please, I'm beg—"

He never finished the sentence as he let out another cry of agony; then more sobbing, and the new pattern repeated itself over and over again.

Like Ledyard, Zeke couldn't take much more of it, either. All he wanted was for this nightmare to end. He pulled the bandana from around his neck and tore off a strip one-inch wide. This he tore in half so that he had two one-inch strips each about four inches long. He rolled each one up into a tight cylinder and jammed them into his ears.

Then he closed his eyes, curled up as comfortably as he could on the ground, and pulled his hat over his face to shut out the light. As tired and hungry as he was, sleep overtook him in a few minutes.

A sharp kick in the ribs brought him roughly awake. He pulled the hat off his eyes and looked up into the grim faces of Two Horses and the other two braves. Pony Woman was with them. The sun was almost down and darkness was setting in.

Two Horses said something Zeke couldn't understand. He removed the earplugs. Two Horses spoke to him again, loudly, as if giving a command. Not understanding him, Zeke turned to Pony Woman just as Two Horses kicked him again. The breath rushed out of Zeke and his side felt like he'd been hit with an ax handle.

"He says for you to get up," Pony Woman said.

Zeke's breath caught in his throat. Had they come for him?

CHAPTER THIRTY

Two Horses said something and the two braves reached down and grabbed Zeke firmly under each arm. They jerked him to his feet as Zeke's legs went to jelly. Their hands were slick and the smell of the rancid grease that coated their bodies repulsed him. The braves dragged him to a large tree and roughly pulled his arms around the trunk so that Zeke was facing it. Then Two Horses produced a rawhide strip and tightly bound his wrists on the opposite side of the tree.

He was relieved to see the three braves walk away, laughing.

"It's getting dark so they tied you to the tree so you couldn't escape," Pony Woman said.

"Do I have to stay this way all night?" he asked, but she was already walking away.

Relief flooded through him. At least that weren't going to torture him—not yet, anyway. But after only a few minutes his shoulders and low back ached something fierce, and the bark rubbed harshly against his face. His side still hurt where Two Horses had kicked him. Craning his neck to see around the tree only made everything hurt worse. He closed his eyes.

A hand gently rocked his shoulder. He came awake slowly, unsure of where he was, but then he saw Pony Woman's face as she stood beside him. She placed a finger over her lips so he would be quiet. Zeke didn't know how long he'd been asleep, but it was dark, and the sky was filled with stars. A nearly-full moon cast eerie shadows over the landscape.

She spoke in a whisper, her face close to his. "Two Horses means to kill you, too. I overheard him talking with Lone Elk and Big Thunder. He is waiting for White Eagle to go to sleep, and then they will come for you. You must leave now, while there is still time." She took the knife from her belt and cut the rawhide binding his wrists.

"Why are you helping me?" Zeke said rubbing the circulation back into his wrists and trying to think. Was she trying to trick him?

"Like me, you, too, have suffered at that one's hands," she said jerking her head in Ledyard's direction. Then she moved closer and said, "Unlike Two Horses, I do not hate all white men."

Zeke stood still, unsure of what to do next.

"You must go!" she said. "Go now, before it's too late. I will go to White Eagle and delay him from going to sleep, but I can only give you a few minutes more, that is all."

Zeke heard Ledyard moaning softly. Then a scream. "They're still torturing him," Zeke said.

"That is only Big Thunder having a little fun. He is keeping watch. Everyone else is bedded down for the night." Her eyes looked into his imploringly. "You must go now!"

He hesitated for a moment, then said, "Let me have your knife."

She placed her hand protectively over the knife at her belt. "No! I have helped you because my father was white, but the Cheyenne are my people and I will not allow you to hurt them."

Zeke watched her move off in the darkness. Then he headed for Betsy. The camp was quiet except for Big Thunder, who was taunting Ledyard. Zeke knew Two Horses and Lone Elk were not asleep, so he moved as quietly as he could keeping to the perimeter of the camp.

The old woman was nowhere in sight. Betsy lay on the ground with her hands now bound behind her back, still tethered to the tree. There was too much moonlight for him to approach her unseen if someone was watching.

He stood behind the big tree and whispered, "Betsy."

She looked up immediately.

"Over here, behind the tree," he said.

She struggled to her feet and walked toward the tree.

"Back up to the tree so I can untie your hands." As she got closer he saw the red welts on her arms, neck, and face from the quirt. "Good thing you're a light sleeper," he said.

"I couldn't get comfortable," she said.

"Are you all right?" he asked as he worked at the knot. He sure wished he had a knife.

"I'll be all right once we get out of here."

The knot refused to budge and he cursed under his breath. They didn't have much time. He moved her wrists to the left so the light fell on the knot as he continued to pry at it. Finally, it gave a little. It took another thirty seconds to work the knot loose, and then she was free.

He placed a finger over his lips. "No talking," he said. "Be as quiet as possible. We have to get to the horses."

"But what ab—"

"Shhhh," Zeke whispered, his finger over his lips again. "Come on."

They headed for the trees where the horses were tethered. Zeke found his horse with the others, tied to a rope strung between two trees as a makeshift hitching rail. He also saw his grandfather's horse, which had been stolen by Two Horses. Both were still saddled.

Zeke looked around to see if they'd been followed. The moonlight cast long shadows everywhere; he couldn't be sure. He pictured Grandpa screaming as Two Horses sliced his scalp away, ripping it free with a vicious jerk. He thought of Ledyard, still staked out helplessly, tortured hour after hour, his cries of anguish still fresh in Zeke's ears.

The still, night air hung heavily, suffocating him. His heart pounded against his ribs, and his palms dampened with a slick sweat he couldn't rub off. They must not be taken captive by Two Horses!

There was no time to waste. Quickly, he released all of the horses, saving his and Grandpa's for last, and untied the rope from the two trees. Holding the reins to both horses in his right hand and the rope in his left, he carefully walked away from the camp as the remaining horses wandered off.

He was thankful for the nearly full moon that illuminated the unfamiliar countryside for them as they made their way along in the semi-darkness. Once they got out of earshot, they could ride away.

They hadn't gone fifty yards when another long, tormented cry of agony cut through the night air. Zeke stopped still in his tracks. He was too far away now to hear Ledyard moaning, but Zeke knew that he was. He knew that Ledyard was still staked out and writhing on the ground with death his only hope for relief, and even that was being withheld as long as possible.

Well, that's not my problem, Zeke thought, as he began to walk away again.

"We can't just leave him," Betsy said.

Zeke did not reply. They went a few more paces, then he stopped once more and looked back through the darkness toward the camp.

It *was* his problem. Should he live the rest of his life like Grandpa did, facing danger head-on, fearing nothing and dying with no regrets? Or should he live like Uncle Billy did, having nightmares about hiding in a hole to escape death, always worrying about what danger might lie ahead, and then end up dying anyway—only dying a coward instead of a man?

Zeke spotted a tree nearby and tethered his horse to it. "You go on, Betsy. Walk until you're far enough away that they can't hear you, then ride for home. I'll meet you there later."

She shook her head. "If you're going back, so am I."

Zeke didn't have time to argue. Two Horses could discover he was gone at anytime. "All right," he said. "If you don't want to leave, then wait here for me. If I'm not back in ten minutes, head for home." He quickly turned and walked away, ending the discussion.

"Be careful," he heard her say as he eased his way back toward the camp, ever so carefully, his eyes straining to see through the moonlight and shadows.

He crept to the edge of the camp where Ledyard was staked out near the fire, which was burning low.

Zeke remembered that Big Thunder was not the brave who had his six-gun. It was Lone Elk who was wearing it earlier in the day and had taken the rifle, too. Maybe Lone Elk gave Big Thunder a gun to use while on watch. There was no way to see from here, but Zeke doubted any Indian would part with a gun if he didn't have to.

He could hear Ledyard clearly now. His breathing was labored and his throat sounded parched. Big Thunder sat a few feet away. Zeke got down close to the ground and looked for something to use against him. He found a rock large enough to fill his hand; then he quietly maneuvered himself into position directly behind Big Thunder, with a line of small bushes between them.

Zeke's heart was beating so hard he was sure the Cheyenne could hear it. He took a deep breath, then stepped through an opening between the bushes and slammed the rock down on the Indian's head before he could turn around. Big Thunder slumped forward and Zeke froze in place, his eyes searching the camp for any sign of discovery. All was quiet.

He rolled the Indian onto his back and saw the knife tucked in his belt. He had neither the rifle nor the six-gun. Zeke took the knife and crept toward Ledyard, who eyed him hungrily. Zeke was out in the open now with the light of the moon and the campfire full on him.

"Kill me," Ledyard said in a garbled tongue barely intelligible. "You got the knife, go ahead and do it."

Quickly, Zeke cut through one of the rawhide restraints.

"Kill me, damn you!"

"Quiet, you fool! You want to wake up the whole village?" Zeke said.

"Gutless lawdog," Ledyard said.

Zeke cut through the last of the restraints and looked about him at the tepees nearby; so far, so good. He helped Ledyard to his feet, seeing the ravaged flesh for the first time. He wrapped an arm around Ledyard to support him, and felt a warm stickiness, as though Ledyard had honey on his arm. Had they staked him on an anthill? Zeke leaned in for a look at Ledyard's arm. Strips of skin were missing and blood oozed from the bare flesh. Zeke felt a wave of nausea and averted his eyes.

They took a few steps, then Ledyard stopped and bent over Big Thunder, the Indian's knife in Ledyard's hand. Zeke was confused for a moment, then remembered laying the knife down when he helped Ledyard get up. Before he could take the knife away, Ledyard plunged it into the unconscious Cheyenne's throat all the way to hilt with a ripping motion.

Ledyard stepped back as a long spurt of blood arced from the gaping wound. He grinned in delight, his face half-shadow and half aglow with the orange light from the fire.

"What'd you do that for? He was already out cold," Zeke said.

"That's one less Indian we'll have to worry about," Ledyard said.

Zeke pulled him away, anxious to leave.

"No, wait, we need that knife," Ledyard said reaching for it.

Zeke pulled even harder. "Never mind that. Let's get out of here."

Scuffling his feet, Ledyard struggled to keep up with Zeke. Concerned about the noise and eager to get away, Zeke threw Ledyard over his shoulder and carried him to the waiting horses. "Can you ride?" Zeke asked.

Ledyard eyed Betsy, surprised at seeing her.

"Can you ride?" Zeke said firmly.

Ledyard shook his head feebly.

"Anybody see you?" Betsy asked.

"I don't think so, but it's only a matter of minutes before Two Horses discovers we're gone," Zeke said as he and Betsy laid Ledyard across Henry's horse and used the rope to tie him on. "Go ahead and mount up, Betsy. I'll ride double with you."

They kept the horses to a walk for a couple hundred yards, then picked up the pace a little when they were away from the camp. Zeke wanted to go faster, but knew Ledyard couldn't take the pounding from the horse as he lay face down across its back.

After a half hour they stopped and Zeke checked on Ledyard; he was wheezing badly. Zeke helped him down from his horse, and the outlaw flopped onto the ground, barely conscious.

After tethering the horses to a tree, Zeke grabbed his canteen and then told Betsy to get some food out of his saddlebags. The raucous chirping of a thousand crickets filled the air, and off in the distance an owl hooted. It was weird how the same piece of land could look so beautiful in the daylight, and yet so eerie at night, Zeke thought.

He sat on the ground and cradled Ledyard in his arm, gently pouring water into his mouth from the open canteen. Ledyard jerked his head away in obvious pain.

Betsy handed Ledyard a sourdough biscuit, but he pushed it away. "Teeth all busted," he mumbled. They both leaned in and took a close look at his mouth, squinting in the poor light. The upper lip was swollen, and there was a vertical line of crusted blood where the lip had been split. Zeke looked past the swollen lip and saw that the front teeth were snapped off, with bloody nerves and vessels hanging from them.

Zeke felt queasy and took a deep breath. "How are your back teeth?"

"I think they're all right."

"You got to get some of your strength back or we'll never make it out of here," Zeke said.

Betsy tore the biscuit into small pieces, then took the canteen and dribbled water over them to soften them up. "Here, put these on your back teeth and chew them as best you can," she said.

With Betsy feeding him one piece at a time, and with an occasional drink of water poured over his back teeth, Ledyard was able to eat two biscuits.

At Zeke's request, Betsy took Ledyard's head and laid it in her lap. Zeke stood up and went to Grandpa's horse to rummage through the saddlebags. He didn't know what his grandfather had packed for the trip, but he hoped the Indians had left him something they could use. His hand found a glass bottle. He removed the pint bottle and scrunched up his face as he looked at it in confusion.

Why would they leave the whiskey? Zeke knew enough about Indians to know that they didn't pass up whiskey. He held the bottle up to the moon. It was full, but it was still only a pint: enough for one man, but hardly enough for three. Whichever one of the braves found it probably put it back without letting on so that he could retrieve it later when the camp was asleep.

Zeke took the bottle back to Ledyard and held it out to him. "You look like you could use a drink."

For the first time Zeke saw a spark of life in the outlaw. He sat up with Betsy's help and snatched the bottle greedily in both hands, screaming in pain as the whiskey poured over the raw nerves of his broken teeth. Still, he drank lustily, as though the liquid was life itself.

Zeke reached down and took the bottle from him. "You can have some more later."

Ledyard grabbed Zeke's shirt clumsily. "Don't let them Indians get me again!" His eyes shifted to Betsy. "I can't take no more." And then he began to weep, softly at first, but then his whole body racked with sobs.

Zeke glanced at the hand on his shirt and recoiled in horror. Betsy gasped and her hand flew to her mouth. Ledyard's fingers were a gnarled tangle of broken bones, the ends blood-encrusted where the nails had been torn off taking pulpy chunks of nail bed.

Ledyard released his grip on Zeke and bent over sobbing, covering his face with his two mangled hands. Now that Zeke had seen Ledyard up close he couldn't take his eyes off him. He was appalled and yet drawn to stare at his mutilated body: the burn marks, the gouged flesh, the ugly welts visible everywhere, the bloody wounds oozing through incomplete clots, and the raw patches of flesh where the skin had been peeled away as one peels a grape.

Until now, Zeke had pictured Ledyard as the epitome of evil, but his deeds paled before the unrestrained savagery of the Cheyenne. Grimacing, he tore his eyes off Ledyard and stood up.

Then he gently helped Ledyard up and said, "Come on, get a hold of yourself. We'll be all right, but we've got to keep moving."

They tied Ledyard on his horse again, mounted up and rode as fast as they dared in the poor light and strange terrain. After another fifteen minutes, Zeke stopped to check his prisoner again. The outlaw was struggling for every breath. Zeke untied Ledyard and eased his limp body off the horse. Still mounted, Betsy leaned over and grabbed the reins to Henry's horse.

"Can you ride anymore?" Zeke asked Ledyard.

The outlaw let out a tired sigh and shook his head feebly. "Ribs hurt...can't breathe...weak...dizzy," he said.

"We'll have to rest here awhile," Zeke said.

"You don't know Indians," Ledyard mumbled.

"What do you mean by that?"

"They're out there somewhere. They can't be too far behind."

"I let their horses go," Zeke said.

The outlaw laughed, then coughed and spat a mouthful of blood. "That only delayed them a bit. They're out there, all right."

Zeke pondered their situation for a moment. "There must be some way to get you out of here and back to Wattersville."

"For what, so I can hang? I'm just slowing you down. Why don't you kill me now and be done with it?"

"I don't have the authority to do that," Zeke said.

"Then why don't you leave me for the Indians? That's

what I'd do." He turned a cynical face to Zeke. "What's in it for you?"

"You ask too many questions," Zeke said. "I need to think." He figured that Two Horses was a proud warrior who would bring Lone Elk with him, but probably not anyone else. Not much glory in bringing half the tribe out to fight one man.

The two Cheyenne warriors would each have a six-gun and a knife, a rifle, and Two Horses may or may not have his bow and arrows with him. Zeke, on the other hand, had no weapon at all, and was responsible for his prisoner and Betsy. The only thing he had on his side was the element of surprise: the Cheyenne would not expect him to lie in wait for them.

But what could he do?

CHAPTER THIRTY-ONE

Zeke took the reins from Betsy, told her to stay put, then led Henry's horse through an opening in a stand of trees and tethered it out of sight. He went back for Ledyard. The outlaw tried to walk but couldn't even stand, so Zeke carried him to some dense bushes about fifty yards from the horse where he could rest unseen.

Betsy had dismounted and followed them, her horse trailing behind with the reins in her hand. "I'll stay with him," she said.

Zeke shook his head. "No, you need to get as far from here as you can."

"Don't you need my help?" she said.

He looked at her for just a moment, admiring her courage. "No, there's nothing you can do," he said. "You know this country well enough to find your way home. We'll meet up with you there."

"But what if the Indians get you?"

"Then you can keep the horse."

"That's not very funny," she said glaring at him. Then she

leaned in and kissed him on the cheek. She quickly mounted up, and rode off without looking back.

Zeke returned to Ledyard and pointed off to the left. "If I don't make it back, the horse is hidden by those bushes over there." Then he squatted next to his prisoner. "Try to be quiet," Zeke said. "If they get me, there's a chance they won't find you."

"You mean you'd let me get away?"

"I mean I don't want the Cheyenne to get their hands on you again," Zeke said.

~

Not knowing how far away the Indians were, Zeke moved about as quietly as possible searching in the darkness for something he could use against his pursuers. After several minutes he came upon a tree split open by lightning and found a fallen branch three feet long and about four inches in diameter at its wide end. He grabbed it at the thinner end like an ax handle and swung it in a wide arc parallel to the ground. A smile crossed his face.

Still holding the club, he climbed into a nearby tree and sat in the branches about ten feet above the ground. Had the light been a little better, he'd have had a clear view of any approaching riders. As it was, he sat on his perch peering through the night, his eyes straining to make sense of the vague shadows that surrounded him.

He ran his sleeve over his face wiping away the cold sweat that dripped from his forehead into his eyes and down his cheeks. His eyes moved about constantly, scanning the direction the Indians would be coming from. He listened intently for their approach, but all he heard were the crickets.

Minutes dragged by, and Zeke was sure the Cheyenne had slipped through unnoticed and had discovered his perch. His imagination running wild, he peered into the darkness half expecting to be shot out of the tree at any time. In his mind he could hear Ledyard screaming again. Zeke's mouth went dry, his body stiffened as his muscles tensed, and his breathing became rapid. "Calm down, calm down," he said softly. Consciously slowing his breathing, he gripped the club tightly in anticipation, still peering into the night.

Pushing aside his fearful thoughts, Zeke pictured his grandfather in this situation: up in a tree with only a branch for a weapon against two armed Cheyenne warriors. Would he be rattled and nervous? Probably not. He might be a little scared, but more than likely he'd be glad to have the branch for a weapon and eager to deal with the Indians that were after him.

Maybe that was the essential difference between Grandpa and Uncle Billy. Grandpa always met situations head-on, whereas Uncle Billy was always on the run. If he were here, Zeke knew what his grandfather would tell him: "Don't be the prey, be the hunter!"

Zeke stiffened. About sixty yards away on the open ground, two silhouetted figures on horseback approached the wooded area where he was perched. Quickly, Zeke dropped from the tree and noiselessly moved toward the line the horses were following. He hid behind a large tree next to where they would pass.

The Cheyenne approached cautiously; even their horses barely made a sound as they moved through the woods. They rode single-file between the trees, and as they drew near, Zeke saw Two Horses in the lead. Zeke ducked behind the tree again and waited as Two Horses passed. They were so close Zeke got a strong whiff of the now familiar stench of the rancid grease that coated their bodies. He gripped the narrow end of his club again with both hands and waited for Lone Elk to pass by.

Zeke felt the weight of the horses treading the ground as they passed, even as his own heart pounded inside his chest. He peeked around the tree just as Lone Elk's horse passed. Now! Zeke stepped from behind the tree and approached Lone Elk from behind. With a mighty swing he brought the club down on Lone Elk's neck and shoulders, knocking him from his horse. The Indian lay on the ground, momentarily stunned.

There wasn't a second to lose. Zeke had to get the gun. Tossing the club aside, he jumped onto Lone Elk. The Indian rolled Zeke over onto his back and instinctively went for the knife on his belt as he straddled Zeke. At the same time, Zeke made a grab for the .44 Remington that was shoved in the brave's waistband.

Zeke got his hand on the six-gun just as Lone Elk grabbed the knife. The blade flashed in the moonlight as he raised it above his head for the strike. In one motion, Zeke pulled the .44 free, cocked the hammer, shoved the barrel into the Indian's stomach and pulled the trigger.

Lone Elk straightened up with the force of the blast, then dropped the knife and slumped onto Zeke, who was still on his back on the ground.

Zeke was trying to throw Lone Elk off of him when the roar of Two Horses' six-gun rang out. Lone Elk's body jerked as the slug slammed into his back. Zeke brought his .44 up as Two Horses fumbled with the hammer to get off another shot.

Taking careful aim and using the dead Cheyenne's body as a shield, Zeke fired at Two Horses. The slug ripped into him above the breastbone and drove him backward off his mount.

Zeke pushed Lone Elk's body aside and moved carefully toward Two Horses, his six-gun cocked and ready. There was no need. Two Horses lay sprawled on the ground with his eyes wide open and unseeing. Zeke rolled him onto his side and examined the wound. The slug had torn through his throat and blown a huge hole in the back of his neck.

Zeke removed his holster and gun belt from Two Horses' body and put them on. He placed the .44 Remington into the holster and then retrieved Ledyard's Army Colt from where Two Horses had dropped it when he fell.

He took one last look around, then went to get Ledyard.

CHAPTER THIRTY-TWO

Judge Fleming was the only lawyer in town, so he convened a hearing to see if a trial was warranted. The hearing was held two days after Zeke brought Ledyard back to Wattersville. News of their return spread through the small community so that all of the witnesses from Chadwick's Restaurant on that tragic night—except for three strangers passing through—were in attendance and ready to testify.

The room was packed. When Marshal Ryan brought in Ledyard, women gasped and covered their mouths. Several averted their eyes. Ledyard's hands were bandaged, and he wore new clothes that covered his arms, legs, and trunk, but his head was clearly visible.

Ledyard's face was a mass of welts and purple bruises, his nose laid off to one side. His lips and his eyes were swollen, the right eye completely shut. He limped on both legs, and two men had to help him as he shuffled to the defense table.

A shriek went up from Mrs. Gordon, and Mrs. Hamilton fainted when a deputy jerked Ledyard's hat off exposing chunks of raw flesh where clumps of hair had been ripped out. One ear was half bitten off, its remnant black and crusted.

And they ain't even seen half of it, Zeke thought from his seat in the back.

Judge Fleming called the first witness, Emma Pitts.

"Were you present when Ray Halstead was shot and killed in Chadwick's Restaurant?" Fleming asked.

"I was."

"If the person who shot him is present in this room would you point him out for the court, please?"

"That's the man right there," she said pointing at Ledyard.

"Did Mr. Halstead have a gun?"

"No, he did not!"

Those were the only three questions he asked the witnesses. Zeke sat quietly in the back of the room observing the proceedings. After the fourth witness in a row testified that Ledyard was the man who shot and killed unarmed Ray Halstead, Ledyard had seen enough.

"All right, so I did it. I'm guilty. Let's get on with it, already," he said, his voice a dry croak.

"STRING HIM UP!" came a cry from the corner of the room. The crowd roared its approval.

Judge Fleming pounded his gavel several times. "ORDER! WE MUST HAVE ORDER!"

Finally, the room quieted down so that the judge could continue. "The court accepts your guilty plea. Doctor Trimble has told me what the Cheyenne did to you, and that there's not much he can do to relieve your pain. He recommended that should you be found guilty, the humanitarian thing to do would be to give you a speedy execution rather than prolong your suffering.

"Accordingly, this court orders that you be taken to the tall elm tree at the edge of town commonly known as the

Judgment Tree, and hanged by the neck until you are dead. Sentence to be carried out one half hour from now under the supervision of Marshal Ryan." He rapped the gavel once.

∼

Zeke leaned against the hitching rail where his horse was tethered in front of Chadwick's. The street was deserted as almost the entire town had followed Marshal Ryan and his prisoner to the Judgment Tree. Zeke heard footsteps on the woodwalk behind him and turned to see Mr. Chadwick come out of his restaurant.

"Zeke! You'd better hurry if you're going to see that killer hang."

Zeke shook his head slowly. "I don't know, Mr. Chadwick. For so long I looked forward to this moment, but now that it's here the thought of it brings no pleasure to me."

Chadwick seemed stunned by this revelation. He stood quietly for a few moments, as though not knowing what to say. Then he said, "Jed Townsend from the land office was in for breakfast this morning. He told me you put your farm up for sale. Is that true?"

Zeke nodded that it was.

"So what are you going to do now?"

"First thing I'm going to do is visit a young lady I met in Colorado. Then I reckon I'll head over to Cheyenne, in Wyoming Territory and have a look around."

"Wyoming Territory, huh?" Chadwick said, then paused a few seconds to reflect on the idea. "Well," he said at last, "good luck to you, Zeke." He stuck his hand out and Zeke shook it. "I better hurry or I'll miss the hanging." With that, Chadwick walked briskly toward the crowd at the edge of town.

Zeke untied his horse and mounted up, taking one last look at his hometown. Then he took the badge off his shirt and pinned it to the outside of his vest, so everyone would know that he was a United States Marshal.

ABOUT THE AUTHOR

John Alexander grew up in the 1950's when Westerns dominated television and the big screen fostering a lifelong love for the genre. He and his buddies roamed the neighborhood with their cap guns and cowboy hats keeping everyone safe from outlaws and marauding Indians.

An Air Force assignment led to living six years at the edge of the Sonora Desert on the outskirts of Tucson. Rattlesnakes, scorpions, tarantulas, and even a mountain lion on the roof required constant vigilance when outdoors. Beautiful sunsets, horseback riding, and visits to Tucson's annual winter rodeo deepened his love for the West.

A former officer in both the Navy and the Air Force, he now writes full time.

Made in the USA
Coppell, TX
05 September 2025